IMMINENT
THREAT

A JAMES FLYNN THRILLER
Book 2

R.J. PATTERSON

IMMINENT THREAT
© Copyright 2015 R.J. Patterson

First Print Edition 2015
Second Print Edition 2017

Cover Design by Dan Pitts

Published in the United States of America
Green E-Books
Boise, Idaho 83714

To Paul Taylor,
for being a supportive friend

Conspiracy theorists of the world, believers in the hidden hands of the Rothschilds and the Masons and the Illuminati, we skeptics owe you an apology. You were right. The players may be a little different, but your basic premise is correct: The world is a rigged game.

— *Matt Taibbi*

IMMINENT
THREAT

CHAPTER 1

FOUR-YEAR-OLD OLIVIA HUFFMAN didn't see the swirling shadows outside her window at dawn on Monday morning, but she was awake. Wide awake—and cold. Livey, her name shortened so her two-year-old brother Parker could say it, twaddled down the hall toward her parents' room. Harold and his wife Claire heard the sound and both groaned. They had five more minutes before they were supposed to get up, but it wasn't happening today. The airy jingle scheduled to awaken them on his phone yielded to their unpredictable alarm clock that sounded like stubby feet stomping down the hall.

Livey jangled the doorknob until it opened. She then raced toward her parents' bed and dove in. "I'm cold," she said, climbing over her mother so she could nestle between them both. "Daddy, will you build a fire?"

He closed his eyes and chuckled. Any twinge of animosity Harold had over losing five minutes of sleep evaporated with her request. She could get almost anything she wanted when she looked at him with her brown doe eyes. He kissed her on the top of her head and tousled her hair. "Of course, Livey. Let me go outside and get some wood."

Livey squealed with delight as she melted into Claire.

"We'll stay warm right here until you get the fire roaring," Claire said.

As Harold stood up, he glanced over his shoulder to catch a glint of a smile on his wife's face.

"At least someone's day is off to a near-perfect start," he mumbled.

Claire laughed aloud and squeezed Livey.

Harold plodded through the house to the mudroom, which was true to its name at the moment. Winters in Idaho Falls were often long and unforgiving. He glanced out the window as he put his boots on.

Great. Another foot of snow.

He immediately started to calculate if he'd have time to thoroughly shovel the driveway. It'd be tight, but there'd be enough time—especially if he quickly got the fire blazing to Claire's liking.

He laced up his boots and pulled on his coat and hat. He opened the door and jammed his hands in his pockets. He slipped outside and left the door cracked to ensure an easy reentry with an armload of wood.

The snow crunched beneath the heavy weight of his footsteps, creating a fresh trail toward the woodshed. It was a trail he'd blazed many times during the winter months only to have Mother Nature erase it with a fresh coat of white flakes—sometimes only hours later.

He collected an armful of logs and some kindling pieces before he stopped. Studying the snow on the roof, he admired his small home. It wasn't the biggest house on the block or even the nicest, but it was his. He never dreamed he'd be able to own a home at age 32, much less be married to a beautiful woman and have two kids. For someone who'd grown up in this eastern Idaho town, he was doing well for himself.

His mild financial success mostly had to do with his steady and consistent job. Having a frugal wife didn't hurt either. When Harold graduated from high school, he pursued a contractor's license to work on H/VAC equipment. Within three months of earning his license, he landed a job with Bengal Heating and Air, a job he'd held ever since.

The money wasn't very good at first, but it got better once his company landed the H/VAC contract with Idaho National Labs, a nuclear research facility some forty miles west in the middle of the desert. His boss trusted Harold to handle INL's account with two of his young employees, though Harold knew it was more about his boss's disdain for the stringent security measures enacted there. Several checkpoints awaited anyone who ventured off the unassuming turnoff to the facility. A distant guardhouse stood a half-mile off the main road with hardly a building in sight. Harold had been to the facility dozens of times and he still wondered what exactly happened there. He signed a non-disclosure form, as did all the contractors who worked there—not that it mattered. He'd seen several bizarre things happen in some of the labs, including lockdowns of the buildings and evacuations. But no one talked about what exactly was happening, at least no one employed there.

About a fourth of the town's professionals commuted through the desert each day to work at INL and remained mum about what they did at the lab. Meanwhile, the rest of the town speculated about the true nature of the lab's business. Harold avoided such conversations, choosing to abide by the contract he'd signed. Yet, it never stopped curious neighbors and friends from baiting him with outlandish comments to lure him in. His neighbor across the street once posited the theory that everything from Area 51 had been moved there and that it was an alien landing strip. One of the deacons at his church told Harold he'd heard that the lab concentrated on genetic testing and that there were monstrous amalgamations of animals hidden in one of their warehouses. A mother at his eldest daughter's preschool said she'd heard the lab manufactured bioweapons and experimented with mind-control drugs. Each time someone floated a theory by him, he remained stoic. He didn't want to give credence to what people were suggesting nor did he want to dismiss them as loons. After all, maybe they were right. He just hadn't seen anything—and if he had, he still wasn't authorized to say a word.

Before Harold tramped back to his house along the path he'd beaten down only minutes before, a familiar voice cried out his name.

"Harold? Is that you?" called his neighbor, Wilson Coleman. Wilson was a private investigator who spent most of his time staking out and chronicling the exploits of unfaithful husbands and wives. When he wasn't on a case, he spent his free time reading conspiracy websites and concocting theories about the INL.

"Yeah, Wilson. It's me."

"Are you going to the desert today? Because if you are, I've got something I want you to check out for me."

Harold rolled his eyes, relieved that Wilson couldn't see into his yard over the fence. "What is it now?"

"Do you remember my uncle who used to come visit from Pocatello?"

"Wasn't his name Donald?"

"That's the one."

"What about him?"

"He told me that he was driving through the desert recently on his way to Sun Valley when he saw some green glow flashing right near where INL was."

A wry smile spread across Harold's face. "Let me guess. You think the green glow is still there and you want me to poke around?"

"Just ask somebody, Harold. You know something fishy goes on out there. See what you can find out."

"You know I can't do that. I signed a non-disclosure agreement."

"Come on, Harold. Don't be such a goody two shoes. They could be breaking all kinds of laws out there or worse—putting us all in danger."

"It's a lab in the middle of the desert. It's not putting any of us in danger." He turned and started walking toward the house.

"Please. Just this once. I won't ever ask again."

Harold didn't stop as he trudged through the snow. "You need a new hobby, Wilson." He smiled and laughed to himself then slid the door open.

His smile vanished the moment after he closed the sliding glass door behind him and turned around. He dropped the wood as it clattered onto the kitchen floor tile.

Three men held Claire, Livey, and Parker each at gunpoint. Another voice emerged from a shadowy figure that stepped out from around the corner.

"If you want to see your family alive again once you return home from work today, I suggest you follow my orders and pay very close attention to what I'm about to tell you."

Harold swallowed hard and nodded. He never thought he'd be so afraid of a woman.

CHAPTER 2

JAMES FLYNN GAWKED at the billboard situated just on the edge of Idaho Falls on U.S. Route 20 as the bus rolled toward Idaho National Laboratory about fifty miles due west. Kim Gates elbowed him to make sure he saw it. She nodded toward the billboard and smiled.

"Get a load of that, will ya?" she said.

He smiled and shook his head. "That's why I'm here, isn't it? To debunk such wild ideas?"

She chuckled. "You mean, you don't think INL is where the military moved everything from Area 51?"

He rolled his eyes and shifted in his seat. But he knew such thinking was exactly why his editor Theresa Thompson at *The National* sent him into the wilderness to get this story. As much as he liked uncovering real conspiracies, half the time he spent exposing fake ones. Today was one of those days.

"I didn't see any alien life as I drove through town," he said.

Her eyes widened as she cocked her head to one side. "Perhaps you weren't looking closely enough. There are plenty of strange men around here."

"Don't you mean 'desperate'?"

She punched him in the arm and giggled. "No, that'd be the women."

"The *women*?"

"How else do you explain that any woman in this town ever marries a man who grew up here? The selection of men is more or less a monolithic crapshoot."

"If it's really that bad, I'm sure you could get a job elsewhere—like D.C., perhaps?" he said as he winked at her.

"I'm not sure I could compete there."

He waved his hand and shrugged. "Big city women are overrated. Women from smaller towns on the other hand—" He let his words hang as he slumped into his seat.

"Well, I know you didn't come here to discuss city life and its dating practices, now did you?"

He shook his head. "Who cares? I'll do anything to pass the time on this ride through the middle of nowhere."

"We might be going through the middle of nowhere, but we're going *somewhere* all right—somewhere that will show your readers that the rumors about the military hiding their Area 51 stuff here is a joke."

Flynn eyed her cautiously. "So, you're going to show me *everything* here?"

A slight grin spread across her face as she looked forward. She didn't say a word.

"I see how it is," he said. "You're only going to tell me what I want to hear."

"Trust me when I say this—there's not much to see or hear. Taking people out here is one of the most boring parts of my job. It's a *lab* for goodness sake."

"Strange things happen in labs." He paused. "Ever read *Frankenstein*?"

"If you see any monsters wandering the halls, be sure to give me a heads up. I wouldn't want to be killed at the hands of a man-made cretin."

He snickered. "You have my word. I'll protect you."

She rolled her eyes. "Oh, good lord," she muttered.

Flynn pulled out his phone and passed the time by surfing the news on the Internet. It was a far cry from how he wasted time while working in the CIA. Instead of perusing government cables, he was looking at the trending stories. The biggest story of the day, aside from an update about some reality TV star's love life, was the news about Russian President Alexander Petrov's latest threat and the growing tension between his country and the U.S. With a scheduled appearance before the U.S. Senate on Thursday, Petrov and his inflammatory comments stoked the embers of a relationship that was simmering at the moment but was subject to boiling over if leaders didn't keep their egos in check. That story rated only slightly ahead of Pyongyang's dispute with Petrov over some oil fields located along the Tumen River. Neither sounded particularly charitable to Flynn yet he presumed it was nothing more than political posturing. *Petrov wouldn't be foolish enough to provoke two nations at once, would he?* Flynn wasn't sure. Petrov's ego wouldn't fit in the bus he was riding in, let alone in the largest country in the world.

After Flynn grew tired of reading articles foretelling the world's impending doom, he turned his attention back toward Gates.

"Why is this place located so far out in the middle of the desert? I mean why not have it near a major city?"

She cut her eyes toward him and shook her head. "They're not exactly making cheese out here."

"So it *is* nuclear?" he asked. "I thought the 'n' in INL stood for 'national.' "

"It does. But there is nuclear activity." She waved dismissively at him. "But you already knew *that*."

"Everybody does. But what I'm interested in is the nature of the nuclear activity."

"Like I told you on the phone before you came out here, I can't answer *every* one of your questions. You're free to draw your own conclusions, but you won't get me to go on the record about such things. I'm merely here to escort you through the facility and show you that this isn't some secret holding facility for all the old Area 51 artifacts."

Flynn said nothing as they rolled along. Five minutes later, the bus swung a hard right and turned off U.S. Route 20 toward the INL facility. Mountains rose in the distance, serving as an imposing backdrop over the handful of one- and two-story buildings dotting the desert landscape in front of them. Their bus rumbled along until it rolled up to a guardhouse and lurched to a stop.

The bus driver exchanged some paperwork with the armed guard standing near the entry point. The iron gate rolled back and allowed the bus to pass. The bus jerked as it gained speed and moved forward along the long road. Flynn leaned into the aisle so he could see ahead. He estimated the nearest building was at least a half-mile farther up the road.

"This is some pretty tight security for a place that makes cheese," he quipped.

She smiled and shook her head. "Do you have to work at thinking up such moronic statements—or does it come naturally for you?"

"I've heard that a good cover for hiding alien spaceships is making cheese."

She folded her arms and stared out the window. "That's why I said we aren't exactly making cheese. Try to keep up."

Flynn liked his host already. Her sarcasm kept him on his toes, though five minutes on the campus and he was already convinced INL wasn't nearly as benign as she portrayed it to be.

I wonder what really goes on here.

Once the bus parked, workers hustled off and headed toward their respective work areas. Flynn remained seated with Gates, who didn't budge until the last employee vanished.

"Shall we?" she said as she stood up.

Flynn followed her lead and headed toward the main entrance. He stopped and whiffed the breezy desert air that carried a hint of burnt plastic to it mixed with the smell of a 1980s-era copier. As he looked around, he scrunched up his face.

"Problems, Mr. Flynn?"

"That smell," he said, whisking the air toward him. "What is that?"

"Ingenuity and invention."

He smiled. "It certainly isn't cheese."

They checked in at the main desk. Flynn underwent several rounds of paperwork protocol. He spent a few minutes perusing the list that outlined what he could and couldn't do.

"No pictures on the tour?" he said.

Gates rolled her eyes. "Please, Mr. Flynn. I told you all this before you came out here."

"How can I prove to readers that this isn't Area 51 without pictures of vacant warehouses?" He flashed a wry grin.

"You almost got me there," she said.

"I think I already did."

He scribbled his name on the paper and handed it to her. The receptionist handed him a badge and he began his tour with Gates.

Flynn tweeted a picture of the facility he'd taken in the parking lot.

"About to tour INL. If the military is hiding aliens here, rest assured I'll find them #Area51"

He shoved his phone back in his pocket and followed Gates. They wound around a long circular corridor until they reached some of the research stations. She showed him some of the projects they were working on, mostly benign. A team of researchers tested fiber optics while others tapped on their keyboards to test "Internet security," according to Gates. After a few minutes of muddling along, he was glad he wasn't allowed to take pictures for he was certain they'd make this mundane story even more boring. Captions like "a researcher tests internet security" underneath the picture of a guy in a white lab coat sitting at his computer didn't exactly make for compelling content. It was clear after a half hour that he wasn't going to find anything compelling on the tour.

He tapped Gates on the shoulder as she continued her torrid pace. "Look, I'm definitely going to be able to tell others there's no Area 51 artifacts here—but only if I get to see some other parts of the facility."

She stopped. "Fine. I can show you a couple more

buildings, but that's it. If you thought this was boring, prepare to be underwhelmed."

Flynn sighed and chased after Gates, who was already six steps into her purposeful gait.

She took them out the back of the main building where a golf cart was waiting.

"Get in," she said, pointing at the vehicle.

Flynn obliged and his butt hadn't even touched the seat before she stomped on the gas. The cart whirred as it eased down an internal access road toward a two-story building about a quarter of a mile away.

"Been here long?" Flynn asked.

"Long enough."

Flynn decided not to press her. Her slumped shoulders and dour expression spoke volumes. They rode the rest of the way in silence.

Once she parked the cart outside the building, she stomped on the parking brake and strode toward the door. Flynn hustled to keep up, grabbing the door as soon as she tugged on it so he could hold it open for her.

"At least there's one gentleman on this property," she said.

Flynn smiled and followed her inside. "So, what is the primary type of research that goes on here?"

"It's something you have to see for yourself." She motioned for him to follow her.

She strode down the hallway past several armed guards, who nodded approvingly at her once she flashed her badge.

"What's with all the muscle and firepower around here?" Flynn asked. "Definitely not a cheese factory."

"That's what I've been trying to tell you."

They continued on for a few more minutes before descending several flights of stairs. Once they reached the ground floor, she led him to a viewing area where they could see inside three labs on each side of the cavernous room.

"What are they doing here?"

"This is one of our nuclear research facilities."

Flynn's eyes widened. "You're showing me your nuclear research?"

"Relax. It's totally benign—unless you ingest it, of course." She snickered and cut her eyes at him.

He studied the team of scientists who scurried around the room.

"Don't worry," she said. "We don't enrich any uranium here or anything like that. No weapons-grade nuclear material."

"It could still kill me."

"If you aren't careful. But we take the utmost precautions around here. This place is safer than Fort Knox."

"So, what are they doing here exactly?"

She wagged her finger at him. "*That*, I can't tell you."

"So, you're going to make me speculate? This could be interesting."

"It's nothing like that."

"Oh, my readers will eat this up."

She sighed and put her hands on her hips. "Fine. I'll tell you—"

Before Gates could continue a loud alarm sounded, echoing off the walls.

She grabbed Flynn's arm.

"What's going on?" he asked.

"Come with me," she said. "We don't have much time."

CHAPTER 3

SENATOR HUNTER THOR took a deep breath and surveyed the room. One side of the table consisted of party
members bent on reducing the U.S. military force to little
more than drone pilots and surveillance satellites. On the
other side sat distinguished veterans who saw it as their duty
to make sure U.S. troops received everything they needed to
succeed—even if the *everything* bankrupt the taxpayers. The
Defense subcommittee for the Committee for Appropria-
tions consisted of regular spirited debates, none of which
seemed to be grounded in logic or reason. Party ideology
governed every member's decisions, though he fancied himself to be immune from such partisan bickering.

With his right hand, he reached for his left ring finger
to twist his wedding ring, a tic he had whenever he was nervous. But it wasn't there, serving as a stark reminder of his
bitter divorce only a few months before. He'd been named
the hardest working freshman senator by *The Washington Post*
in a poll conducted by the newspaper, yet it served as little
consolation for him. His dedication to his position on Capitol Hill didn't impress his wife, who grew tired of the long
days and weekends spent being entertained by lobbyists. In
an effort to save his family, he told his wife he decided to

step down after his term ended. She decided a relationship with a masseur was what she needed more—and she took their girls, Emily and Courtney at ages six and four, with her when she filed for divorce. Despite a fierce custody battle, she won out since she had a parcel of secrets on a handful of people in the court system. Every attempt he made to influence a favor was met with resistance until he figured out his wife's game—one he couldn't beat her at without great risk to his own political future. That's when he really threw himself into his work.

With the sting of betrayal still fresh, Senator Thor put aside his aspirations for a second chance at a happy family. Now his life was about creating a happy America, a place where the future was bright and the borders were safe. It was about making sure that the dream imagined by the country's Founding Fathers could actually become a reality for the American people. Government reach had grown far beyond manageable, creating instead an unhealthy dependence on an approach to governance that crept toward socialism. And he wasn't having any of it.

Led by Senator Norton Queen, the committee meeting commenced—and Thor braced himself for the budget review process. It seemed to be a never-ending process, one filled with favors, trades, and promises.

He sifted through the stack of papers in front of him, combing for details to question, contest, or confirm.

If the American people knew this is how their government ran, they'd storm Capitol Hill and the White House with bayonets if they had to.

The committee was Thor's least favorite, but he felt an obligation to be there before the doves stripped the country of its world power status in an effort to regain favor in the world's eyes. Serving on this committee, he never balked at spending suggestions—only reductions. But his eyes blazed when anyone sought to reduce or remove funding, particularly when it had no basis. Yet he didn't expect his compatriot and fellow party member Senator Colt Ryan to be the one hoisting the axe on a handful of programs Thor deemed vital to national security.

"This missile defense program needs to be seriously reduced, if not eliminated all together," Senator Ryan said, his voice gruff and gravely as he tapped his cane on the floor. "I hate to see the American taxpayers fleeced for something that will remain inoperable for years to come—if ever."

Thor banged his fist on the table. "It's that kind of thinking that's going to get us bombed back into the Stone Age. Our enemies are getting smarter and more technologically advanced every day. We must stay ahead of the curve, and cutting this program would be a severe miscalculation on our part. We need to be vigilant in our defense of the American people, using our resources to keep them safe from any and all threats."

"Nobody has ever lobbed missiles at us."

"That day's coming sooner than you think," Thor said. Then under his breath, "But I doubt you'll be around to see it."

Ryan slowly turned toward Thor. "I might be deaf in my left ear, but I can still hear your snarky comments loud and clear."

Senator Queen cleared his throat. "Gentlemen, let's remain focused on the task at hand." He paused and peered over his glasses at the sheet in front of him. "I tend to agree with Senator Ryan on this issue. The missile defense program has stalled out and serves only as a deterrent rather than an actual tool to defend this nation. I'm of the notion that it should be reduced only to a subsistence level until we can perform more viability studies. Under the current economic conditions, I feel like it would be wasteful spending. We need to be paring this program down and focusing on other things, not ramping it up."

Thor sighed loudly. "You're going to regret this. We need this program right now, more than you'll ever know. Shuttering it won't shutter the resolve of our enemies to destroy us however they can."

One senator's phone buzzed and he slipped away to a corner of the room to answer it.

"They may try to destroy us anyway they can, but firing missiles across a large body of water isn't how they're going to do it," Queen retorted.

The senator who'd stepped away, returned to his seat and shook his head. "You might want to reconsider that last statement, Senator Queen. Terrorists just attacked one of our facilities that makes plutonium in Idaho." He paused and reiterated for effect, "On our own soil!"

CHAPTER 4

SVETLANA YURKOVICH NEVER TOOK pleasure in watching men squirm under her control. While she knew others who did, she deemed it a distraction to her mission. For her, it was about the money, which only came after accomplishing the task. Delighting in a position of power over another man might result in failure or worse—death. "Never underestimate your opponent," she preached to her team before every assignment. And the fact that her foot was on the throat of a tied-up Harold Huffman meant nothing more than she was inching closer to accomplishing a difficult undertaking.

An alarm buzzed in the facility while lights flashed. She peered out of the closet and watched white-coated researchers scurry for the exit.

"Niko, I need your help again," she said into her radio. "We're not going to be able to blend in here."

"On it," he said.

She looked down at Harold, who pleaded with his eyes that she not kill him. With his mouth gagged, it was all he could do. She sighed, growing tired of his begging.

"Finish him," she said to Vladimir Gurkin, one of her hired musclemen for the mission.

"Gladly," he said before picking up Harold and breaking his neck with his bare hands. He chuckled as he watched Harold slump to the floor.

"Niko? You still there?" she said.

"Almost got it," he answered. There were a few more clicks on his keyboard until he spoke again. "OK, ready?"

"Still waiting on Boris," she said.

"Not sure you can do that based on the lab's protocol. You need to get moving—and here's what you need to do."

Niko guided Svetlana and Vladimir through the research labyrinth undetected. They heard shots fired but kept moving.

"Do you think that was Boris?" Vladimir asked.

"Don't have time to think about it. Let's keep moving," she said.

Niko led them to a washroom where they could suit up like the other researchers and walk out without drawing suspicion.

"Think you can hide the plutonium under your lab coat?" Niko said.

"Of all the things I've done today, that might be the easiest," she said.

In a matter of minutes, they'd slipped into white lab coats and made it out of the building. They found an empty golf cart with the keys in it and drove toward the main parking lot, almost invisible amidst the chaos. They passed several security cars and two fire trucks.

"Must've been some kind of accident back there," Vladimir said.

Svetlana laughed. "It won't be anything compared to what's going to happen with this plutonium once we get it out of here."

They disappeared around the backside of the main building where Niko was waiting in Harold Huffman's truck.

"Ready?" she shouted before she'd even pulled the cart to a complete stop.

"Let's do this," Niko answered.

Svetlana slid into the driver's seat and turned the ignition as the truck roared to life. She rammed the gearshift into drive and was about to step on the gas before she felt a cold piece of metal jammed into the back of her skull.

"I wouldn't do that if I were you," said an unfamiliar voice.

She took her hands off the steering wheel in surrender.

"That's it. Nice and easy," said the security, who shifted his position so he could now see all three of the fleeing suspects snug in the front seat of the truck cab. "Keep those hands where I can see them." He paused. "Now, get out."

Svetlana didn't move. "Why exactly are you pointing a gun at us?"

"Don't insult my intelligence. I know what's going on here."

"I doubt you do," she quipped. "This stuff is way over your pay grade."

He forced a smile and cocked his head to one side. "You fit perfectly in my pay grade. Just be lucky I don't have an itchy trigger finger."

Svetlana threw her head back and laughed while reaching for the gun in her boot as she stepped out of the truck. In one smooth motion, she pulled her gun out and peppered the security guard with three shots. He staggered backward before falling to the ground. He dropped his gun and put both hands on his chest. Blood pooled around him as he gasped for air.

She looked down at him. "You're right. I do feel lucky you didn't have an itchy trigger finger." She reached down and took his gun and cell phone before climbing back into the truck.

"Now, let's see if we can make a clean getaway this time," she said before stomping on the gas.

She grabbed the guard's cell phone and punched in a phone number.

"Hello?" answered a man in a hushed voice

"I'm just calling to check in with you. We have the package."

"Excellent. News has already reached Capitol Hill and people are panicking here."

"Time to move on to Phase 2 of the plan."

"Already in motion." She hung up and sped toward the guardhouse and the man who stood firm in the road with his gun trained on them. He kept screaming at them—right up until the second she clipped him and sent him flying through the air.

Niko and Vladimir both turned around, eyes wild with delight.

"That was incredible," Vladimir said.

"I've never seen anything like that," Niko said.

A grin spread across Svetlana's face. "And we're only getting started, gentlemen."

CHAPTER 5

DR. MELISSA WATSON ADJUSTED the radio dial on her rusted Camry. She could only move the dial about an inch, which was fine with her since it remained stuck at the left end of the spectrum. Public radio heaven. She flipped between 90.9 and 89.3 FM—often a difficult choice for her. Classical music versus jazz. Her car lurched to a stop at a red light, where she took the chance to sway while sawing on her air violin as Rachmaninoff Symphony No. 2 blared on her speakers.

She didn't stop until she noticed the man in the car next to her staring and smiling. She shot him a look and looked straight ahead, smoothing her hair back in her ponytail. It wasn't the first time she'd been caught and she doubted it'd be the last. But she didn't like the attention or the fact that she was someone else's amusement. She gripped the steering wheel and pursed her lips in anticipation of the light turning green. When the red light blinked off, she stomped on the gas and quickly pulled ahead of him.

As she neared the next intersection, the radio host concluded the hour of music by introducing the news. She almost twisted the knob to the jazz channel until something the newswoman said arrested her attention.

"A growing concern about biological warfare has prompted the Department of Homeland Security to tighten its restrictions on liquids for flights originating from or landing on U.S. soil." The newscaster continued. "In an about-face from several years ago, Homeland Security has credible intelligence that there is an imminent threat and that this is one way to prevent it."

Watson rolled her eyes.

What is this world coming too? Next thing you know, my kale smoothie will be considered a threat to national security.

"Only medicines in labeled containers of less than two ounces and baby milk will be permitted through security checkpoints," the woman said. "Homeland Security apologized for the inconvenience this new regulation might cause, a regulation which begins effective today."

Not only will half the stuff out there not kill you—it won't even hurt you.

She clicked on her turn signal and waited for the next light to change so she could enter The Goldstein Group. It wasn't well known to the general public but it was highly regarded in research circles, which led to Watson choosing to work here over a slew of other offers. After her Ph.D. defense of her thesis on HIV and vaccinations, she emerged as one of the nation's brightest young minds in her field after graduating from the University of Maryland's acclaimed Institute of Human Virology. She had her pick of research institutes across the country, but she loathed the thought of moving again and relished the idea of staying in the same area and working at The Goldstein Group. It wasn't what she ever dreamed of when she entered Maryland's program, but it surpassed her expectations in every way. Cutting edge research, the most up-to-date technology—and the pay? She couldn't complain about it, though she refused to spend hardly any of her swelling bank account.

A knocking noise in her car's engine attracted unwanted attention as she threw the gear into park.

"You might want to get that looked at," Gary Mosley said as she got out of her car. "It won't be long before you're stranded along a shoulder in rush-hour traffic."

"Good morning to you, too, Gary," she said, ignoring his comment.

"I could take a look at it for you," he said.

"You've got better things to do in your evenings, I'm sure," she said, stepping out of the car. "Besides, I'd rather buy another used car than sink money into this thing again." She paused. "I think I'll just drive it until it dies."

"Suit yourself. You know how to reach me if you change your mind."

Watson waited until he turned away until she rolled her eyes and shook her head. If Gary had tried once to put the moves on her, he'd tried a hundred times. He was 45, single, and desperate—two of three major strikes that went against him. Then, when Watson considered the fact that he worked with her, he struck out completely. She concluded long ago that a workplace romance wasn't anything she desired—no matter how handsome the specimen might be.

Before she'd even put her things down, The Goldstein Group director, Dr. Harrison Franklin, stormed into her office with a folder in his hand.

"Good morning, sir," she said.

"No time for pleasantries, Dr. Watson," he said sharply. "I need your help on this antidote. Some other researchers have made progress, but I know you'll be able to help speed up the process."

She took the folder from him. "Why the urgency? I haven't heard of any report about this virus, other than what you've told me."

"Just trust me. It's coming to the U.S. soon and we need to be ready."

"And you think I'm the one to do this?"

"It reacts similarly to HIV in the way that it attacks the body's immune system." He pointed at the file. "Just read it and tell me what you think. I've got some samples that you can begin work on right away."

"Like that?" she said. "You think I can figure out a vaccine with the snap of my fingers. These things take time."

"Time isn't on our side, but you won't be starting from ground zero. A team of great researchers has been working on this for a while, but they can't seem to solve it. There's credible evidence from Homeland Security that the U.S. is going to suffer a biological attack from this virus in the very near future."

"How near?"

"Days, weeks. We're not sure. But if we're not ready when this thing hits the U.S., this virus could turn into a pandemic in a matter of days. Good enough for you?"

She nodded. "I'll get to work on it right away and see what I can do."

Once she settled into her chair, she started to read the documents Dr. Franklin handed her. Her eyes widened at the pictures showing how the virus devastated its victims. After she finished reading the report, she started to peck away on her computer. About an hour later, she got up and entered the lab where she greeted Dr. Mosely.

"Has the director got you working on this, too?" he asked.

She nodded but didn't look up. Instead, she stared at the slide in front of her and carefully carried it to the microscope near her workstation in the lab. She peered through her microscope and gasped at what she saw. "Have you looked at this?" she asked.

Dr. Watson looked up in time to see her associate shove a needle into the arm of a monkey caged in their lab.

"What are you doing?"

"What does it look like I'm doing? He's got me working on a cure, not a vaccine."

She crept closer as the monkey's eyes began to bleed. "What did you do?"

"I injected it with the virus."

The monkey started to spasm and then went into what looked like a seizure.

"Oh my—"

He stepped back and stared at the animal. "I'm told it works much slower on humans than monkeys, but I'd prefer never to find that out myself."

"You and me both," Watson said as she scurried back to her desk.

CHAPTER 6

JAMES FLYNN DIDN'T MIND sharing tight spaces, particularly with Kim Gates—though he would've preferred other circumstances. Flashing lights and blaring sirens proved to be counterproductive to any kind of romantic notion he had toward her.

"Why are we hiding in the closet again?" Flynn asked. "Don't we need to get out of here if there's some kind of nuclear disaster?"

"That sound is a different kind of alarm—one I thought I'd never hear outside of a drill."

"And what sound is that?"

"The sound of a breach."

Flynn peeked out of the closet door as scads of researchers hurried toward the exit. "Shouldn't we be following them?"

"Yes, but—" She stopped.

"But what?"

"I'd rather just hide in here. No telling what awaits outside this door."

"I never took you for a fearful woman."

"My father was killed during a terrorist attack overseas a few years ago. If he had stayed put instead of trying to be a hero, he'd still be with us today."

"Well, a lot more people are going to die if we don't get out there and figure out what's going on." Flynn pulled the gun out of the holster that wrapped around his back.

"You have a gun?" she said.

"No one frisked me. Besides, I've had a difficult time leaving my former CIA life behind. If I can help it, I never venture outside without my piece."

Her breathing turned short and shallow. "What are you going to do with that thing? Shoot somebody?"

Flynn peered into the hallway through a cracked door. "If I have to, yes." He paused and turned and looked at her. "Just calm down. Everything's going to be all right."

Before she could protest, he flung the door opened and fired at a trio of people toting guns storming down the hall.

"What are you doing?" she squealed.

"Trying to stop some terrorists."

He slammed the door as he exited the closet and chased after the three people who looked out of place in the research facility. He sprinted down the hallway and slid as he turned to the right. Nothing. Any terrorists had vanished down the hall. He kept running, the burn in his lungs creating a sharp pain in his chest. Flynn ignored it and continued on.

He turned again to the right and caught a glimpse of one of the terrorists. Without hesitating, he hoisted his gun up and opened fire.

Yes!

He hit the trailing man among the trio with a shot to his upper right back. The man crumpled to the ground.

Flynn rushed toward him but the other two vanished down the hallway.

He stood over the man bleeding out. "What were you doing here?"

The man glared up at Flynn and spit at him.

"I asked you a question," Flynn said as he jammed his knee into the man's chest and knelt down close. "What were you doing here?"

The man spit at Flynn again.

Flynn flipped the man over and jammed the barrel of his gun into the man's back. The man screamed a few distinct phrases Flynn understood.

"Oh, so you're Russian?" he said. "What brings you to Idaho National Laboratory today?" He paused and added more pressure to his gun. "Or should I squeeze it out of you?"

The man wailed in pain yet refused to answer Flynn.

"Fine. Have it your way." Flynn grabbed the man's arm and broke it, eliciting more shrieks of pain. "Like that? Want some more?" He grabbed the man's other arm.

"Okay, okay. I'll talk. What do you want to know?"

"That's more like it," Flynn said. "So, what are you doing here?"

The man paused and turned up to look at Flynn. "Pissing off an American asshole."

Flynn shoved his knee into the man's back again with swift force. More screams.

"I'm not going to ask again."

"Good," the man said before he passed out. Blood continued to pool around his limp body.

Flynn rolled the man over and took a picture of him

with his cell phone. He texted the image to Todd Osborne, his remaining contact and lone friend at the CIA. Then he called Osborne.

"So, I'm guessing this call has something to do with the picture of the dead man you just sent me," Osborne said as he answered.

"He's not dead yet."

"Just give me a second as I upload this to our database and try to get a hit."

Flynn glanced around the room but didn't keep his eyes on the man. Before he knew it, he'd grabbed Flynn's gun and pulled the trigger, shooting himself in the head.

"What was that?" Osborne asked.

Flynn glanced at the man and shook his head. "It doesn't matter. We won't get any answers out of him now. He's gone."

Kim slumped to the floor, her back against the hallway wall. She sobbed heavily.

"Let's get you out of here," Flynn said. "You don't need to see this."

He helped her up and ushered her outside to a golf cart. "Go back to the main building. I'm sure it'll be safe there. I want to make sure nobody is still inside."

He went back inside and raced down the hall where the other two people had disappeared. Nothing. INL was under attack—and Flynn was no closer to knowing the answer now than when it all started.

CHAPTER 7

SENATOR THOR STORMED into Senator Ryan's office. He noticed the elder statesman's hands shook as he towered over him. Ryan glanced at him before looking back down at his papers.

"Can I help you?" Ryan asked.

"Perhaps you better start by telling me what the hell you think you're doing in there?" Thor said as he stamped his foot. "Our national security is on the line, something the American people elected us to uphold—and you're acting like you don't even care. Are you even aware of the elevated threat level since plutonium was stolen from a lab on American soil earlier today?"

Ryan continued to sift through the papers in front of him, acknowledging his junior counterpart with nothing more than the slight rise of his eyebrows.

"What's wrong with you?" Thor continued. "Where's the fire you once had? Where's the man who fought valiantly for this country and nearly sacrificed his own life to save others? What happened to *that* guy? Because that's the guy I wanted to partner with on this committee. When you find him, will you tell him to give me a call?"

Thor spun and strode toward the door. As he put his hand on the knob, Ryan finally spoke.

"Do you want an answer or do you want to just yell at me?"

Thor turned around, walking back to Ryan with measured steps. He put his knuckles on the desk and leaned forward. "Why don't you stop playing games?"

Ryan glanced back down at his papers and remained quiet.

"So, I guess you can't give me an answer, can you?"

Ryan slammed his fists on his desk and stood up. "You know what the problem is with all these younger generations? You all think the world owes you something. Entitled little punks today think we need to give them high-paying jobs for brainless work. Corporate entities believe they deserve to be handed interest free money so people don't lose their jobs—and they don't lose their precious retirement pensions. And you? You think you deserve an answer for how I acted in a meeting today. The only difference between you and all the other entitled snots out there is that you actually *are* entitled, pretending like you're serving the people when you're only serving yourself." He paused. "I doubt you even know—or care—about how people out there feel today. You have no idea of the struggles people in this country went through to gain the enormous freedoms we have today. You have no idea of the struggles some people still face on a daily basis. I bet you've never even served in your life, except maybe scooping beans on a plate in a soup kitchen for a photo op."

Ryan sat down and mopped his brow with a handkerchief.

Thor smiled. "There's that fire—but it still doesn't explain why you're working against me on getting our defense department properly funded."

"We are engaged in a game, Senator Thor. And if you intend to win, you must never tip your hand too early."

"And what exactly is in our hand?"

Ryan shook his head. "I'm not sure what's in your hand, but I know what's in mine—and I'm going to win." He stopped and took a deep breath. "We're going to win. *America* is going to win."

"Win what, sir?"

"The war on terror."

"There *is* no war on terror, but there is a war on terrorists and the real live missiles those lunatics will be hurling toward us if we don't stop them."

Ryan sniffled and stared past Thor in the direction of the office's lone window. "I suggest you stand down, Senator Thor. This isn't a battle you're going to win—not in a committee meeting or in a court of public opinion. I have a plan and just because I haven't made you privy to it, doesn't mean we're on opposing sides."

"Then I suggest you fill me in."

"I suggest you get control of your righteous indignation and be a good team player. Who knows what might happen to you if you continue to row against our team."

"Are you threatening me?"

Ryan let out a hearty laugh. "I might be old—and partially deaf—but I'm very well connected. And I can assure you that you don't want to cross me."

Thor's eyes narrowed as he pursed his lips. He walked around to the back side of Ryan's desk and leaned over him. "Watch your step old man," he said, kicking Ryan's cane to the floor. "Your time to pass might come sooner than you'd like."

CHAPTER 8

THERE WAS NO EASY WAY out of the Idaho wilderness for Svetlana and her team. The I-84 route ran east and west and was the major thoroughfare through the state. But the element of surprise was on her side, as the law enforcement forces that would be pursuing her would have no idea where she was headed.

Straight north was Canada, a seven-hour drive if they cut through Montana. The Oregon coast was a twelve-hour drive west, the Utah desert a four-hour trek. And while they were all good places to disappear, they weren't optimal locations for getting plutonium out of the country—that designation rested with the Idaho port city of Lewiston, a destination not likely to be searched.

"Did you see that guy flip into the air?" Vladimir asked. "I've never seen anything like it."

Niko shook his head. "A new experience for me."

Svetlana smiled as she adjusted her rearview mirror and pressed harder on the gas. They needed to hurry up and make it to the next town so they could ditch Harold's truck and get a different ride.

After nearly an hour of hard driving, Svetlana slowed down as they approached the small farming community of

Carey. She instructed Valdimir and Niko to keep a low profile, as attracting any attention in such a small town might alert law enforcement of their location. She parked the truck behind a Family Dollar store and got out. She left Vladimir and Niko in the truck while she walked down the street about a block away in search of a new vehicle. It didn't take long before she found an unlocked truck parked along a side street with the keys in the ignition. She jumped in and turned the ignition as the truck roared to life. After revving the engine several times, she waited to see if anyone came out after her. Nothing. She turned the truck around and picked up her two team members.

"Did you get the bolt cutters?" she asked.

Vladimir nodded and threw the tool into the back of the pickup.

"Good work," she said as they headed back toward the main route.

They soon veered off onto a dirt road that headed northwest across the state. They bumped along for a little over an hour before a shirtless man laboring under the burden of a backpack flagged them down in the middle of the road.

He motioned for Svetlana to roll down her window.

"Mighty nice of you to stop," he said as he leaned on the door. "Where are you folks headed? Portland? Seattle?"

Svetlana eyed him cautiously but said nothing.

"Well, aren't you folks gonna say something?"

"We're going to Lewiston," Vladimir said.

Svetlana reached across and punched him in the chest.

"I detect a different kind of accent there. Where are you guys from? Minnesota? Wisconsin?"

"We're from shut-the-hell-up," Svetlana said.

The hitchhiker put his hands in the air in surrender. "No need to get ugly—I'll just wait for the next truck to come along."

"No need for you to know where we're going either," she said before raising her gun and putting a bullet in his forehead. The man slumped to the ground.

Svetlana ordered Niko and Vladimir to drag the man's body into a ditch along the side of the dirt road. Less than a minute later, they were back on their way toward Lewiston.

"I hope nobody finds him for a while," Vladimir said.

Svetlana rolled her eyes. "You and your big mouth. Let's keep it shut next time." She recoiled and bashed him on the head with the butt of her gun. "I can put a bullet in your head, too."

They rolled on for several hours until they turned off the dirt road and headed north along the Interstate

"It won't be much longer now," she said.

CHAPTER 9

SERGEANT DAN THATCHER CHECKED his coordinates as he ventured north into the Afghanistan mountains north of Lake Kowl-e Chaqmaqtin. He'd grown tired of the reconnaissance missions and welcomed the opportunity to actually take out some enemy targets. Contrary to celebrated announcements to the American public, U.S. troops were still very much on the ground in Afghanistan, acting on intelligence the military hoped would be used to weaken the Taliban and bring more stability to the region. However, as his squad neared the small village tucked in the foothills of unforgiving mountains, they saw little and heard nothing.

"What've you guys got?" Thatcher said as he radioed the other half of his squad approaching the village from the north side.

"Nothing, sir," came the response.

"Be careful. This could be an ambush."

After losing a half-dozen friends to Taliban ambushes, everything made Thatcher jumpy. If something seemed to be too easy, he always assumed it was because the bottom was about to drop out on his troops. He kept them alert—and vigilant. The last thing he wanted was to see one of his guys taken home in a body bag.

"We've made visual contact," said Sgt. Bellman over the radio. "But they don't look like a serious threat."

"What do you mean?" Thatcher asked.

"I mean, it looks like they're just sitting around, like they're tired or sick or something. I can't tell what's going on."

"It might be a trap. Be careful," Thatcher said.

A gunshot echoed through the mountains.

"Did you fire?" Thatcher asked.

"No," Bellman said. "They did."

"At you?"

"Negative, sir. It looks like they're shooting their own."

Thatcher furrowed his brow and shook his head. "Proceed with caution."

The team from the north reached the village a few minutes ahead of them. Several shots rang out as Thatcher moved his team closer to follow-up.

"What do you see, Bellman?" Thatcher asked.

"More of the same, sir. We're still hanging back, waiting for your command. But if they have seen us, they don't look interested in engaging us in combat. I see one man staggering around shooting everyone. Most of the combatants are writhing on the ground, begging for the lone standing gunman to shoot them. I'm not sure this is a trap."

"Mercy killing, perhaps?"

"From where I stand, that's what it looks like."

"Get your team ready. I'm still leery of these fighters. I wouldn't put it past them to stage something like this to draw us in."

"Copy that."

Thatcher moved his team from the south toward the

village. They stopped about a hundred meters from the entrance to the targeted compound, crouching behind several boulders. He gawked as he slipped around the corner to study the scene ahead through his binoculars.

"What is it, sir?" one of the other men asked.

Thatcher withdrew and rested with his back against a rock. "It looks like they've all gone mad."

"Think it's chemical?

"Could be. Masks on, everyone." Then into the radio. "Bellman, make sure your guys have their masks on."

"Already on, sir. Whatever is doing this to them looks nasty."

"Are you transmitting video back to command?"

"It's live now."

"Good. They're gonna want to analyze this."

Thatcher pulled his mask taut and checked the rest of his team's masks. They hadn't encountered any biological warfare since their latest tour began—and he didn't want to take any chances. Losing one man was one too many for Thatcher, who prided himself on a perfect return rate for his troops.

Thatcher addressed the men before they stormed the compound. "I'm not sure what we're about to encounter, but stick to your training. There could still be other armed men in the compound based on the intelligence we received."

"Bellman, are your men ready?"

"Affirmative."

"On my mark. Three, two, one—go."

The two teams descended on the compound from opposite directions at the same moment. Thatcher braced for a gunfight that never happened. The bodies of the men they were supposed to kill were already dead. Puss oozed from their faces along with what appeared to be chemical burns. Some of the men were still alive, but barely. They didn't move, instead moaning something unintelligible to Thatcher.

"Be careful around these bodies," Thatcher instructed his team. "They might be contaminated."

As Thatcher secured the wall near the front entrance to the compound, the gunman Bellman described earlier stumbled around the corner toward him. Thatcher raised up his gun. The man threw down his weapon.

"Shoot me, please," he said in a broken English accent. "I don't have the strength to do it myself."

One of the other soldiers circled back to assist Thatcher. "You need any help, sir?"

Thatcher shook his head. "No, stay with the others. I want to ask this man a few questions first. Secure the area."

"Yes, sir," the soldier said before dashing toward the center of the compound.

The man collapsed to the ground, flat on his back with his eyes closed. "Please, shoot me. You wouldn't have hesitated before."

Thatcher knelt down next to him. "What did this to you?"

"*Iblis*," the man muttered.

"The *devil*?" Thatcher asked, unsure if he'd heard the man correctly.

"In my pocket," the man said without moving.

Thatcher fished around in the man's pants pockets until he retrieved a vial with a series of numbers and Asian characters printed on it. He held it up in front of the man.

"This is what did this to you?"

The man nodded. "Now, shoot me."

Thatcher still had more questions. "Where did you get this from? Who gave this to you?"

"It was for the American soldiers, but we never got a chance to use it. A devilish trick, for sure—now will you please shoot me?"

Thatcher put the barrel of his rifle on the man's forehead. The man reached up and grabbed it, jamming it further into his head.

"Do it!"

Thatcher looked away and pulled the trigger. He'd never had any qualms about killing anyone in combat before, but this was different.

The man's body fell limp as blood pooled around his head. A fly landed on the man's nose and wandered into his mouth.

Thatcher looked at the empty vial and shoved it into his pocket. Then he froze. He heard a sound he usually welcomed but this time the sound made him uneasy.

"Fall back! Fall back!" Thatcher yelled. "Now. Bellman, get those men out now."

Thatcher looked up and had his suspicions confirmed—two drones armed with missiles were headed straight for them. And before he could say another word, one of the drones fired on their location.

He jumped over a wall along the side of the compound and took cover behind two boulders. He closed his eyes and prayed, wishing he could plug his ears from the cries of his fellow troops. Their screams seemed surreal, almost haunting, as missile after missile rained down on the compound.

The attack lasted no more than thirty seconds before the drones banked left and turned around to head back to their base, mission accomplished.

Thatcher took a deep breath and peeked out from behind the rock at the rubble before him. He rushed back into the compound to search for survivors. One by one, he found and identified his troops. He wanted to dog tag them, but he stopped. He was certain this attack was purposeful, orchestrated by someone high up within the U.S. military. And if they had the power to do this, if they knew he was alive, they would stop at nothing to find him and kill him, too.

A tear streaked down his face, stopping at the bottom of his mask. A pool quickly formed there.

He stumbled over the rock in search of any survivors until he heard a faint moan.

"Over here."

Thatcher hustled toward the direction of the voice and began shoveling chunks of rock and other shrapnel off the body of a fellow soldier. It was Bellman. He had a metal rod protruding from his stomach. His face was charred and bleeding.

"Sarge, I know I'm not going to make it, but tell my wife and kids that I love them—and find the sonofabitch who did this to us."

Thatcher nodded. "You have my word. You did good, soldier."

Bellman's body went limp, his stare vacant. Thatcher reached down and closed Bellman's eyes.

Thatcher stood up again as his tears continued to flow. But it didn't take long for them to turn from tears of sorrow to tears of rage. Whoever did this was indeed the devil. Thatcher determined to find out what was going on and expose the devil himself to honor the brave soldiers—even if it cost him his own life.

CHAPTER 10

JAMES FLYNN WATCHED as a pair of FBI agents hustled away from the INL helipad. The agent in front was a woman, who moved with precision. Behind her was a buff man in his mid-thirties. Both of them looked like they could handle themselves—though Flynn had already started wondering if he could handle her.

Flynn stood to the side as the two agents met with INL officials, who briefed them with additional information since their last conversation on the phone. After a cursory investigation, INL security ascertained that the only thing missing was Plutonium-238. It wasn't weaponized and was used primarily to power devices that required long battery life.

"This doesn't make sense," said the woman. "Why storm the castle for something so benign?"

Flynn stepped forward. "It's not benign—and Russia stopped producing Plutonium-238 several years ago. It's a hot commodity on the black market."

She cocked her head to one side. "And you're an expert on black market trade?"

Flynn shrugged. "Expert might be overstating it a little, but I've got my ear to the ground."

"Is that what they do when they let you out of the lab?"

He laughed. "Oh, I'm sorry—you must have me confused with someone who actually works here."

She stared at him, squinting as she pursed her lips. "You *do* look familiar?"

"Perhaps you've seen me on television? CNN? Fox News? *The Today Show*?"

She shook her head. "Nope. I'm pretty sure it was on an episode of *The Mole*. I think you were eliminated in the first show one season."

Banks' partner, Frank Lang, grew disinterested in their banter and continued to speak with the INL officials. Flynn was pleased to get all of Banks' attention.

He was used to being recognized in public, but not for his appearance on the now-defunct reality TV show that barely lasted longer on the air than he did on the episode. "It was a long time ago."

"That was you—wasn't it? You're some kind of writer, aren't you?" she asked.

"It's what brought me out here today. Just working on a story about conspiracy rumors regarding this facility."

She smiled and shook her head. "Well, your editors ought to love this then. Nothing stokes the embers of conspiracy like more mystery."

"It's not like that—"

She waved him off. "Whatever. We're not here to discuss anything your twenty readers living in their parents' basements will care about."

"Oh, they'll care about this deeply. I'll probably have fifty theories in a half hour once I post this to Twitter."

"That'd be fifty more than our team came up with."

"So, why don't you let me help you?"

She laughed and punched Lang in the arm. "Did you hear that, Frank? This guy is going to crowd source our investigation to get an idea of where these thieves are headed."

Flynn sighed. "I never said that."

"You didn't? I could've sworn you just said your readers would—and I quote—'have fifty theories in a half hour once I post this to Twitter.' "

"I did say that, but I never said they would give you an idea of where the thieves are headed."

"Oh? What use are they then?"

"It doesn't matter."

"And why's that?"

"Because I know where they are headed."

"Do you now? Why don't you fill us in first?"

"Look, I appreciate the banter—I really do. But you need to take me seriously when I say this—and you need to take me with you."

Banks rolled her eyes and Lang laughed.

"And why do we need your help?" Lang asked. "We've got this under control."

"Not if you don't know where the Russian thieves are taking nuclear material."

He stretched as he glared at Flynn. "Play nice before we make you a suspect."

"I can find them for you," Flynn shot back.

Banks, who had recovered from Flynn's stinging comment, rebounded. "What are you? A blood hound? You'd only slow us down."

"I'm not just a writer, you know. I used to work for the CIA."

"Your special talents never seem to end."

Lang's phone rang. "Excuse me while I take this." He stepped a few feet away.

Flynn turned back toward Banks. "So, you think I'm lying?"

"I think you're crazy—and I can't see how taking you along would help."

Lang stepped back into their conversation. "It looks like we're going to find out how he can help whether we like it or not."

She shot her partner a look. "What do you mean?"

"That was Goldman. He said we have to take Mr. Flynn with us. He said he'd prove to be a valuable asset."

Flynn smiled and winked at Banks.

"Looks like you have some high-powered friends, Mr. Flynn," she said. "And unfortunately, you're coming with us."

"I doubt you'll see it as misfortune once you end up being the heroes of this story and have commendation medals pinned on your chests."

"I'll be happy to throw you a bone with my acceptance speech," she said.

Flynn clapped his hands together two times. "Well, let's get moving. We're wasting time because they're getting away—albeit slowly."

"What are you suggesting?"

"I'm not suggesting anything. I'm telling you straight up that these men aren't rushing to get out of the country, nor are they intent on getting their Plutonium-238 across the border quickly either. It's going to be a slow chase—so settle in for a long ride."

CHAPTER 11

A FEW SELECT SENATORS serving on the defense committee were summoned for a special briefing regarding the security breach at INL. Up until the meeting, all that Senator Thor knew was what he read online and what his aides gave him from social media reports. And details were sparse.

He settled into his seat next to Senator Ryan.

"Are we all on the same page again here?" Thor asked.

Ryan cut his eyes toward the junior senator and grunted. "Are we all done with the bravado?" He stamped his cane on top of Thor's foot and ground it in for a few seconds before releasing it.

Thor refused to give the old man the satisfaction of grimacing, even though he wanted to cry.

Brian Westfield, a senior White House official, helped lead the briefing.

"I know you've all heard the initial reports about a terrorist attack on one of our facilities that handles nuclear matter. So, I wanted to let you know what we know and what we're doing to get this under control."

He took a long pull on a water bottle at the edge of the table before continuing.

"This morning just after 8:30 Mountain Time, the

Idaho National Laboratory was attacked by a gang of four people. Based off surveillance footage and the body of one of the assailants, we believe them to all be of Russian origin. At this time, we're not sure if this was an attack coordinated by the Russian government or if it was a group of independent mercenaries. Until we're able to apprehend one of the suspects, we won't be able to definitively determine that. The reason being is that Plutonium-238 is manufactured there—one of only two locations in the world that are currently processing Plutonium for purposes unrelated to nuclear power or nuclear weapons.

"We have a pair of special agents who are working in cooperation with Homeland Security and the CIA to apprehend these criminals as soon as possible. Three people were killed in their attack, including one of the criminals. At this time, we're choosing to keep the nature of their attack classified so as not to create a public scare. However, we are releasing photos of the suspects in an effort to get the public's assistance in locating them. Rest assured we are working on this."

Senator Thor raised his hand.

"Senator Thor?" Westfield said.

"Have we identified the dead assailant yet?"

"Not at this time. We should know something very soon, which will help us in apprehending the rest of the crew."

"Do we know how they entered the country?" another senator asked.

"Not yet. That's something we're still looking into."

Senator Ryan cleared his throat and stood up. "This is exactly why we need to make securing the borders a priority."

Westfield put his hands up. "Let's not make this a political issue. The security of this nation may be at risk, but we don't need to let this escalate to partisan talking points."

Ryan sat back down.

"That's exactly why we can't keep cutting the defense budget," Thor snarled in his ear. "The next time something like this happens, it could be on you."

Westfield dismissed the meeting and Thor scooped up the classified briefs and headed toward the door. He stopped before he exited and turned around to look at Ryan, who was just getting up from his seat.

Thor stared at him. "I'm watching you, Senator."

***

KYLE KRAMER STOOD over the body of his latest victim and took a picture. He then carefully checked the room for prints, more specifically for his own prints. His assignment was simple, though the execution of it was far more complicated. Kill a foreign dignitary, make it look like a suicide or natural causes, and escape without ever being noticed.

"God bless the U.S.A.," he said as he stepped over Julio Rodriguez, the Mexican governor of Chihuahua.

His phone buzzed and he concluded his search for prints. He peeked through the windows to make sure he was still alone. The apartment of his mistress wasn't watched by his security detail. He was more afraid of his wife somehow finding him by some loose-lipped guard than he was of one of the cartels. But neither was his undoing.

"Kramer," he answered.

"What are you doing?"

"Tying up some loose ends."

"I need you stateside as soon as possible."

Kramer groaned. "What is it this time?"

"A couple of FBI agents I need you to take care of for me." The man paused. "But I can find another agent if necessary."

"No, I'll do it. I was planning on being back for my kid's six-year-old birthday party."

"Some things are more important."

"God bless the U.S.A. Send me the details. I'll handle it."

He let out a long breath and went over the scene one more time. Dead mistress upstairs in the bedroom along with her husband. Dead governor on the floor in a crumpled mess after shooting himself in the head. All deaths committed with a gun that could be easily traced to one of Chihuahua's most powerful cartels that often got into public spats with the governor.

Perfect.

He smiled and closed the door behind him. He had a plane to catch—and some more people to kill.

CHAPTER 12

THE SUN HADN'T YET set over Lewiston, Idaho, when Svetlana pulled into town. She went through a drive-thru to grab a few burgers at a local dive just inside the city limits. They sat in their car and ate after she found a place to park outside a grocery store.

"American food," mumbled Niko as he picked a tomato off his burger.

"It's better than your mother's borsch," Vladimir said laughing.

A wry smile spread across Niko's face. "Why do you think I left home in such a hurry?"

Svetlana shoveled fries into her mouth and stared at the customers walking mindlessly in and out of the store.

"Do you think these people have any idea that their own government plots against them?" she asked.

"Of course they do," Niko said. "Every Hollywood movie is about an American spy who's betrayed his country."

"Do you think they care?" she said.

Vladimir chuckled to himself. "Not as long as they are fat and happy. They will have no idea what hit them."

"I hope they like borsch," Niko said.

"Shut up, you two," Svetlana said. "I'm serious. These people must be awakened from their slumber."

Niko squirted a packet of ketchup onto his burger wrapper. "We're going to take care of that. They'll be wide awake after we're through delivering the package."

Vladimir grunted. "I don't care if they're awake or asleep, just as long as I get paid."

"Just do your job, Vladdy," Svetlana said. "You'll get paid soon enough."

The trio sat in silence for a few minutes until they finished eating.

Svetlana threw the truck into drive. "Ready to get dirty, boys? We've got some more work to do."

She used a circuitous route to reach their final destination. If someone was watching, she wanted to be sure they would be looking in another direction when she crept in.

She turned the radio on and flipped between channels until a man's voice arrested her. With the wave of her hand, she silenced Niko and Vladimir's debate about the best Russian cuisine. "Listen. I think they're talking about us."

Be on the lookout for a white Ford F-150 headed east across the state and into Oregon or Washington. The three Russian terrorists are armed and dangerous—and they should not be confronted. If you see them, please alert the authorities immediately. To view pictures of the three assailants, please visit our website.

Svetlana turned the radio off and banged the steering wheel with her fist.

"Did you think this was going to be easy?" Niko asked.

"No, but I didn't expect they would be able to catch onto us so quickly," she said.

Vladimir chuckled. "Look on the bright side—we're not driving a white Ford F-150."

"That's not the point," she said before taking a deep breath. "Oh, never mind. We've got a job to do. Let's just get to it."

She threw the truck into park as they came to a stop a block away from the Port of Lewiston. Located near the convergence of the Snake and Clearwater Rivers, it served as Idaho's primary commercial port, a place almost forgotten amidst terrorism concerns. Using the Columbia River between the border of Oregon and Washington, it was possible to take a boat using the waterway lock system more than five hundred miles into the U.S. interior without first setting foot on solid ground until Idaho. It was the least conspicuous way in and the least conspicuous way out—as long as law enforcement didn't start combing the waterways. Yet despite the radio bulletin about Svetlana and her team, she still felt safe.

They waited until the sun disappeared before heading toward the docks. Svetlana decided to walk on Vladimir's arm, while Niko remained behind. Perhaps they would draw less attention as two star-crossed Russian lovers than as the trio the newscaster had warned about.

After a short walk, they arrived at one of the staging areas for the shipping containers that were loaded onto barges and floated to Portland. News of an impending strike created a flurry of activity by Idaho and eastern Washington farmers, who all preferred transporting their crops on cost-effective barges rather than semi-trucks. It also made for an easy way for the trio to transport their Plutonium-238 out of Idaho and toward its final destination—at least as far as they were concerned.

"What container are we looking for?" Vladimir asked.

"Number 235," she said. "He said it would be in the far corner of the yard." She scanned the area. "Aha—there it is." She walked stealthily toward it.

Vladimir followed her, attempting to keep a low profile—something easier said than done while holding a pair of bolt cutters.

"Do your thing," she said.

But before he could open the container, a German shepherd lunged toward him. The dog clamped down on his arm and refused to let go. Vladimir tried to shake the dog loose, but to no avail. He then grabbed the dog's tail and yanked, leading to a sharp yelp and just enough time for him to free his arm. He reached into his pocket and fished out a few treats, which he knew he needed from an earlier reconnaissance mission. Within seconds, the dog stopped.

"Rex, where are you?" came a man's voice.

Svetlana watched as his flashlight flashed in their direction. The beam grew brighter with each call out to the dog. "Rex! Rex! Where are you? For goodness sake, get back over here."

The dog put its head down and sulked back toward its owner.

"What's that in your mouth?" the man said. "You been eatin' dandelions again? I declare, you're one stubborn dog."

Svetlana held her breath as she watched the light dissipate.

"Are they gone?" Valdimir asked.

"We can come out now," she said. "Let's make this quick."

Vladimir approached the container, looked over his shoulders, and then satisfied he was in the clear, he clamped down on the bolts; they sprang open. He pulled the door open slightly and helped Svetlana ease inside, where she slid the container of Plutonium-238 into a metal box attached magnetically to the top of the shipping crate.

Once back outside, she rammed the security bolt into place and let Vladimir re-seal it.

He tossed the bolt cutters into a vacant lot covered with trash during their short walk back to get Niko.

"It's done," Svetlana announced as she leaned against the truck window.

Niko nearly dropped his laptop. "Don't sneak up on me like that again. It's not nice."

"Grab your stuff, it's time to go." She waited until he got out of the truck with his gear. "We're going to walk one at a time down to the docks. I'll go first and have a boat waiting. Once we get out on the water, they'll never be able to catch us."

Vladimir flashed a smile and nodded; Niko remained stoic.

Svetlana punched Niko in the arm. "Cheer up. It's almost over."

"This is too easy," he said. "I'm concerned."

"It's always easy when you know what you're doing and you're dealing with fools." She grinned. "I'll see you in a few minutes."

She gave him a hug and then turned around to blow him a kiss as she walked away. "See you soon," she said before disappearing from underneath the yellow glow of a street light.

CHAPTER 13

DR. WATSON INSERTED a handful of vials into the centrifuge and waited. It was nearly ten o'clock at night, and she hadn't made much progress. She glanced down at the previous report generated. Nothing but dire news. Despite Franklin's directive for her to create a vaccine for this mysterious virus, she joined forces with Mosley. Yet her hard work and persistent testing failed to halt the virus' advancement in the monkey suffering in a room just a few feet away.

"How's it coming along?"

Watson looked up to see Mosley fumbling with a petri dish as he ambled toward her. "Fine. Are you getting anywhere with this?"

"Nada." He dropped his papers on the counter next to her. "I can't make heads or tails of this."

"I hate working under all this pressure. That little monkey is going to die in there if we don't figure something out."

He nodded. "Wait until it's an outbreak stateside. You won't know what pressure is until that happens."

She shrugged. "Fortunately, that's not the case."

"It may be sooner than you think."

She looked around the room and leaned toward him. "*What* are you talking about? Is Dr. Franklin being straight with us about this virus?"

"I heard that it's part of some biological warfare developed by the North Koreans," he whispered. "I didn't catch the entire conversation, but I heard him talking with some other suit about it earlier as I crept up on his office."

"Entirely unintentional on your part, I'm sure." She smiled.

He put his hand on her back and smiled as he shook his head. "I would *never* do anything like that."

She punched him in the arm. "You can't fool me."

He laughed. "So, what have you got here?"

Watson showed him her research and the results of her testing so far. He didn't have any answers.

"I'm going to check on the monkey," he said.

She watched as he entered into the room. Mosley wasn't the most dashing man, but he was compassionate. Her lips curled upward while she observed him trying to feed the lethargic monkey a banana. The monkey refused at first, but then relented once Mosley took his gloves off.

If only he'd ask me out …

She disregarded the three strikes she'd given Mosley and thought she should look at him in a different light. Before she knew it, she began fantasizing about becoming Mrs. Dr. Mosley. It was a short-lived dream, one that shattered and snapped her back to reality when the monkey drew back and lunged at him. The monkey sunk his teeth into Mosley's wrist and clamped down. Mosley tried to shake the monkey off of him but couldn't until a few agonizing seconds passed. Instinctively, Mosley scrambled out of the room and locked the door behind him. He looked down at his arm, bleeding profusely.

He grabbed a vial and scooped some blood into it. He put a cork on it and then looked around for a bandage.

Watson rushed into the room. "Are you okay?"

He held up his hands. "Get back. I might be contagious."

"Surely, you aren't."

He offered the vial to her. "Test this. If there are any traces of the virus, let me know. I'll wait in quarantine until you give me an answer."

She wiped a tear from her eye. "It's going to be okay."

"I know it will—especially with you working on this."

Watson took the vial and began testing. Several minutes later, she returned to the quarantine area with a dour look on her face.

"It's positive," she said.

"Are you sure?"

She nodded. "How much time do you have?"

"About twenty-four hours—same as him, I suppose," he said, gesturing toward the monkey. "I know you can do it."

Watson took a deep breath, gathered her papers, and marched toward Dr. Franklin's office. She flung open his door, somewhat surprised to see that he was still there. In one cohesive motion, she slammed the folder of papers down on his desk and slowly looked up at him.

"Can I help you, Dr. Watson?" he asked.

"I want to know what the hell is going on—and I wanna know right now!"

Franklin looked up at her, his brow furrowed. "So testy? Perhaps you've had too much coffee to drink today."

She seethed, her eyes narrowing. "My anger is due to the fact that I'm being kept in the dark about the origin of this virus—and now Dr. Mosley has it. I'm afraid I won't be able to save him if you don't start talking."

He smiled and laughed. "Concerned about Dr. Mosley, are we? That's cute. But the workplace is no place for romance."

"This has got nothing to do with romance—this is about the decency of caring for another human being." She put her hands on her hips. "Isn't this the reason why you've got me working on this in the first place?"

He folded his hands and pursed his lips. "Perhaps. But it has more to do with the fact that I was assigned to oversee this case."

"By whom?"

"That's none of your concern, Dr. Watson. And if you continue this line of questioning, perhaps I need to assign this to someone else?"

"Who else is going to take this? Dr. Mosley? He's now dying in quarantine. You know I'm your top virologist—and I suggest you start treating me as such."

"I'll start treating you as such once you starting acting as such and hand me the vaccine. Otherwise, this conversation is over." He shooed her away with his hand. "Now run along before Dr. Mosley dies on your watch."

She didn't move. "I wanna know what this is really all about."

He stood up and spoke in a measured pace. "Do your job. Can I be any clearer?"

Watson collected her papers and exited Franklin's office, slamming the door behind her. She could feel the blood surging to her head, her face red with heat.

She determined to develop a cure and save Mosley—and then she was going to find out what was going on.

CHAPTER 14

THE FBI HELICOPTER TOUCHED DOWN at the Lewiston airport just after eleven o'clock. Flynn went all in with his hypothesis that this is where the terrorists were headed. Trying to make it to Canada in an eight-hour trek, not to mention dealing with customs would've been a risky proposition. Driving into the wasteland of Utah might be a possibility, but it still doesn't solve the problem of how to get the nuclear material out of the country. Heading west toward Portland or Seattle also could've worked, but their odds decreased over time. That left Lewiston.

There were other ports along the Clearwater and Columbia rivers, but this just made the most sense to him. He looked at a map of the area and concluded that the fastest way to disappear—and escape with Plutonium-238—was by water. At least, that's how he would've done it.

"You better be right about this," Banks said as they hustled to clear the helicopter.

Flynn winked and mouthed, "Trust me," to her.

Once they made it to the terminal, a black SUV was waiting for them. They wasted no time in heading toward the port. Banks climbed into the driver's side.

"If you're right about this, I'm going to question that

the CIA ever simply let you go," Lang said.

Flynn, sitting in the middle seat of the second row, leaned forward. "There's not a day goes by where they don't regret firing me—I can promise you that."

Banks shook her head and smiled. "You know, I don't know if I've ever met anyone who carried himself with such humility."

"That's funny," Flynn answered. "I haven't met anyone as humble as me either."

"There's part of me that really hopes you're wrong," she said.

"I hope it's only a tiny part, since you've staked your reputation at the bureau on this," Lang snapped. "He can call himself the greatest secret agent in the history of the world, for all I care—just as long as we catch these bastards."

"Let's don't get carried away with all the superlatives," Flynn said. "We actually have to find them first."

They drove on in silence until they reached the Port of Lewiston. The three got out and headed inside the shipping yard where the port manager met them.

"How can I help you?" the manager asked.

"We want to find out if there's been any suspicious activity around here tonight," Banks said, taking the lead.

"Suspicious how?"

"Maybe three Russians toting some nuclear material," Lang said.

The manager laughed. "Surely, you're joking, right?"

No one said anything.

"You are joking?" he asked again.

Banks shook her head. "I'm afraid we aren't."

"Well, you'll need to talk with the locker operator and

see if he noticed anything suspicious. He would've seen anything that's happened around here tonight, suspicious or otherwise."

The lock operator was engrossed in a news report about a troop of Americans who were killed in a firefight with the Taliban in a remote region of Afghanistan. He got up and introduced himself as Greg McClendon, offering to shake after he put down his doughnut and wiped his hand on his pants.

Banks and Lang simply nodded, while Flynn touched his index finger to his forehead as a salute.

McClendon withdrew his hand. "So, what can I help you with tonight? Is there some major drug bust going down? Is this gonna be on television?"

"Mr. McClendon," Banks began, "I need you to focus for me and think back about all the people you've allowed through the docks tonight, perhaps in the past few hours. Did anyone seem a little off to you?"

He squinted and cocked his head to the side. "Off in what way?"

"Like perhaps they weren't your normal clientele?" Lang responded.

"Hmmm. Nothing out of the ordinary as I recall off the top of my head." He paused. "I did have a yacht come through, which doesn't happen every day, but I know who that guy is—Frank Yankoski. He owns half of the town."

"Anyone else, Mr. McClendon? It's very important that you think hard about this," Banks said.

McClendon took a deep breath. "Well, there were these three foreigners who came through the locks on a speedboat."

"Foreigners?"

"Yeah, I don't know. They had an accent of some sort."

"And that's unusual?"

"Mostly just fishermen or rich people or their spoiled kids use this waterway. It's rare that I hear anyone with an accent."

"Did you get a look at them?"

"Not much of one. Just two men and a woman. They looked like they were out for a good time. Very serious, though. I chalked that up to being from another country. Not everyone is as easygoing as the folks around here."

"If you had to guess, what kind of accent would you say they had?" Lang queried.

"Well, I've never been to Moscow—except the city just north of here," McClendon said with a chuckle. "But if I had to guess, I'd say Russia."

"And what time was that?" Banks asked.

"Maybe about two hours or an hour and a half ago—I can't be sure."

"What kind of boat was it?" Lang asked.

"It looked like a Bayliner."

"Thank you for your time," Banks said.

"Is that all you need?" the manager asked.

"It's all for now. We've got your number and we'll call you if we need anything," Lang said.

The manager split while the three stepped outside to discuss next steps.

"It has to be them," Flynn said. "Do we have access to a boat?"

Banks shook her head.

"Well, we'll have to commandeer one," he answered.

Before she could protest or suggest an alternate action, Flynn raced toward the docks and found a speedboat. From surveying the contents of the boat, he assumed the people were into skiing—and going fast. The twin 150 horsepower engine on the back told him as much. It made for the perfect boat to pursue the terrorists.

"You can't just take this boat," Banks shouted as she ran down the dock.

"We can ask for forgiveness later—and I can assure you everyone will be far more forgiving once we've apprehended the terrorists," Flynn said.

Lang stormed down the dock and grabbed Banks by the arm. "Screw protocol. We need to catch them before they escape the country with plutonium."

Flynn prepped the boat before he hot-wired it.

"How do you know how to do that?" Banks asked.

Flynn shot her a look.

"Never mind. I don't wanna know."

Flynn backed the boat slowly out of the dock.

Without reservation, Lang put his hands on the wheel. "Here. Let me drive. I spent my summers ripping up and down rivers like this one."

"Be my guest," Flynn said.

He sat down next to Banks near the front of the boat.

"Still afraid we're barking up the wrong tree?" he asked.

"I'm more afraid that you're right."

"Afraid?"

"If terrorists can sneak into this country and steal out of here with nuclear material, I'm very afraid. How much longer until they decide not to leave the country and use it on our own people?"

"Until it happens, it's nothing more than an unfounded fear."

"That's what they said about nine-eleven."

"True—but terrorism these days seems to be about making a point, not simply terrorizing people. It's an art."

She sighed. "It sounds like you almost admire these people."

"Don't get me wrong—anyone who has the guts to storm a nuclear facility and take off with Plutonium has my respect. But I despise terrorists. They're like cockroaches though—you stomp on one and three more appear."

"It's why I chose the FBI over the CIA."

"Yet, here you are."

She smiled. "Yes, here I am."

They rode along for several hours, nothing but the hum of the outboard engines and the boat cutting through the water to fill the air. Four hours, then six. Nothing.

The dawn started to break just after 5 AM. Banks had fallen asleep, using Flynn's arm as a pillow. He nudged her.

"Hand me your binoculars," he said.

Startled, she rubbed her eyes and gave them to him. "What is it?"

"I don't know, but there's another boat up ahead."

"Fishermen?"

"Could be. But they're flying down the river pretty fast."

"Looking for their spot, perhaps?"

Flynn motioned for Lang to throttle up. "I think that's them," he said.

The boat lurched forward, shoved into another gear by Lang.

Flynn studied them closely through his binoculars. He wasn't close enough to make out many details yet, but he knew they soon would be.

"That looks like a Bayliner, the kind McClendon said they were driving," Flynn said.

"Two men and a woman?" Banks asked.

"I can't tell yet."

Flynn peered through his binoculars as they drew closer to the boat. Despite the low light, he was finally able to make out one of the men aiming a gun in their direction.

"Everybody get down," he said.

Before he could say another word, the boat broke hard to the right. Flynn glanced over at Lang, who was clutching his chest.

"I'm hit," Lang said, trying to hold the boat steady.

Flynn crept back toward Lang but got hit in the arm with a bullet. He hit the deck as he heard several more bullets pepper the water near them.

"Lang, are you okay?" Banks said as she rushed toward him.

"Stay down," Flynn yelled.

She dropped to her her hands and knees but kept crawling toward him. Noticing the blood dripping from Flynn's arm, she looked at him. "Did you get hit?"

"Yeah, but I'll be okay," he answered. "I need you to drive the boat."

"But what about Lang?" she said.

"We'll tend to him when we get a chance, but I need you to navigate the boat closer toward them. We can't let them get away."

Bullets sprayed the water around them as they neared the boat ahead. Flynn said a little prayer under his breath. Their long night was far from over.

CHAPTER 15

SERGEANT DAN THATCHER never broke protocol, except in the rare case where the life of one of his troops was in danger. He needed an evacuation—and protocol called for him to radio command for help. But this time, *his* life was in danger and the last place he wanted to contact for help was the same place that apparently tried to kill him.

He wiped the sweat off his brow while he rested with his back against a rock.

Think, Thatcher. This had to be a mistake. They wouldn't try to kill you and your troops, would they?

He couldn't make sense of anything. While his survival instincts kicked in, what he really wanted to do was sit there and cry. He'd lost some great friends—not at the hands of enemy combatants, but at the hands of the side they fought for.

Perhaps the real enemy is my own country.

He shook his head, unwilling to believe it. Somebody, somewhere messed up an order. It was a costly one, but an error nonetheless. That's what he had to believe. His own country wouldn't purposefully try to kill him—would it?

He stood up, his head spinning just as much as his mind. Still at a loss for what to do, he surveyed the smoldering rubble. The only sign of life was the birds that had started to peck away at the bodies—and a stable of pack mules.

He raced down a short incline toward the stable, which was about 200 meters east of the compound. Feverishly working to untie the mules, he assessed which two might be best suited to get him over the mountains and up the ridge toward the nearest outpost. If he hurried, he might be able to make it there before nightfall.

Thatcher gathered what supplies he could find for the journey and saddled up. He looted the bodies for munitions and weapons, just in case. But he was cautious about appearing combative with an additional mule laboring under the burden of enough firepower to wipe out a small settlement. He hoped he wouldn't have to use it.

With the threat of a return visit by the drones, he wanted to vacate the area as quickly as possible. If they had a satellite overhead, it wouldn't matter. They'd already know he survived. But if not—he still had a chance to escape.

He started his journey quickly, distancing himself from the site. But after thirty minutes of riding his mule as hard as it would go, he settled into a more comfortable pace.

As he began to ascend into the mountains, he looked back on the valley behind him. It was mostly barren and dry, but from afar it appeared serene, almost quaint. After having trekked through it, however, he knew no matter what it looked like, it was a valley of war.

With the sun starting to slip beyond the horizon, Thatcher arrived at the outpost. With little more than tents and a couple of permanent structures, the area looked more like a temporary campsite than a permanent dwelling. Goats roamed freely in the common areas, searching for anything they could eat. Sheep huddled together inside makeshift fences. The people cooked evening meals over open fires— a chore from which they stopped to inspect the stranger invading their settlement.

Thatcher started to set up camp away from the other villagers. After he hoisted his tent, one of the men approached him with a bowl of soup. Thatcher took it and thanked the man with a kind gesture. He had no idea if it translated, but these people spoke a language he'd never heard. Without any other way to communicate, he smiled and bowed often, trying to remain humble that they might allow him into their encampment, if only for a night.

He settled into his sleeping bag and stared at the stars. He wanted to sleep, but didn't know if he could trust the people. Inside his bag, he gripped a knife. After all that had happened in the past twelve hours, he couldn't trust *anyone*— not even his own government.

Around 1 AM, Thatcher heard someone rummaging around near one of his mules. He slipped up on the man, who spun around and slashed toward Thatcher with a knife. Thatcher withdrew and avoided any contact before striking the man on his arm. The man lunged toward him again, but Thatcher darted to the side and jabbed the man again, this time in his leg. It was enough to make the man retreat, hobbling as he went.

The next morning, he awoke to a surprising sound— a small single-engine airplane buzzing the community. He sprang to his feet and went outside his tent in time to watch it fly off.

A few meters away, he noticed the man who'd delivered him soup staring up in the sky with a wide grin on his face.

"Will that airplane come back?" Thatcher asked.

The man shrugged and furrowed his brow.

Thatcher asked again, this time with hand gestures that seemed to communicate the gist of his question.

"Ah," the man said before continuing on in his native tongue. He gestured back what Thatcher took to mean that the airplane would return later.

Thatcher broke camp and waited and waited. He passed the time watching the young boys play a game with a stick and some rocks. After intensely observing them for a few minutes, he asked if he could play. Before he knew it, he was running around like a kid and laughing. It provided a brief respite from the pain he felt every waking moment since he mounted his mule.

When Thatcher heard the familiar buzz of the airplane, he dropped his stick and ran toward what appeared to be a makeshift landing strip. The plane touched down and rolled over toward a small wooden shed with a windsock attached to the top of it.

The pilot walked toward the villagers, speaking to them in their native language. But he froze when he saw the soldier.

"Lost your way, soldier?" the pilot asked.

Thatcher broke into a grin at the sound of the man's voice. An American pilot. "Boy, am I glad to see you."

The pilot looked at him cautiously. "And why's that?"

"I need a ride outta here."

"This is not a military transport vehicle," the pilot said. "We only fly humanitarian missions. I'm sure someone else could come and pick you up."

Thatcher leaned in closer. "What's your name?"

"Jason Roberts. And you are?"

"Staff Sgt. Thatcher. Now, Jason, I really need your help."

"How come you're out here by yourself."

"It's a long story—but the short version is that American drones fired on our position and killed everyone in our squad except for me."

Roberts scratched his neck and adjusted his cap. "That doesn't sound right."

"Exactly. So right now, I'm trying to get somewhere safe so I can figure out what's going on."

"Tomorrow's load is light. I might be able to get you tomorrow. But I'm all full today."

Thatcher shook his head. "That won't work. Last night a guy almost stabbed me."

"I can put in a good word for you with the people—but I can't make any guarantees they won't try to do the same again tonight."

"Can't you make another trip back?"

"These are three-hour trips one way—and we don't fly at night. There's no way I'd be back in time even if I got permission. Just be ready tomorrow."

Thatcher nodded. "Okay, if that's the best you can do."

Roberts slapped him on the arm. "I'll put in a good word for you with the leader—but in the meantime, why don't you help me load this plane. I sure could use those muscles of yours."

Thatcher helped stuff the small Cessna with goods the people had made, which Roberts said he helped transport to other countries where they'd be sold at a substantial markup. Wool hats hand-woven, leather sandals, purses and handbags—all packed into scores of boxes.

"Do you come out here often?" Thatcher asked.

"Once every two weeks," Roberts said. "Sometimes more, if necessary."

Before Thatcher could hoist the next box to Roberts inside the plane, chaotic yelling arrested their attention. They both looked in the direction of the noise where several people were running toward the plane, waving their arms.

Roberts began to converse with them and within seconds, an elderly woman was excitedly talking and pointing toward a younger man staggering toward the plane.

"What is it?" Thatcher asked.

"Start unloading the plane. We've got an emergency."

Thatcher started ripping off the boxes to create space in the plane, while Roberts gathered more information. Roberts pulled out a stretcher from the back of the plane and he helped some of the locals put the man on it.

When Thatcher came over to help lift the injured man into the plane, the man's eyes widened. He started yelling something at Roberts.

Roberts looked at Thatcher. "It seems like they're more afraid of you than you are of them." He pointed at the man's wounds. "Is this your doing?"

"I was only defending myself."

"Well, it's your lucky day."

Thatcher's brow furrowed. "What do you mean?"

"This is a new humanitarian mission. I'll come back tomorrow and get their things, but this man is in critical need of medical care. And now I'll have room for one more passenger."

"Are you serious?" Thatcher said.

"Let's get you somewhere safe, soldier."

CHAPTER 16

"GET ME CLOSER!" Flynn said over the hum of the engines and the relentless wind beating against them. He crouched low and positioned himself near the edge of the boat. Another smattering of bullets hit near them and he pushed Banks' head down.

"What do you think you're going to do?" she asked.

"Just get me close enough and keep it steady. Then peel away."

"You're going to jump into their boat?"

"Do you have any other ideas?"

Flynn watched one of the men aboard the other boat begin to reload his gun.

"If we're gonna do this, we have to do it now. Gun it!"

Banks pushed the throttle forward and the boat's nose tilted upward.

"Good work. We're almost there."

Flynn watched as the man located another clip and prepared to jam it into the gun.

Ten meters, five meters.

"Steady," Flynn said.

The boat held steady for three more seconds, just enough time for Flynn to leap into the other boat and tackle the gunmen. With both men holding on to the gun, Flynn jerked it upward and held down the trigger, harmlessly emptying the clip. The man then tightened his grip on the gun and ripped it away from Flynn. He used it as a battering ram, trying to jab Flynn in the head with it.

Flynn danced out of the way of the oncoming behemoth, unholstering his gun and shooting him twice in the back before the man fell headlong into the water.

And then there were two.

Flynn eyed the remaining assailants—a familiar-looking woman driving the boat and another man in the back of the boat. He'd never seen the man before, who acted cagey. Flynn decided to take care of him first as the woman didn't seem interested in engaging in a fight just yet.

For a second, Flynn looked toward Banks to see where she was. That was all the time the man in the back of the boat needed to gain the upper hand, using an oar to smack Flynn's arm and knock the gun out of his hand. The gun splashed into the water while Flynn tried to regain his edge. He rushed toward the man, who went low and almost flipped Flynn out of the boat. Flynn slid down the back and nearly into the water. Clinging to the inside, he clawed his way back in as the man bashed his fingers with the oar.

Flynn took another pass at the man again, this time grabbing him as he went by and pulling him to the ground. Then the man pulled a knife out of his sock and tried to stab Flynn.

As this was happening, the woman trained her gun on Flynn. She went to pull the trigger when the boat lurched to the side. She looked up to see Banks driving her boat hard into hers. And it was enough of a distraction to help Flynn gain control of the knife and stab the man. He shoved the man's body out of the way and walked toward the woman.

"Svetlana?" Flynn said.

"James?" she answered.

"It doesn't have to end like this," Flynn said.

"True. You can jump in the water now so I don't have to kill you in front of your lady friend over there." Svetlana waved at Banks and continued down the river at top speed.

"That's not what I mean," he said.

"Of course it isn't, but those are your options at this point. Let me go and live or try to capture me and die. One of those things is going to happen."

"I beg to differ," he said.

"Of course you beg—like you did that night in Prague."

"If things were different—"

"But they're not."

"Why are you stealing Plutonium-238? Who hired you? What is it for?"

"I don't want to kill you, James."

"I'm not going to ask again."

"Good," she said with a laugh. "This is getting old fast. Can't we just move on to the place where you jump in the water and I speed away and you tell the American government that I outsmarted you—or will your ego not let you do that? I always told you that your ego would be the death of you."

"Not today it won't." He grabbed the wheel and yanked it hard right, forcing the boat into a spin.

Svetlana reached underneath the wheel and pulled out a gun. Before she could get a shot off, Flynn ripped it from her hand and put a knife to her throat as he steadied the boat and powered down the throttle. The boat rocked in its own wake as he pressed the knife closer to her throat.

"You know I will never betray my country," she said.

"I'm not so sure this is about your country, is it?"

She said nothing and swallowed hard.

"Who hired you, Svetlana?"

Nothing.

"Tell me now!"

She reached for his knife and rammed it into her own throat.

"Svetlana! What have you done?"

Gasping for air and coughing up blood, she looked up at him and grinned. In a whisper, she said again, "I'll never betray my country."

Her body went limp.

Flynn began pillaging the boat, looking for the Plutonium-238 canister. He searched through the pockets of the dead man at the back of the boat and found one interesting item. After a few minutes of searching, he looked up to see Banks edging her boat closer to them.

"Is everything under control now?" she asked.

He shook his head. "They're all dead—and no one would say anything."

Banks looked at Lang. "We need to get Lang to a doctor quick. He's not doing so well and he might bleed out if we don't hurry."

"Go on without me," Flynn said. "I'll deal with this mess and see if I can find the Plutonium."

"You don't see it?"

"No. And I don't think it's here either. Perhaps they

hid it somewhere else in the boat, but we'll need to get a team out here to verify it one way or another."

"Where is it then?"

Flynn held up a few short metal pieces. "Do you know what these are?"

She shook her head.

"Bolt seals for shipping containers."

"You think they hid it at the port in a container?"

"That's my working theory, but I don't want to give up on this boat yet."

Banks nodded. "Okay, let me get him some medical attention and I'll be back soon." She let out a long breath and revved up the boat's engine. She looked back at Lang. "Hold on tight, partner. We're going to get you some help."

As she was turning around to look toward the front of the boat, Lang's chest exploded.

"What the —"

Flynn tackled her into the water. When they came up for air, their heads barely bobbed above the surface. Hidden from plain sight between the two boats, she stared at him, her brow furrowed.

"What just happened?" she asked.

"Someone's trying to kill us."

"I thought we already neutralized the three assailants who escaped from INL."

Flynn smiled. "We did." He paused. "Apparently they're not the only ones who want us dead."

"Who even knew we were out here?"

Flynn shook his head. "The number of people who know about our mission is probably far more than you imagined. But the number of people who could actually locate us? That's a much smaller number. Someone doesn't want us to find that Plutonium-238."

"Or find out who's behind it," she added.

"Unfortunately for whoever that person is, we're going to solve both of those burning questions."

She nodded resolutely. "Let's do this."

"How good of a swimmer are you?"

"First in my class at Quanaco."

"Stay underwater until we reach the opposite bank. There's a cove we can duck into there and we can go and get some help. But don't come up under any circumstances until we've reached the other side. Whoever shot Lang is still out there, and I guarantee you he's waiting for us. So, let's go. We don't have much time."

Flynn and Banks dove down into the cold river water and swam furiously, struggling against the current. It took them about three minutes to reach the other side and disappear into the forest.

They both turned to look back at the boats when an explosion sent shockwaves along the water and the vessels splintered across the river.

Flynn tugged on Banks' arm. "Come on. We don't have much time."

***

KYLE KRAMER WHISTLED WHILE HE packed up his weapons. He paused and smiled as he looked out at the boat still in flames, shrapnel littering the river. After taking another brief moment to admire his work, he finished packing and called his employer.

"It's all taken care of," Kramer said.

"Are you sure?"

"Unless they could survive a missile launcher that obliterated their boat from two hundred yards away, I'm sure."

"Good to know you were being discreet."

"No one was around."

"They soon will be."

"That's why I'm packed up and about to disappear."

"Okay. Good work. I'll be in touch when we need you again. The funds should deposit in your account within the hour."

"One more thing," Kramer said.

"What's that?"

"There were three people in the boat, not two. I took care of all them, but they had some help."

"Interesting. Thanks for letting me know."

"Thank you for your business." Kramer hung up and collected the last of his belongings. He stood up and took one final look at the havoc he wreaked—and the scene of his latest victims.

He closed his eyes, took in a deep breath, and grinned.

I love the smell of pine trees and the warm sun on my face.

Then he opened his eyes, horrified at what he saw— his two victims scurrying up the riverbank and disappearing into the woods.

His work wasn't finished yet.

CHAPTER 17

SENATOR THOR SAT ON one end of a bench in the national mall, admiring the early Tuesday morning reflection in the water. It appeared so calm on the surface, much like him—though he doubted the water below was churning half as fiercely as his stomach was. He'd become deft at remaining cool and collected in certain situations. His passion drove him, but it could also become a liability if he didn't control it.

At half past eight, a man settled onto the opposite end of Thor's bench. The protocol for such meetings remained awkward, yet Thor preferred it to secretive meetings behind closed doors. He reasoned that a public appearance always reduced the opportunity for someone to accuse him of darker deeds. However, he was certain someone would consider what he was doing to be on the shadier side of political activities. But he convinced himself that as long as his conscience was clear, it didn't matter what others thought. Besides, what he was doing was for the good of the country.

"Did you do what I asked?" Thor said, barely opening his mouth.

The man opened up a magazine and pretended to read as he flipped the pages. "Mmm, hmmm."

"Did you find anything?"

"Nothing of consequence yet."

"Keep trying—and keep me posted. This thing is starting to get out of hand."

"Would you like for us to move into phase two of the operation?"

"Not yet. We still have quite a bit of work to do before we can go there."

"The General is getting antsy."

"Just tell him to relax and that everything is being handled. We'll have some answers soon."

The man flipped some more pages and kept his head down as he talked. "Good. I'm not sure how much longer he can hold it in."

"You must not let him talk. Once he does, the entire operation is blown and we'll all be exposed."

"I can assure you that won't happen."

"I appreciate your assurances, but they mean nothing. I've learned that if someone is determined enough to talk, they will—and there's nothing you can do about it."

The man rubbed his forehead with his right hand before flipping some more pages. "I've always found cutting someone's tongue out is a very effective way to keep them silent."

"Look, I don't want any of that kind of behavior. Let's use persuasive means that don't include threats, intimidation, or mutilation."

"I guess I can't make any guarantees then."

Thor took a deep breath. "I'm okay with that as long as you stay on top of things. We're going to be ready to move to phase two very soon, but we need the General on board if that's going to happen. Otherwise, everything becomes too risky."

Silence lingered for a few minutes before Thor spoke again.

"I have another meeting later this week, if not sooner. I should know more by then."

The man closed his magazine, slid it into his briefcase and stood up to leave. "Have a good day, sir." He nodded and tipped his bowler cap.

Thor clasped his hands together as he leaned forward and stared back at the water again. He felt his stomach churning. They were almost there—as long as everyone could hold it together.

CHAPTER 18

DR. MELISSA WATSON RUBBED her eyes and sighed. The numbers on the printout in front of her delivered more bad news. Nothing was working. She'd tried numerous approaches to coming up with an antidote that worked, but none of them seemed to have any effect on the infected monkeys. She even considered forgoing the trial on the monkeys and testing one of the sample antidotes on Dr. Mosley—the one she figured to have the best chance of clearing the virus. But she couldn't bring herself to do it.

What if something happened to him? She'd never forgive herself if she expedited his death when she had a chance to save him. But time was vanishing more quickly than her ideas.

She took a break and peered at him in the quarantine chamber.

"How are you holding up?" she asked through the speaker.

He forced a smile. "I'm still alive."

"I hope to keep you that way."

"Well, can you hurry it up? My cellmate here is struggling."

Watson watched one of the monkeys on the floor. The

primate was in a lethargic state, grunting and moaning.

Mosley shook his head. "I don't want to suffer like he is."

She took a deep breath. "Just hang in there. I think I might have an idea."

Watson rushed back to her workstation and worked busily for the next half hour. Observing the monkey on the floor gave her an idea. It wasn't much of one, but it was better than banging her head against the wall.

The phone near her workstation buzzed. She ignored it, continuing to create a sample antidote and carefully recording all her steps. The phone buzzed again, this time using the intercom system.

"Stop ignoring me," Dr. Franklin said. "I know you're down there, Dr. Watson. If you had saved Dr. Mosley by now, you would've both surely been in my office. But as it stands, all I can assume is that you've done nothing but fail."

"I'm still working, sir. When I know something, you'll know something." She slapped the button on the phone to end the call and muttered to herself. "I swear, once this is over, I'm putting together my resume and getting out of here."

After a few more minutes, Watson was satisfied with her antidote. She smiled as she swirled it around in a test tube. "Make me proud," she said.

She drew some of the liquid into a syringe and suited up in her hazmat suit. Once she went through the entry chamber, she entered the quarantine room.

Mosley stood up and rushed toward her. "Do you have something?"

"I think so. But I wanted to try it out on this monkey first. I've got enough for both of you if this works."

He put his arm on hers. She looked at him and smiled.

"Don't worry," she said. "I'm going to save you."

Watson plunged the needle into the monkey's arm and emptied the contents into his body—and waited.

In the initial moments after the antidote was administered, the monkey lay motionless on the floor. But after a few seconds, he began to writhe around. He screamed and screeched, flailing his arms and kicking his legs. Then the primate became aggressive. He lunged toward Mosley and jumped onto his back, beating him with both his fists. Mosley flung the monkey to the ground and backed away. But the monkey stood up and resumed his assault, racing back toward him and latching onto his leg. With his teeth showing, the monkey hissed at him before attempting to bite him. Mosley beat the monkey in the head with his fist, but it didn't prevent the monkey from taking a bite out of his upper thigh. Mosley screamed and fell to the floor. The monkey climbed on top of him, dancing on his chest.

Watson watched terrified. She wanted to help, but she didn't want to attract attention to herself. If the monkey could overpower and knock down Mosley, what could it do to her? She wasn't interested in answering that question.

The monkey began pounding on Mosley's chest with his fists until he stopped almost as soon as he started. His arms dropped to his side before he rolled over and fell onto the floor. Dazed, Mosley scooted away from the animal.

Watson's breathing turned shallow as she reached to check the monkey's pulse. She needed to know if the antidote worked or not—and if her test subject was still alive. She tried to get a pulse. Nothing.

"He's dead," she said, looking in Mosley's direction—

but he wasn't there.

Where'd he go?

She stood up and spun around in time to see Mosley flying toward her with a syringe.

"What are you doing?" she asked, fighting him off.

He didn't answer until he worked off part of her hazmat helmet and sunk the needle into her neck. "Properly motivating you."

Her mouth dropped as she glared at him. "What did you do?"

"Now, maybe you'll work a little harder since *your* life depends on it."

Watson staggered out of the quarantine unit and locked the door behind her.

"There's no use keeping me in here," he yelled. "You're the one contaminating the rest of the lab now."

She turned and shot him a nasty look before proceeding with the decontamination process in the entry chamber. She took off her suit and proceeded into her office.

She didn't know what was worse—Mosley's betrayal or the fact that she now carried a virus that would kill her soon enough. Yet she couldn't separate the two. They were intertwined, both causing her great distress when she needed to be as clear-minded and focused as she'd ever been.

Watson looked at her watch: 10 A.M. She set a countdown on her phone for twenty-four hours. If she didn't find a antidote, it was all the time in the world she had left.

CHAPTER 19

WHEN THEIR PLANE TOUCHED DOWN at Washington National just after four o'clock, Flynn and Banks rushed to the parking lot to get Banks' car and try to beat the rush-hour traffic. It was a lesson in futility. They had a better chance of capturing every single member of Al-Qaeda than they did of escaping the clutches of the Beltway.

During their commute to Langley to debrief with Osborne, Flynn suggested Banks check in with her superiors.

"If anything, find out if there's been any update while we were in the air," he said.

"Fine. I'm sorry if I'm a little jumpy right now. It's just that *someone* had to tell that sniper that we were there. And there's no way he was part of that team."

"I think you're right. We need to be careful, but we need to play along. If we act suspicious to the wrong people, we may seal our own fate soon enough."

Banks picked up the phone and dialed her supervisor, Carl Jacobs. She put the call on speaker.

"How was your flight?" Jacobs asked.

"As well as expected. I was just calling to check in. We're back in D.C."

"Good." Jacobs paused. "My condolences on your

partner. He was a good man."

"He was—and I want to nail these bastards to honor his memory."

"Don't worry. We will."

"Any new developments?"

"Well, your hunch was right."

"Oh? Which one?"

"The one about the Plutonium-238 being on one of the shipping containers at the Lewiston Port."

Flynn shot her a look and furrowed his brow. He mouthed "Really?" to her. She put her head down sheepishly and refused to look at him.

"I'm glad you trusted me," she said.

"It's been paying off for me for a while now."

"So all of the nuclear matter is accounted for?"

"Thanks to you, it is."

"That's a relief. Anything else happen while we were in the air?"

"Nothing major, but I would like to see you in here tomorrow for a debriefing. We've got a few things to discuss."

"Like what?"

"Oh, nothing to worry about. Just standard protocol."

"Okay, I'll see you in the morning." She hung up and glanced at Flynn. "What do you think that's going to be about?"

He shook his head. "I don't know, but I wouldn't tell him too much. I think you're right about something going on. This whole thing doesn't sit well with me either."

"Do you trust your contact at the CIA?" she asked.

"Implicitly." Flynn paused. "They might have kicked me out for exposing them a while back, but Osborne has never failed me. I trust him with my life—and have several times."

Once they arrived at Langley, Banks accompanied Flynn to Todd Osborne's office.

Osborne gestured for them to sit down while he closed the door behind them.

"Good work, Flynn," Osborne said. "You too, Special Agent Banks."

She smiled and nodded.

Osborne leaned on his desk and scanned both of them with his eyes. "So, tell me about this sniper who tried to take you both out."

"I couldn't tell much at the time since he was shooting at us almost the entire time, but it was like he knew we were coming."

"What do you mean?"

Banks leaned forward. "What he means is that it's unlikely that this team positioned a sniper up on the river bank to shoot at anyone who might have been trying to kill them once they passed. For a team that seemed to be one step ahead of us most of the time, this seemed like a stretch."

Osborne stroked his chin. "I see. And this is how you feel too, Flynn?"

Flynn nodded. "It would've taken some incredible luck for one of their own guys to be doing—" He paused and stared out the window.

"What is it?" Banks asked.

Flynn spun around. "They certainly wouldn't have blown up the boat if they knew what was in it though. So either it *was* one of their guys *or* it was someone else entirely different who had no knowledge of what was going on."

"Or it was both," Osborne added.

"Both?"

Osborne nodded. "Perhaps someone knew what they were doing and what you were doing—and was willing to go to great lengths to cover it up so nobody found out the truth."

"It's working so far," Banks said.

"Yes, but we're still alive—for the time being. And we still have a chance to find out who was behind this."

Osborne shook his head. "But it just doesn't make sense if it wasn't one of their team members. Why would anyone else want to kill you—especially someone who might have had knowledge of your location and objective?"

"That's a question I've asked myself a hundred times if I've asked it once," Flynn quipped.

"That's why I don't prefer the field," Osborne said.

"Well, I think this is some kind of an inside job," Flynn said. "And no one is safe if that's the case."

Osborne threw up his hands. "I don't know. I just can't make heads or tails of this one yet. All I know is that something isn't right."

"Thanks, Captain Obvious. Would you also like to tell us how summers are generally hot and winters are usually rather cold?"

"Knock it off, wise guy. You know what I mean. It feels like you've been compromised in a way."

Flynn pointed at himself then Banks. "Me or her?"

"Her, but you're involved now."

"Just keep my name out of any official reports," Flynn said, glancing at Osborne then Banks. "Both of you. Understand?"

"They both nodded. You'll remain nameless in my reports, though I can't help but wonder if the sniper doesn't already know who you are—or at least that you're involved. He shot an FBI agent first."

"Low-hanging fruit," Flynn said.

Osborne furrowed his brow. "Come again?"

"Lang was almost dead, so he took him out and made sure that he wasn't going to survive. Banks was likely next—but I doubt he was counting on me."

Banks looked at Flynn. "You're the only one I can count on right now."

"Ditto. And we need to stick together if we're going to figure out what's going on."

Osborne threw his hands in the air. "What about me? Am I chop liver?"

Flynn laughed. "No, but you're the man with no answers right now. Keep digging and let us know what you find."

Osborne opened the door and gestured for them to exit. "I'll keep you posted once I find out anything else."

Just as Banks was about to step out into the hallway, several agents ran past her. "What's that all about? Is that how people *walk* down the hall at Langley?"

Osborne chuckled. "Oh, everyone's in a hurry today. Some soldier survived the Taliban attack the other day and went on television about an hour ago telling everyone that the U.S. government was behind the attack that destroyed his squad. He was the lone survivor."

"Sounds intense," Flynn said.

"It is—pretty intense accusation," Osborne said, waving his hand. "I'll believe it when I see it."

CHAPTER 20

KYLE KRAMER SAT IN HIS CAR a half a block from Jennifer Banks' condo in downtown D.C. The sun sparkled just above the trees, a last gasp before it disappeared until morning. He'd been there a half hour and no sign of Banks or the man he'd seen escaping with her down the river earlier that morning on the other side of the country.

"Ah, modern travel, isn't it great?" he said to himself.

He pretended to read *The Washington Post* but kept his eyes trained just above the top of the paper on the parking garage for her building. Still nothing.

Out of the corner of his eye, he noticed an elderly woman hobbling down the street with a load of groceries. She tripped on a manhole cover on the sidewalk and tumbled to the ground. He jumped out of his car and helped her up, gathering all of her groceries quickly and stuffing them back into her sacks.

"Here you go, Miss," he said once he handed the last bag to her.

She smiled at him. "Why, that's just so kind of you," she said. "And some people think there aren't any decent people left in this world." She reached up and pinched his cheek. "You keep proving them wrong." She grabbed her walker and flashed another smile at him before turning and shuffling down the street.

He hustled back to his car and refocused his attention on the parking garage. Nobody had gone in that looked remotely like his target.

His phone buzzed and he glanced down at the number. He took a deep breath and answered it.

"Yeah."

"I thought you said you took care of those two FBI agents," the man said.

"I thought I did, too."

"Well, you didn't."

"I know. I'm in D.C. right now, camped outside Banks' parking garage."

"Do you even know what she drives?"

"That'd be helpful."

"A black two-door Toyota Camry model from two years ago. I'll text you the license plate number."

"Great."

"But there's another problem."

Kramer took another deep breath and let it out. "Oh?"

"Yeah, she's working with another guy. Did you see him?"

"I saw someone with her. He didn't seem like much of a threat."

"Well, appearances can be deceiving. And besides, he obviously survived the best you threw at him already, didn't he?"

Kramer seethed at the insinuation that someone outsmarted him. "Who is he?"

"James Flynn, former CIA operative."

Kramer chuckled. "The same conspiracy theorist who's on television all the time?"

"Don't take him lightly. He's trained and he's dangerous."

"You want me to take him out, too?"

"I'll double your fee if you do."

"Double? Are you serious?"

"I don't joke about anything. Take him out." The man paused a beat. "But it's got to seem like a viable accident. Nothing suspicious. He's got a following that could create pressure for the feds to investigate if it looks wonky."

"And the girl?"

"Take her out by any means necessary. I don't care. Just get her out of the picture."

"I'll handle it."

"You better handle it—and it better be handled more swiftly and completely than you handled things on the Columbia River."

Kramer would've punched the man in the face if he were standing right in front of him. He was a professional—and everyone had an off day, even an expert like himself. But it wasn't a battle he intended to lose. "You have nothing to worry about."

"And Kramer?"

"Yes?"

"Don't underestimate Flynn. He might be a journalist, but he's got skills. He's far more resourceful than you might think."

"Understood. You have nothing to worry about."

"I know I don't." The man drew a deep breath, one that Kramer could hear. "If you don't, I'll send someone after you."

Kramer hung up and slammed his phone into the passenger's seat. He wanted to scream. He wanted to kill someone.

His phone buzzed and he glanced at the text message containing Banks' license plate.

Then he looked up, just in time to see a black two-door Camry pull into the parking deck with Banks at the helm—and another man in the passenger seat.

Well, isn't this my lucky day.

He laughed and popped his trunk.

CHAPTER 21

DR. WATSON GLANCED at her watch and returned to looking at the slide on her microscope. Hours seemed to tick past like seconds. She felt weak and shaky. Despite the fact that she took ten minutes to devour a takeout pizza she'd ordered and had a security guard leave outside her door, she was still famished—but she couldn't justify eating more. Some things were more important, such as her life.

She heard some faint banging coming from the quarantine ward. She stopped what she was doing and rushed to see what the commotion was all about.

It was Dr. Mosley.

"Let's go, Melissa," he said. "I don't have all day, much less all night."

She drew a deep breath and waved him off and started to walk away. "I'm doing the best I can."

"It isn't good enough."

She stopped. "Perhaps you could give me some suggestions, maybe your final words."

"We're in this together," he said. "Just use your head." He collapsed to the floor, sweat beading up on his forehead, blood oozing from his nose. Then he screamed.

"What's wrong?" she asked, pressing her face to the glass.

"Everything. I think my organs are starting to shut down."

Organs?

Watson disappeared, dashing back to her workstation. His comment gave her an idea. She scurried around the lab to prepare another antidote—potential antidote—one she hoped would work this time.

With just two hours left to save Mosley, Watson had only two more infected monkeys to work with. After that, she was on her own. She might even have to start testing on Mosley, but she hoped to avoid reaching such a desperate place.

Though she knew she likely had the virus based off Mosley's injection, she still dressed up in a hazmat suit to enter the quarantine chamber.

He rolled his eyes. "Still pretending, are we?"

She narrowed her eyes. "Just hold him down," she said, gesturing toward the monkey.

Mosley grabbed the monkey while she administered the antidote. She retreated to the other side of the quarantine chamber and watched through the glass. The monkey seemed to become more alert after a few minutes before he convulsed and shook—and died.

"Come on," Mosley screamed as he slammed the glass. "You can do better than this."

She swallowed hard and looked at the clock. Only one more monkey left—and only ninety minutes left for Mosley.

CHAPTER 22

SENATOR THOR COULDN'T WAIT to talk with Staff Sgt. Dan Thatcher as soon as he saw his face plastered across the television screen. Cable news programming went crazy with the story. Everyone from his mother to his aunt to his second grade teacher was being interviewed as a character witness to Thatcher's alleged account. Psychologists and therapists broke down his recorded interview with a German television station to determine if he was lying—and the conclusions were split. No matter what side anyone took, there were holes, gaping holes to his story. Nothing made sense.

But Thor knew better.

"Get me Staff Sgt. Thatcher on the phone," he said to one of his aides as he snapped his fingers. "Like yesterday."

The aide stared at him, mouth agape. "Really? You think he'll talk to you?"

"I know he will. Now get moving."

In a matter of minutes, Thatcher answered the phone. "Senator Thor?"

"Yes, Staff Sgt. Thatcher. It's me. How are you?"

"All things considered, I'm alive."

"That's it? You're just alive."

"Sir, I don't mean you any disrespect, but I have no

idea who I can trust anymore. I didn't even want to take your call, but I was curious as to why you'd be calling. I couldn't resist."

"Curiosity killed the cat, right?"

"I'm hoping it doesn't kill me."

Thor laughed. "No, no, Sergeant. It's not going to kill you." He paused. "As long as you tell me the truth."

"If you've been watching these news reports, you've heard the truth already. I've got nothing to hide."

"Oh, I think there's more to the story than what you've said. You attack a Taliban outpost based on intel, and as you move in a U.S. drone attack wipes out the entire compound, including your troops."

"That's it."

"I'm not buying it. There's more to your story than that. I can see it in your eyes."

"Senator, I mean you no disrespect, but I don't know if you're cleared to hear any more."

"I've got top-security clearance and serve on the defense committee, but that's irrelevant at this point. Someone was trying to kill you—and you want to know who."

"Exactly."

"And so do I." Thor took a deep breath. "So, tell me what really happened."

"I already have, sir. If you've seen the news reports, you've heard all there is to hear. We were in a firefight with the Taliban in the mountains of northeastern Afghanistan when a pair of U.S. drones honed in on our position and annihilated us. I was the only survivor—and I'll be damned if I don't know why."

"Are you sure it was U.S. drones?"

"As sure as I am standing here."

"Hmmm. Well, that does sound strange. And I understand your reason for breaking protocol. I'd be suspicious myself if something like that happened to me."

"I wasn't just breaking protocol, sir. I was saving my life."

"Well, I'd be careful if I were you. If you think breaking protocol and sharing your story to a global audience is going to save you, I'd suggest that you rethink what you're doing. If someone wants you dead, they're not going to care about what anyone thinks—they simply want you dead. And they're going to stop at nothing to ensure that happens."

"Are you threatening me, senator?"

"On the contrary—I'm warning you to be on the lookout. Be vigilant for anything out of the ordinary." Thor went silent and waited for a moment before he resumed speaking. "But I know there's more to your story. Drones wouldn't just hunt you down for no apparent reason. I'm not sure what it is that you're not telling me, but I'm smart enough to know when someone is withholding information." Thor broke into a chuckle. "Hell, I work on Capitol Hill with a bunch of professional liars."

"You know everything I know, sir."

"Suit yourself. I can't protect you if you don't tell me the entire truth. But I suppose you've already been told that your commanding officer was lost today."

"What? How?"

"A roadside IED. He was on a routine sweep and he and his entire company were killed by insurgents in the ensuing firefight."

"I had no idea."

"Of course you didn't, Sergeant. You were too concerned with making sure the world heard *your* story. But there's more to this than you think. So, if you change your mind, it's easy to find me."

Thor hung up and stared out his window at the twinkling lights of D.C. The young sergeant had undoubtedly been through a lot, but he knew there was more to his story—and he intended to find out everything, no matter what it took.

***

THATCHER STARED AT THE PHONE and slumped into the chair at the U.S. consulate in Stuttgart. He contemplated remaining at the television station and catching a commercial flight home, but he didn't want to appear too combative. Despite his growing cynicism toward the U.S. military, he figured he could find at least one or two allies. Perhaps Senator Thor was one of them; perhaps he wasn't. At this point, he couldn't be sure of anything. He didn't even know if he believed Senator Thor when he said that his commanding officer had died.

When Thatcher hatched his plan to tell the world—mostly for selfish survival reasons—he figured upon Stuttgart. It was one of Germany's large metropolitan areas and had a U.S. base. However, he didn't think he'd leave so soon, but the military police at the door suggested otherwise.

"You have a flight to catch, Sergeant," one of the officers said. "It's time to go."

Thatcher stood up and put his hands on his hips. He

surveyed the office one more time before grabbing his coat and following the officer.

Thirty minutes later, Thatcher climbed the steps of a C-130 headed across the Atlantic for the U.S. The pilot offered his hand as he stepped aboard.

"Ready to go home?" the pilot asked.

Thatcher nodded. "You have no idea."

The pilot laughed. "Buckle up. It should be a rather uneventful flight—especially since there's no in-flight entertainment."

Thatcher forced a smile. "I'm sure I'll be fine."

"Just make sure you buckle in just in case we face some turbulence."

"You got it."

Thatcher settled into his seat and snapped the five-part harness into place. He gave the captain a thumbs-up signal before watching the pilot disappear into the cockpit. Two other military passengers sat in jump seats across from him.

"You Staff Sgt. Thatcher?" one of the men asked.

Thatcher nodded.

"That took a lot of courage to do what you did today."

Thatcher shook his head. "I wish I could say I was courageous, but it was more out of fear."

"What are you afraid of?" the other passenger asked.

Thatcher thumbed the sharp blade with his right thumb in his pocket. He rubbed the vial in his left pocket with his other hand. "You don't know what I saw out there."

"Care to enlighten us?"

Thatcher shook his head. "It's probably not a good idea. I don't want to scare you."

The man laughed. "I'm a Navy Seal. You can't scare me."

"I'm not so sure about that."

"Try me."

Thatcher waved him off. "Maybe another time."

After a few minutes, the plane began to move, lurching forward. All the passengers jerked in the direction of the cockpit. The engines revved up and the plane began to gain speed, heading down the runway.

"Hold on tight," the Navy Seal said.

Thatcher smiled as the nose of the plane tilted skyward and placed them all in an awkward position, leaning toward the ground. The plane continued to gain altitude for several minutes until it finally leveled off.

Thatcher remained lost in thought, wondering what his family might be thinking now. Would they disown him? Embrace him? He couldn't be sure, especially coming from a third generation military family. He tried not to think about it—until he drifted asleep.

When he first heard a noise that startled him, he couldn't be sure how long he'd been asleep, but he awoke, eyes wide. In front of him, he watched the Navy Seal moving toward him with a knife. He glanced at the other soldier, who appeared to be slumped over and bleeding, perhaps even dead.

What the—

Thatcher worked to get his harness off, but couldn't do it in time. He thrust his feet out to thwart the oncoming man, who was wielding a knife. It bought Thatcher a few moments—just enough time to work his harness free and stand up. He reached for his knife, but couldn't pull it out in time before the Navy Seal bowled him over.

The man straddled Thatcher and drew his knife over

his head, preparing to strike. But some turbulence created a challenging environment. As the man went to strike, Thatcher rolled to the right, just avoiding the blade as it became lodged in the back of his seat. Thatcher shoved the other man off of him and reached for his knife. When he did, the plane experienced more turbulence and his knife fell to the floor, sliding toward his assailant.

Before Thatcher could regain his footing, the Navy Seal rushed Thatcher, crashing into him and sending him to the ground. Thatcher head butted him and scrambled to his feet. He punched the button, opening the transport hatch in the back of the plane. But Thatcher didn't see the man flying toward him, both feet forward.

Thatcher tumbled backward, clinging to the cargo net, which flapped around on the cargo deck.

"Who sent you?" Thatcher asked.

The man didn't say a word and just grinned. He knelt down and started to knife through the cargo hold.

CHAPTER 23

FLYNN STEPPED INSIDE BANKS' apartment and watched her secure the door with a series of deadbolt locks. She turned toward the wall and armed the security system before looking back at the door and sliding the final chain lock into place.

"Rough neighborhood?" Flynn asked.

She cracked a faint smile and shook her head. "You can never be too careful around here—especially with what just happened to us."

"I've seen you in action. The bad guys should be afraid of you."

She waved him off. "You haven't *really* seen me in action—otherwise, you'd be afraid of me right now." She gestured for him to have a seat.

"I've been thinking," Flynn said.

"Me, too. And I think we need to take this to the director of the FBI."

Flynn's mouth fell agape. "Are you crazy?"

"We need someone to know the truth about what's going on here, about what we've seen and what we know."

"Sure, but from what I've seen so far, someone high up on the food chain in our government doesn't want that truth to get out. It seems like they'll go to great lengths to stop us."

"But if someone knows, at least it provides us with some protection."

"What we need to provide is proof. All we have right now are our own hunches. We don't know who that guy was who was shooting at us."

Banks let out a short breath. "It certainly wasn't one of their people."

"We don't *know* that for sure, even though it seems most likely that he wasn't part of the terrorist group."

"Perhaps the CIA is different, but the FBI is full of reasonable people who are trained to make logical deductions. I think they'll agree with us before we have solid evidence."

Flynn sat forward on the edge of the couch. "It doesn't matter if someone agrees with your hunches because if this thing goes all the way up the chain of command like we think it does, it'll be a daunting task. We need to know how high up it goes and who's behind it all before we mount any type of offensive to protect ourselves." She reached into her bag and slid her iPad along the coffee table in front of Flynn. "It's all right there. One of my colleagues sent me dossiers on all of the terrorists they found."

Flynn scrolled through the images and files for a few minutes in silence. "This isn't much to go on."

"It's *something*, which is more than we had a few hours ago."

"Let me see if I can get Osborne to look into this for us."

Before Banks could respond, a loud knock at the door

startled both of them.

"Were you expecting any visitors?" Flynn asked.

Banks shook her head.

Flynn put his index finger to his lips and slipped behind a wall just off the entryway.

"Who is it?" Banks asked.

"I've got a delivery for a Jennifer Banks. It requires a signature."

"Okay. Just a moment."

Flynn dashed across the room and peeked out of her second-floor window onto the street below. He rushed back to Banks. "There's no delivery truck down there," he whispered before he slid behind the wall again.

"What delivery company did you say you were with again?" she asked, peering through the peephole. The man sported a dark brown shirt and a pair of brown cargo pants. But she remained leery of him.

"UPS, ma'am. I had to park in the garage. New city ordinance," the man answered, almost as if he were reading her mind.

"Sorry, I'm a little skittish right now. She started to unlock the doors. Flynn waved at her, trying to get her to stop, but it was too late. She released the last lock, but before she could slide the chain lock out, the door rattled and slammed her in the head as the man charged in.

Banks stumbled backward and fell to the ground. She scrambled to get to her feet but couldn't get any further than on her hands and knees before the man jammed his gun into the back of her head.

"Don't make another move, Miss Banks."

CHAPTER 24

THE LIQUID MIXTURE SPILLED onto the counter next to the test tubes. Dr. Melissa Watson's hands wouldn't stop shaking. She used her left hand to grab her right in an attempt to steady it. She started to shake all the more violently, creating a mess all over her workstation.

Watson balled up her fist and slammed it on the table, letting out a slew of expletives.

I can't even stop shaking long enough to test the antidote, let alone get it into a syringe to inject it into me.

She looked upward and threw her head back, unleashing a scream. Noticing a tray of empty test tubes nearby, she snatched them up and slammed them on the floor. The sound of splintered glass tinkling across the floor was followed by another scream.

"Rough day, Dr. Watson?" came the voice through the intercom.

She looked toward the observation window leading to the outer hallway. Standing outside next to the door was her director, Dr. Franklin. The smirk on his face infuriated her.

Watson rushed toward the door and turned the handle. It didn't budge.

Dr. Franklin wagged his finger at her and clucked his

tongue. "Now, now, Dr. Watson. You know better than to try and contaminate my research facility—at least I thought you did. Good thing I locked this door."

"How did you know?"

He laughed. "A little birdie told me. Now I suggest you quit throwing temper tantrums and find a cure like your life depends on it, because, well, it does."

"Dr. Franklin, I can't do this by myself. I need help."

He shook his head and shrugged. "Sorry, I can't help you. This is a problem you're going to have to solve on your own."

She banged on the glass. "Dr. Franklin! Dr. Franklin!"

He turned and started to walk down the hall, waving at her once his back was to her.

She punched the glass again, causing more pain to her hand. If anything, it got her mind off the impending doom she sensed, as she felt no closer to creating an antidote now than she had a day ago.

Before she returned to her workstation, she noticed Dr. Franklin had stopped and was in an intense conversation with another man in a suit. They were looking at pictures in a folder, but she couldn't make them out. She put her ear to the glass to hear what they were saying.

"Do you think these could help the doctor find an antidote more quickly?" the man asked.

Dr. Franklin shook his head. "I'd rather not give these to her. It won't help. Besides, we're probably going to have to start over again soon anyway." He turned around to look back toward the lab and his eyes locked with Watson. He shooed her away with the back of his hand.

"If you can help me, Dr. Franklin, you must!" she

screamed.

The man in the suit furrowed his brow for a moment before spinning on his back heel and walking away.

"Dr. Franklin!"

She pounded on the glass several more times. She glanced up at the clock, which seemed to be churning through the minutes like they were seconds.

She beat on the window once more before collapsing to the floor.

CHAPTER 25

STAFF SGT. DAN THATCHER CLAWED his way up the netting as the soldier sawed through the rope netting. He couldn't advance more than one or two strands before the turbulence lifted him up and slammed him back down onto the ramp. Each time, Thatcher fought through excruciating pain.

After a minute of inching his way up the netting, he clambered to his feet with the help of the rope. Only a few more feet and he'd be clear of the ramp. He looked up to see the Navy Seal grinning as he held the final rope strand in his hand.

"Where do you think you're going?" he said as he almost finished cutting through it.

Thatcher looked up to see the co-pilot standing behind the Seal. The co-pilot tapped him on the shoulder. He spun around to see a gun pointed in his face.

Thatcher took advantage of the opportunity to climb up the ramp and get on an even surface.

Meanwhile, the Seal didn't hesitate, reacting by shoving his knife into the co-pilot's leg. When the co-pilot went to grab his leg, the Seal ripped the gun out of his hand and trained it on him. He cocked the gun and prepared to fire.

Before he could pull the trigger, Thatcher walloped the Seal in the head with a fire extinguisher and sprayed him in the face. Thatcher kicked at the man, sending him backward down the ramp. He grabbed onto the netting, still flapping up and down on the ramp, and shot at Thatcher.

Thatcher dove out of the way, unknowingly exposing the co-pilot. The shot ripped through his chest, killing him.

Thatcher rolled to his right, grabbed the knife and threw it at the remaining strand still holding the netting in place. The knife severed the netting and sent the Seal flying out of the cargo bay.

Thatcher staggered to his feet, closed the cargo bay, and headed toward the cockpit.

What's going on?

He looked down at the pilot, who turned around in horror.

"Where's my co-pilot? Did you do something to him?" the pilot asked.

Thatcher shook his head and tried to catch his breath. "One of the passengers back there tried to kill me."

A voice came over the radio, telling the pilot that he was clear to land. The pilot held up his finger. "We're about to begin our descent into D.C." He adjusted a few controls and then turned toward Thatcher. "Now, where's my co-pilot."

"He's back there—dead."

"One of your passengers—I think he told me he was a Navy Seal—killed the other soldier and shot your co-pilot."

"And where is he now?"

"Floating in the Atlantic. I just shoved him out through the cargo bay."

"Well, have a seat and buckle up. We need to set this bird down before we can sort all of this out."

Thatcher followed the pilot's orders, strapping himself into the co-pilot's seat, which was still warm.

"I told you not to trust anyone," the pilot said.

Thatcher chuckled as he looked out the cockpit. "Yeah, I should've listened to you."

"Yeah," the pilot said. "You really should have."

Thatcher turned to look at the pilot, who had a gun trained on him.

CHAPTER 26

FLYNN PEERED AROUND THE WALL at the man who stood over Banks. He was standing at such an angle that he couldn't see who was behind him.

"Where is he?" the man roared.

Banks shrank lower and lifted her hands in the air. "Where is who?"

"You know who I'm talking about. I saw you drive into your parking garage with another man." He bent down and got in Banks' ear. "Now, where is he?"

Before Banks could answer, Flynn flew at the man, knocking him against the wall and shaking the gun loose from his hand. The man tried to get up, but Flynn kicked him the ribs. Instead of flinching, the man grabbed Flynn's foot and twisted it, spinning Flynn to the ground.

Now with the advantage, the man put a knee in Flynn's chest and began pummeling him. He laid several licks on Flynn before Banks collected herself and pulled out her gun.

"I think this has gone on long enough," she said, straddling in front of him. "Now get up."

The man got up slowly with both hands raised. Flynn squirmed free but stood up in between Banks and the man, giving the man the split second he needed.

The man shoved Flynn toward Banks and sprinted toward the window, diving through it. He landed on the hood of a car parked on the street below. Flynn and Banks watched as he slowly rolled off and crossed the street. He quickly got into a car and drove off.

"Did you get the license plate number?" Banks asked.

"Got it up here," Flynn said, tapping the side of his head.

"Good. We need to find out who he is."

"We've got his gun, too," Flynn said, holding it up with a pencil.

"I doubt we'll be able to get any prints off of it."

"If you try, be careful who you give it to."

Banks smiled. "Give me credit for being smarter than that. I know a guy."

Flynn winked at her. "It's always good to know a guy." He paced around for a moment. "Speaking of which, I might know someone, too, who can help us get information—someone that won't draw any attention in either agency."

He picked up his phone and called his editor, Theresa Thompson. *The National*'s fearless leader always made time for her prized reporter.

"Where have you been?" Thompson said as she picked up. "I've been worried about you. I haven't heard anything since that incident in Idaho."

"I told you I was okay," Flynn said.

"But no follow up? I was starting to get worried."

"It's been a rough two days," he said. He glanced at his watch. "And it hasn't even been two full days yet."

"So, you're all right?"

"Fit as a fiddle," he said, clutching his sore ribs. "Maybe some day I'll write a book about it."

"What exactly happened to you?"

"Never mind. It's not important right now. But what is important is that there's far more to this story than a simple nuclear heist."

"How so?"

"I'm not sure yet, but I'm working with an FBI agent to figure it out. Everything is leading us to believe that this was an inside job."

"You mean someone in the government orchestrated this attack."

"Yes, and used Russians to misdirect everyone. But I need to confirm a few more things before I start spewing this information."

"And you need to be more careful about saying this on an open line."

Flynn rolled his eyes, glad that Theresa couldn't see him. "Anyway, I was wondering if you might be able to hook me up with that guy you told me about."

"The hacker?"

Flynn snapped his fingers as he tried to think. "Yeah, Black Magic or something like that?"

"Black Magic is the guy's name. I'm not sure I want to have this conversation on our phones, you know with the NSA tapping media's landlines."

"And you think your cell is safe?"

"My encrypted burner phone is."

Flynn chuckled. "I never took you to be so overly cautious."

"It's impossible to be overly cautious in this day and

age. Give me a sec and I'll call you right back."

Seconds later, Flynn's phone buzzed.

"Okay, here's his number," she said before rattling it off. "Tell him I said to take good care of you."

"Do we have enough in the story budget to pay this guy?"

"He's on retainer. Call him. And call me when your story starts to take shape. I'd love to help if I can."

"You got it." Flynn was about to hang up when he heard some squealing in the background. "Theresa? Are you still there?"

"Yeah, I'm here."

"What's going on? It sounded like I heard some high-pitched screeching in the background."

"You did. A couple of staffers are reacting to a news bulletin."

"That exciting, huh?"

"Have you been following that story about the sergeant in Afghanistan, the one whose entire troop was obliterated by U.S. drones? At least, that's what he claims happened."

"Just bits and pieces."

"Well, it looks like he just parachuted out of a transport plane over the Potomac River."

"Are you sure?"

"There's only one way to find out."

Flynn took Banks by the arm and started nudging her toward the door. "We're on our way right now."

CHAPTER 27

DR. WATSON COULD HEAR everything but refused to even twitch. In her right lab coat pocket, she held a rag soaked in chloroform. She waited and waited. With her ear to the floor, she heard every click of every step on the floor. The muffled voice of Dr. Franklin outside seemed somewhat calm as he gave orders.

After about ten minutes, two men finally entered the room.

"Doc said to drag her into the quarantine room," one of the men said.

"Do you think it's dangerous?"

"Nah. They're just being overly cautious."

"Good. I hate wearing this mask."

They each grabbed one of Watson's arms and started dragging her across the floor toward the quarantine room. Then she clutched the man on her left, digging her fingers into him.

"What the—"

She pulled him close and head butted him, stunning him temporarily. He grabbed his nose while she went to work on the other man. She grabbed the back of his head with her left hand and shoved the chloroform-soaked rag into his face with her right. He gasped and struggled to get away but not before the chemical knocked him out.

The man she head butted was still holding his nose when she jumped on his back and shoved the chloroform over his face. He went down within seconds.

That was far easier than I thought it was going to be. She smiled. *Maybe I should've been a spy.*

With the two men out of the way, Watson scurried down the hall to another room. She grabbed several of the microbes she needed for her latest attempt to create the vaccine, working with one eye on the door, which she'd locked and bolted after dragging the men's bodies out into the hall. She didn't have much time to mix her latest concoction and test it.

While waiting for the cells to incubate, she meandered toward the quarantine chamber. Mosley looked up at her, nearly defeated, the bags under his eyes sagging.

"Help me," he groaned.

She shrugged and pressed the intercom button to speak to him. "I'm trying. Your little stunt didn't make it easier for me."

"I'm sorry," he said. "I was desperate."

She stamped her foot. "So you kill us both?"

He shook his head. "I know it was wrong. I'm sorry. But I know you'll figure something out. You always do."

The centrifuge stopped whirring and she hustled over to check it out. She mixed the antidote and loaded it into a syringe. She wanted to give it to Mosley first and observe how he reacted. But she was running out of time—and her self-preservation mode kicked in. Without another thought, she jammed the syringe into her own armed and waited. She said a quick prayer and waited some more.

A few seconds later, she crumpled to the floor.

CHAPTER 28

SENATOR THOR GLANCED at the notecards in his hands and took a deep breath. He shuffled through them several times and rehearsed what he was going to say underneath his breath.

"You're going to be fine, Senator," one of his aides said while he swept lint off Thor's jacket with the back of his hand. "Just let the people know what's at stake. It will be an easy sell."

Thor closed his eyes. "I hope you're right. Because if the American people buy the spin machine out there that says we should remain isolationists—"

"They won't," the aide answered. "The American people often vote for a candidate by thinking the best about him. But when it comes to safety, they always believe the worst."

Thor tapped the cards against his leg, straightening them out. "Do you believe the worst?"

The aide looked down and rocked from his toes to his heels. "I rarely believe anything anyone ever says," he said after a few moments. "Except for you, of course."

A thin smile spread across Thor's face. "I don't even believe that."

A member of the cable news crew popped her head

into the room. "We're ready for you in thirty seconds, Senator Thor," she said before darting outside again.

"Knock 'em dead, sir," the aide said and slugged Thor in the arm. "They need to hear this."

Thor tugged at the bottom of his sport coat and strode toward the door. "Wish me luck."

"Always," the aide said.

Thor opened the door and walked into the lobby to meet the large gathering of reporters in desperate search for a fresh angle on the news breaking that Staff Sgt. Thatcher was attacked by U.S. drones. Legal analysts had already debated whether such acts could be considered murder and what was the burden of proof required to make such an accusation. Others bantered about the news that he was a disgruntled soldier, one who had been passed over more than once for promotion. And every other view on the spectrum found time on the airwaves.

But the ultimate conclusion to Thatcher's fate didn't concern Thor. All he wanted was to seize upon the opportunity to show the American people that their precious safety hung in the balance if they didn't do something about it.

He strode to the podium, laboring under the weight of microphones, and started to speak.

"Over the past twenty-four hours, a couple of stories broke that should have all of us—as American citizens—concerned." He flipped his first card and glanced at it before looking directly into the camera in front of him. "Our precious liberties are not to be taken for granted, not now, not ever. The day we begin to presume upon them is the day they start to vanish. And I think it's safe for me to speak for countless Americans when I say this: We're not interested in losing any liberties at the hands of rogue nations or terrorist sects, lest we make the sacrifice of tens of thousands who've fought valiantly for this great nation meaningless."

He took a deep breath and continued. "Earlier today I sat in a meeting with U.S. senators from both sides of the aisle to discuss how we might better fund our troops to protect us against outside aggression. Unfortunately, I was in a minority. Some people felt beefing up our military equated to a provocation of war. Others held the belief that there are better things for us to invest in domestically than the military. And I couldn't disagree more with either viewpoint. Protecting ourselves is of utmost importance if we intend to remain a free nation. And if that action provokes our enemies, so be it. I have no doubt the American resolve will ward off any such threats from those countries that would like to see us removed as one of the world's superpowers."

Cameras clicked and flashed as Thor continued.

"The American people need to send a message today to those who have sworn an oath to uphold the constitution as they represent the citizens of this great nation. And that message is this: Don't let political ideology be the altar upon which we sacrifice our freedoms. Don't let Washington politics get in the way of keeping Americans safe. And don't let us become a toothless nation, unable to protect and defend not only ourselves but also others."

Thor looked sternly at the camera in front of him and nodded. "Thank you for your time."

He exited to a flurry of questions called out by the press corps, none of which he intended to answer. His speech spoke for itself. It was the first of many salvos he intended to fire at those senators stonewalling suggested military spending.

Thor closed the door behind him, his heart still pounding. He leaned against the door and let out a long breath. "So, how'd I do?"

His aide broke into a big grin. "You nailed it, sir. If I wasn't working for you, I would've gone and signed up to join the military."

"That convincing?"

"If you'd have gone on any more, the networks may have billed the military for commercial airtime."

Thor frowned. "I wasn't trying to be a cheerleader—just a prophetic voice in a world determined to hear what they want to hear."

"You definitely accomplished that."

Before Thor could continue the conversation, the door flung open. It was Senator Ryan.

"Just *who* do you think you are, standing in front of the cameras and scaring the American public like that?" Ryan said as he slammed the door behind him.

"Isn't the answer obvious? I'm a man doing my civic duty to inform the people of the chicanery happening behind closed doors on the taxpayers' dime."

"You think you're helping, but you're not," Ryan growled.

Thor walked over to the aging senator and put his arm around him. "We're on the same team, you and me. We need to stick together, not be torn apart."

Ryan shook free of Thor's arm and stepped back. "We're not on the same team, not in the least bit—especially if you insist on shooting off your mouth about what's taking place in our committee meetings."

"The American people have a right to know—"

"The American people have no such rights. They have the right to believe what we tell them."

"That's why it's high time we start with the truth."

"The truth isn't a miracle worker. In fact, it often betrays the good of the whole. You'd know this if you'd been on the Hill longer than a few years and weren't so green behind the ears."

Thor sauntered up to the senior committee member and stared at him, cocking his head to one side. "It's that kind of thinking that's put us all at risk. A war is coming— and if we're not prepared, we're all going to die. You may not care about that since your best years are behind you, but what about your kids, your grandkids? Don't they deserve to live in a country that's as grand and wonderful as you once believed it to be?"

"It still is."

"Not if you think neutering our military is the way to go about it."

Ryan poked his cane into Thor's chest. "That's not what is taking place here—you've gotta believe me."

"Then what *is* going on here? Maybe you can start there and clue me in since you want us to be on the same page so badly."

"You'll see in time."

Thor walked toward the window and shook his head. "No, no, I won't. Your cloak and dagger approach isn't something I'm willing to wait on. I'm being proactive about this. By the end of this week, Americans will be so whipped into a frenzy that everyone on that committee will be looking to me—not you—for leadership. They'll see me as a visionary."

"I wouldn't bet on it."

Thor laughed. "Is denial a trait that every elderly person is born with?"

"Is stupidity a trait that every young person gets at birth?"

Thor pointed at the door. "Get out. And don't try to stop me. I know what this country needs—and it's more honest politicians, not deceptive ones like you."

Ryan hobbled toward the door and opened it. He looked back over his shoulder. "A war is coming all right—and you better watch it or you might become its first casualty."

CHAPTER 29

BY THE TIME FLYNN and Banks reached the site of Thatcher's landing spot in the Potomac, a slew of Metropolitan Police Department squad cars were scattered throughout the area. They walked toward the scene, where Thatcher slogged through the water toward the bank while TV camera crews and news helicopters tried to capture the event as it unfolded.

Flynn ignored one of the officer's calls to stop, marching toward the action. One of the police officers handcuffed Thatcher before he set foot on dry ground and shoved him toward land.

"Is this really necessary?" Flynn said.

"Save it, Flynn," one of the officers said. Then he paused. "And who let you in here anyway?"

Banks flashed her badge. "He's helping with an investigation."

The officer rolled his eyes. "And this is an FBI investigation how?"

"It's our jurisdiction."

"Bullshit," the officer shot back. "This has got nothing to do with you and you know it."

"You keep telling yourself that, buddy," Banks

snapped. She read the officer's name off the nametag plastered to his shirt.

"Until I hear otherwise, this stunt man will remain in my custody."

Banks held up her finger. "Hold that thought." A quick conversation with her supervisor led to a call on the officer's phone.

"Officer—Davids, was it?" she asked.

"Who's asking?" he said.

"I think the person on the other end of your phone call."

Davids rolled his eyes and answered his phone. He remained silent while the person on the other end rattled off a list of instructions. "I understand, sir. Will do."

"He's all yours," Davids said, shoving Thatcher toward her.

"It was a pleasure doing business with you," she said.

He waved her off and signaled for the other officers to vacate the premises.

"That was easy," Flynn said with a wink.

"I have that effect on people sometimes." She grabbed Thatcher and uncuffed him.

"Thank you," Thatcher said. "That guy was starting to get on my nerves."

"You learn to deal with him."

"So, what do you plan to do with me now?" Thatcher asked.

"Let's talk about it in the car." She pointed toward her vehicle and started walking.

Thatcher turned toward Flynn. "Hey, aren't you that guy on television?"

Flynn flashed a smile. "More often than not, I'm mistaken for George Clooney on the silver screen, but who exactly are you talking about?"

Thatcher stopped. "No, wait a minute. I know I've seen you before. You're that conspiracy theorist guy, aren't you?"

Flynn shrugged. "I've been called worse."

"I knew it," Thatcher said, clapping his hands. "I don't watch television all that much, but I knew I recognized you from somewhere."

Flynn cocked his head to one side. "You sure it wasn't in a movie?"

Thatcher shook his head and smiled. "Stop playing games with me."

"Get in the car," Banks said.

Thatcher got into the backseat, while Flynn joined Banks in the front.

"I don't think I could've had a more perfect person to pick me up than you," Thatcher began as he buckled up.

"Why's that?" Flynn asked.

"Because you'll actually believe me."

Flynn wagged his finger. "I wouldn't jump to hasty conclusions. Just because I investigate conspiracies doesn't mean I believe them all. It's why I *investigate* them."

"Well, this one is worth investigating."

"How so?"

Thatcher slammed his fists down on the seat next to him. "Are you kidding me? My own government—my own military—tried to have me killed for what I saw."

"Are you sure that's the reason?"

"If you saw what I saw, there'd be no doubt."

Flynn turned around in his seat and studied Thatcher. "So, what did you see?"

Before Thatcher could answer, a loud pop echoed in the car as glass from the back window shattered, spilling into the car. Instinctively, Thatcher and Flynn both ducked while Banks started to weave the car back and forth.

Pop. Pop.

Two more shots found their target, hitting the body of Banks' car. She whipped the car onto a side street and stomped on the gas, disappearing from what she presumed was a sniper perched nearby. She drove for a few minutes without anyone saying a word. Not another shot.

"What the hell was that?" Thatcher said.

"Someone doesn't want you talking," Banks said, eyeing him in the rearview mirror.

"Well then, it's probably because of this," Thatcher said, holding up a small vial containing a clear liquid.

"What is that?" Flynn asked.

"I was hoping one of my friends could tell me."

CHAPTER 30

DR. MELISSA WATSON AWOKE to find herself in the quarantine area, lying next to Mosley. She grabbed her back as she rolled over and tried to stand up. Mosley, eyes wild and face pale, looked up at her. Then he sprang toward her, pushing her back against a table.

Withdrawing, Watson stared in disbelief. "What's wrong with you?"

Saliva oozed out from the corners of his mouth. "Did you find a cure?" he asked.

She pushed him away. "I hope so. Give me a few minutes to run some tests."

"If you didn't succeed, bring me a gun," he growled.

Watson hastened into the lab and drew a sample of her blood. While she waited for the blood to spread over the slide, she glanced at Mosley, who clutched his stomach and writhed in pain. She shook her head and returned her attention to the slide. A smile spread across her face while she studied it. "I did it!" She paused. "We did it!"

She stared intently at the blood then heard a slow clapping sound, causing her to look up.

"Well done, Dr. Watson," Dr. Franklin said as he approached her. "I knew you could do it."

"No thanks to you."

"Oh, I think there's every bit of thanks due to me." He settled onto a stool next to her. "I found you—and the monkeys." A slight grin. "I also found Dr. Mosley."

The mention of his name reminded her that she needed to get him some antidote as soon as possible. She pushed her way past Franklin and started to mix some more antidote for Mosley.

"You really think that can save him at this point?" Franklin said, motioning toward her chemical construct.

"You got any better ideas?"

"I wouldn't waste my time with him," Franklin said.

"Saving a life is never a waste of time." She filled up a syringe and glared at Franklin as she walked toward the quarantine chamber.

"I've got something for you," she said.

Mosley groaned, muttered something unintelligible, and rolled over.

"That's it," she said. "Just be still. Don't move."

She slid the point of the needle into his arm and forced the rest of the liquid into him.

After helping Mosley sit up and handing him a glass of water, Watson returned to finish her conversation with Franklin.

"You know what I don't understand?" she said.

He shook his head.

"Why us? Why this lab? I mean, I don't even know what this virus is other than this generically assigned XC-47 listed on this vial here. If this is really as big of a deal as you say, why are we the only ones working on it?"

Franklin folded his arms and took a deep breath. "I'm

afraid I can't answer all of those questions."

"Can't or won't?"

"What's the difference? You don't get to know all the answers, Dr. Watson. Some things will always be a mystery—to both you and me."

"I'm not sure I'm buying that."

Franklin smirked. "I'm not selling anything to you but the truth. If you don't believe it, just log on to the Internet where you'll find someone somewhere spouting off something that you agree with—truth be damned."

"Truth isn't relative."

"Well, that's your interpretation of it, isn't it?"

"Are we done here? I need to check on Mosley and then get home so I can get some much-needed rest." She stood up only to watch Franklin slide in front of her path toward the quarantine room.

"Mosley will be fine—as long as you are."

Watson tried to push past him, but he didn't budge. "I *need* to check on Mosley."

"What you need to do is sit down and remain under observation by a few other fellow scientists before we let you go charging back out into the world."

She looked him up and down. "You're not wearing anything to protect you from the virus, so it's pretty safe to say that you're confident my antidote worked."

"For now. But we must observe you regardless."

"While you roam free? You may be carrying it and not even know it."

"Highly unlikely given what we know about the virus."

Watson huffed. "We hardly know anything, according to you."

He picked up a thick folder and threw it onto the table next to her. It landed with a thud as papers spilled out. "We know more about it than you think. Read for yourself."

Her eyes narrowed, but only slightly. "You mean to tell me that you had more information on this virus all along but chose not to give it to me?"

"I told the director you wouldn't need it."

She threw her hands in the air. "Are you out of your mind? Withholding this kind of information cost several monkeys their lives."

"I didn't realize you were a member of PETA?"

"If I was a gun-toting member of the NRA, I'd still be upset about this—if anything, from a professional standpoint. You can't just go around withholding vital information from me that could prevent me from doing my job."

Franklin loosened his tie. "Yet it had no effect on you. This information would've only bogged you down and slowed down your research."

"It's inhumane."

He winked at her. "Good thing we weren't dealing with humans then, eh?"

Watson rubbed her face with both hands. "Look, I just need to check on Mosley and get outta here. Can you let me do that?"

He shrugged. "Check on Mosley? Yes. Get outta here? No. I need you to stick around for at least another hour or two."

"My blood's clean."

"Let's verify that first before we let you out to infect half of D.C."

She growled. "I'm losing patience with you."

"I thought you might appreciate my respect for protocol. Nevertheless, it's what must be done." He headed for the door before he stopped and turned around. "And Watson? I expect to see a formula for the antidote on my desk before you leave. This is an issue of national importance."

She forced a smile. "How convenient. I'll leave you one. Just don't let any of those people—whoever these mystery people are—wait around to verify me. I'm itching to get out of here."

"I bet you are," he said, turning back toward the door.

Watson didn't move until she heard the ding of the elevator and waited ample time for the doors to close. She rushed over to the windows and peeked down the hallway just to make sure he was gone. Satisfied that he was, she raced back into the quarantine room to see how Mosley was doing.

"Mosley? Mosley?" she said, shaking him. "Are you awake, Mosley?"

He squinted his eyes and opened them, turning away quickly due to the sudden influx of light. "I am now," he said, looking to one side at the ground. "Did you find a cure?"

She knelt down and took his hand. "I don't think you'd be here if I hadn't."

"That bad, huh?"

"Worse than you know. Here, let's get you to your feet." Watson grabbed Mosley's arm and helped him up. "Have a seat so I can check you out."

Mosley slumped into his seat, still groggy. "How'd you solve it?"

"That's my secret, for now."

He started to roll up his sleeve so she could take a blood sample. "The whole world will need to know soon enough."

"Why? For an outbreak that hasn't happened yet?" She shook her head. "I doubt that."

He shrugged. "Why else would we be working on this?"

"I'm not sure, but once I clear you, I'm going to punch you in the face."

Mosley laughed. "Now, now. Don't be so angry. You weren't properly motivated before—otherwise, I'd be dead."

"We both could've been dead," she said, roughly jamming the needle into his arm to draw the blood.

"Owww! Watch it there!"

"What? You don't like people ramming needles into your arm when you aren't expecting it?"

He glanced up at Watson and didn't say a word.

"That ought to do it," she said, pulling the needle out of his arm and stuffing a cotton ball on top of the entry wound bubbling with blood. "Sorry I don't have any cookies and juice for you."

He stared at the floor. "Look, I'm sorry about what I did, okay? I wasn't thinking straight."

"You weren't thinking at all. And if I didn't feel so sorry for you, I'd sock you between the eyes right now."

Mosley forced a smile and clapped as he stood up. "But it all worked out, right? No harm, no foul?"

"This will take me a while to get over."

"How about getting over it over dinner tonight?"

She shook her head. "I'm too tired. Plus I'm not sure I trust you after that little stunt you pulled."

"I said I'm sorry."

Watson noticed the color had returned fully to his face. "Now go get some rest while I create a report for Franklin."

"Sure I can't help?"

"You've *helped* enough for tonight. Now, get outta here."

He grabbed his briefcase and headed toward the door. "If you change your mind—"

"Go," she said, waving him off. The second the door shut behind her, she wondered if she'd made a mistake. Maybe she should've gone with him to dinner, though she wasn't sure if she wanted to slap him or kiss him at this point. She needed time—and answers, though she doubted she'd get what she was looking for out of Franklin.

She returned her attention to the report and finished filling it out for Franklin. She was careful to leave out one element that made the antidote work. As uneasy as she felt, she figured she could chalk it up to being tired and barely having survived the virus herself.

No need to give them everything just yet, is there?

She made a copy, taking a picture of the formula on her phone. She kept the missing ingredient in her head.

I'll never forget this—nor is anyone else smart enough to figure it out.

The short walk upstairs to Franklin's office gave her more time to process the events of the past forty-eight hours. It had been a blur, but a painful one. For all that she gained from working for Franklin, she'd willingly give it up for normal—whatever that looked like.

When she entered Franklin's office, he was on the phone. She tossed the file folder on his desk. "Here's your report."

He put one hand on the receiver and turned toward her. "Excellent work, Dr. Watson."

"Am I clear to leave now?"

"Sure. See you in the morning."

Dr. Watson ambled down the steps to the parking garage and climbed into her car. She turned the ignition as her Toyota Prius awoke with something akin to a mild purr. Before putting her car into gear, she tweaked the rearview mirror so she could see herself. Bags under her eyes, frazzled hair, sunken cheeks. She wanted to go home and watch one of those makeover shows while gorging herself on ice cream. It wasn't the ideal life she imagined for herself when she graduated from college, but she couldn't turn back time no matter how much she wished she could.

She readjusted the rearview mirror and put the car into drive. She pulled out of her parking space and headed toward the exit.

Headlights flashed behind her.

Is someone following me?

She shook her head and smiled.

I get so paranoid sometimes. It's probably nothing.

She turned on the radio and started humming along to Dmitri Shostakovich's Symphony No. 5.

She failed to notice those same headlights following her down the street.

CHAPTER 31

FLYNN WATCHED BANKS MANEUVER through D.C.'s evening traffic with ease. She effortlessly whipped her car down several different side streets, avoiding major jams throughout the city's main veins.

"Do you know where you're going?" he asked.

"You gave me the address, didn't you?" she said, flashing a smile at him. "I'll get us there. Don't you worry. I don't need a GPS, nor would I ever use one taking someone to a safe house."

Flynn rubbed his face. "Guess I'm a little rusty."

"I'll say."

Several minutes later, Banks had her car out of D.C. and headed for a safe house in the Virginia hills.

"Promise you'll forget this place?" Flynn said.

She crossed her heart with her right hand. "Hope to die."

Flynn glanced at their passenger in the backseat. Staff Sgt. Thatcher hadn't said a word since they got into the car. Flynn wondered if he was still in shock from the fact that someone was still trying to kill him—someone in high places. Regardless of the reason, it didn't matter. Processing that information would be difficult for anyone, especially a sergeant in the U.S. Army who was willing to sacrifice everything for his country.

Flynn turned around to look at Thatcher in the eyes. "Want to tell me about that vial you showed us?"

Thatcher looked around the vehicle. "Is it safe to talk in here?"

"Safest place on earth," Banks answered, watching him in her rearview mirror.

"I don't know. I'd rather talk about it when we get there."

"Fair enough," Flynn answered.

Thirty minutes later, Banks pulled off the interstate and turned onto a state highway leading into a wooded area. "I always wondered what was out here," she said.

"Trees," Flynn said. "Lots of trees."

"And safe houses, apparently."

He put his finger to his lips. "Not as many as you might think."

They wound up and down the road, turning several times until they pulled into the driveway of the house. Flynn jumped out and punched in the security code for the garage door to open. Once the door revealed an empty space, Banks roared in and parked her car.

Flynn opened Thatcher's door. "Say hello to your new home for the next few days."

Thatcher headed inside without a word.

"Think he's okay?" Banks whispered to Flynn.

Flynn nodded. "Just give him some time. I'm sure he'll be fine."

Thatcher had already settled into the couch. He looked relaxed—and tired.

"Wanna talk?" Flynn said, handing Thatcher a glass of water.

"About what?"

"Why don't we start with that vial in your pocket? It seems that might be the reason someone's trying to kill you?"

Letting out a long breath, Thatcher rolled his head around, cracking his neck. "I don't even know anymore. I'm just scared."

"Well, I'm here to help you," Flynn said, locking eyes with Thatcher. "It's not just a line—and I'm not just doing this for a story. If there's something corrupt taking place in our government, I want to expose it. It's why I was kicked out of the CIA in the first place."

Thatcher cocked his head and furrowed his brow. "Yet, here we are in a supposed CIA safe house?"

Flynn pulled out his phone and started recording their conversation, gesturing toward it until Thatcher nodded and gave a thumbs-up signal.

"It's complicated," Flynn continued. "But there are some people there who still trust me—and are distrustful of others in the agency. It's a mess, I know."

Thatcher stared at his feet. "I just don't know what to do or what to make of anything that's just happened. Our own military ordered an apparent drone strike on our location when they knew we were there. I had to fend off not one, but two people who wanted to kill me on a transatlantic flight just to parachute out. I even had to break the pilot's arm and take his gun just to get away. Otherwise, I'd be boxed up somewhere, never to be heard from again."

Flynn leaned forward in his seat. "But you're not. You're here with—with a chance to turn the table on these bastards. So, why don't you tell me why you think they want you dead."

Thatcher dug into his pocket and fished out the vial. The clear liquid swirled around as he moved the cylinder in a circular motion. He stopped and held it up, waving it around for Flynn and Banks, who'd settled onto the couch next to Flynn. "Whatever is in here holds the answer."

"What is that?" Flynn said.

Thatcher shook his head. "I've got no idea. But whatever it is, it was making those insurgents crazy."

Flynn furrowed his brow. "Crazy? How?"

"They looked like they were being tortured by something. One guy was marching around the compound, shooting his own soldiers on demand. I wasn't close enough at the time to hear anything, but it appeared like they were asking him to shoot them. A lot of writing around, foaming at the mouth." He paused and took a deep a breath. "Quite frankly, I didn't want any part of it. I've done scores of missions like these, but I've never seen anything quite like this—especially in Afghanistan."

"What do you mean?" Banks asked.

"Chemical weapons like this are almost non-existent. The Taliban aren't sophisticated enough. They rely on intimidation, fear, and guerilla warfare. But this was like another level."

"Maybe they purchased some off the black market?" Banks said.

Thatcher shrugged. "Possibly. But I've never seen any intelligence report anywhere suggesting that the Taliban in the area where we were fighting had ever gained access to something like this." He held up the vial again and stared at it. "And even if they did, the most puzzling question for me would be why they used it on themselves."

Flynn folded his arms. "Maybe they didn't use it on themselves. Maybe it was an accident."

Thatcher shook his head. "What I saw was no accident—it was clearly an intentional attack."

Flynn stretched and yawned. "We'll get it analyzed soon, but let's sleep on this. We have a lot more to talk about, but I think a good night of sleep would do us all a world of good."

"Agreed," Thatcher said.

As they were shutting off the living room lights, Flynn froze. "Did anyone else hear that?" he asked, drawing his gun.

Banks and Thatcher both shook their heads.

Flynn put his index finger to his mouth and moved stealthily toward the door. "Banks, take him to the back of the house. I'm going to check this out."

He stepped out onto the porch and crouched down, peering into the dense vegetation surrounding the house. Nothing.

I could've sworn I heard something.

Flynn waited a few more minutes before he crept back into the house and locked the deadbolt behind him.

CHAPTER 32

KRAMER PEERED THROUGH THE BUSHES at the small cabin tucked deep in the Virginia mountains. The FBI agent and her friend had given him more trouble than he cared for, dragging him across the country to this quaint spot.

At least it will be over soon enough.

He checked his watch. According to the information he'd received from his contact, this was the safe house his targets would be staying in.

Much easier than trying to shoot them out of the water.

He adjusted his night vision goggles and prepared to sneak into the house. He had plenty of advantages—knowledge, weapons, skill. Most of all, he had the element of surprise on his side. The term "safe house" gave people a false sense of security. This wasn't the first one he'd breached and he doubted it'd be the last.

He moved swiftly through the woods and reached one of the windows on the side of the house. With the help of a stump, he looked inside and noticed the room was empty and the door was shut.

Perfect.

He gave the window a little nudge and it didn't move.

He pushed again. It was locked.

Perhaps I'll take a more direct approach.

The locked window presented Kramer with a problem in more ways than one. If he tried to jimmy the window open, he risked setting off the alarm and losing his surprise attack. If he went in through the front door, he'd likely be met by gunfire. Either way, his prospects at pulling off a successful mission dwindled.

He slumped against the house and contemplated his next step. The direct approach was the best. After all, he was the best shot in his class at Quantico before he was directed toward other opportunities for service. And the body armor he wore beneath his shirt emboldened him for the final push he needed to charge into the house.

He kicked the door down and rushed in, waiting for the lights to come on and people to scatter about.

Nothing.

What the—

He crept through the house and didn't see anyone. He barely saw three beds in the cabin, much less three people.

How am I supposed to do my job with intel like this?

He looked in every room in the house and there was no sign that anyone had even been there in days. Before calling his superior, he went outside and looked for a cellar—anywhere they could be hiding.

Still nothing.

He pulled out his phone and dialed his contact.

"There's no one here," Kramer said.

"No one?" the man asked, incredulous.

"Are you deaf? I said NO ONE."

"Are you sure? That's the safe house assigned to them."

"Maybe they thought better of it."

"Or maybe it's a trap. Watch your back—and don't let them catch you alive. I don't want to have to explain this one."

Kramer kicked the chair in front of him, sending it sprawling across the kitchen. Based on the month and year of the magazine on the table and the level of dust he gathered with the swipe of his finger, he figured it'd been a while since anyone had even visited the house, much less spent a night in it.

"How am I supposed to do my job?" he growled.

"If you would've done your job right the first time, we wouldn't be in this predicament," the man hissed.

Kramer hung up and shoved his phone into his pocket. He stormed out the front door and galloped down the steps. Without another thought, he screamed, his frustrated cry echoing through the woods.

CHAPTER 33

FLYNN DIDN'T NOTICE when Thatcher swiped his phone and took it to the bathroom as everyone was getting ready for bed. Banks volunteered to stay up for the first shift.

Thatcher logged into his Facebook profile and looked up his former classmate, Dr. Melissa Watson.

If anyone can help me, she can.

He felt a twinge of guilt as he sent her a message. It's not that Flynn and Banks seemed suspicious to him, it's just that he'd already experienced firsthand what could happen when he blindly trusted someone. For all he knew, they might hack him to death in the middle of the night and steal the vial from him. And he wasn't about to let that happen.

He brushed his teeth and reviewed in his mind everything that had happened over the past twenty-four hours. The warm welcome in Germany. The near-death experience on the transport plane over the Atlantic multiple times. And the way he surprised the pilot and wrestled the gun out of his hand before leaping out of the back and into the Potomac.

If only I had a cool car and a hot girl.

The reality was he had neither, though he fancied Banks. He preferred blondes—and women who couldn't go toe-to-toe with him in a fight. For the time being, he was glad to have her on his side. He didn't know if she'd feel like protecting him once he stole her car.

He finished brushing his teeth and saw a reply from Dr. Watson pop up on the screen.

Let's talk. I just watched the news and saw what happened. Are you OK?

He hammered out a response.

I'm fine. What's your address? I need to see you.

A few seconds later, she responded with her address. He committed it to memory and then deleted the message. He looked up her address and memorized directions before deleting it as well.

Once he exited the bathroom, he slipped down the hall and put the phone back where he found it. As he closed his door, Thatcher heard Flynn talking to himself. "There you are. I thought I already looked there for you. I must be losing my mind."

Thatcher smiled to himself—and waited.

After about an hour, he opened the door and slipped into the hallway. He glanced in the living room toward Banks, whose head bobbed every few seconds. As he kept an eye on her, he slid her keys off the table and crept toward the back door. She didn't flinch as he opened the door and exited the safe house.

He jumped off the porch and raced to the SUV. Before he started the vehicle, he checked everything around him, ensuring that he'd make a clean getaway. Nothing stood in his way. He put the SUV in neutral and pushed it down the driveway until it gained momentum and headed downhill. A few seconds later, he pumped the brakes to stop before entering the road and inserted the key.

With the twist of his right wrist, the SUV purred. He eased onto the gas and crept down the driveway with the headlights off. He looked behind him.

At least no one is streaking after me.

He smiled as he wove around the two-lane road. In a matter of minutes, he was on the highway, cruising toward Watson's condo.

The fact that Watson wasn't working for a non-profit shocked him. Her stance against big corporations made her a pariah in some circles. Her anti-war position riled many of his friends from military families who insisted that their sacrifices protected her rights. Yet here she was—working for The Goldstein Group, a big corporation that had military ties. However, her duplicity didn't bother him. He'd already recognized that there were plenty of sides to every argument—and to try to sort them out would be a lifetime of wasted energy. All he wanted to do was serve his country, just like his father and grandfather before him. Yet now he was questioning everything, even what his country stood for.

His mind whirred as he roared down the road, contemplating St. Thomas Aquinas' Just War Theory and wondering if it applied to his country's situation in the Middle East. Thoughts pinged around in his mind until he finally resigned himself to the fact that it didn't matter—safety and security mattered most, regardless of early Christian philosophies.

He glanced at the vial on the passenger seat next to him. The Korean symbols served as a stark reminder that the global world he lived in wasn't always black and white. It was complex, convoluted, and complicated.

Thatcher hit the steering wheel with his fist. He

preferred the simple life, the one where good and evil stood in opposition to one another and it was easy to tell who was on which side. But this was a far cry from it. Gray hovered over black and white—and it was impossible to distinguish the difference, depending on one's perspective. This wasn't a problem he was going to solve today or tomorrow or the next day—maybe ever. But with a little luck and some help from Dr. Watson, maybe he could figure out who was behind the biological attacks that ravaged a compound of Taliban fighters and ultimately cost his troops their lives.

He turned on the radio and listened to an oldies station piping 80s songs over the airwaves. George Michael's "Careless Whisper" filled Banks' car and reminded him of one stark truth: The truth always comes out.

How fitting.

It was up to him to discover the truth—and make sure it came out.

Thatcher turned off the interstate at the exit he'd memorized and drove for several minutes until he came to Watson's condo. He pulled into a parking spot along the street and hustled toward her apartment, clutching the vial.

Ahead of him by a few yards was another woman heading toward the same building. She entered in her code and the door buzzed open. Thatcher quickened his pace and caught the door in time.

I'm sure she won't mind if I knock instead.

He slipped inside and headed for the apartment number she'd messaged him.

Thatcher stepped into the elevator and waited as the mechanism hummed and started to hoist him upward toward her condo on the fifth floor. It wasn't long before the elevator dinged and he exited and began an immediate search for her door number.

First left and then right before he noticed the pattern on the wall. Number five hundred forty-two. It was to the left. He shot down the hall until he came upon her door, which was wide open.

"Melissa!" he cried.

He pushed the door open with his fingertips and entered. Sounds of struggling came from the kitchen.

"Melissa!"

He rushed toward the room and found a man wrestling her to the ground. She tried to call out, but he held his hand over her mouth. When the assailant caught sight of Thatcher, he froze. Clearly, Thatcher's presence was unexpected.

Watson slapped at him, trying to break free. But it was a useless attempt, one he quelled with one hand.

Without wasting another second, Thatcher rushed the man. He jumped in the air and delivered a forearm shiver that connected with the man's head. He fell backward, releasing Watson. She scrambled away, while Thatcher landed on top of the man and commenced to beat him. In a matter of seconds, the man was subdued. Thatcher then picked up the man's body and shifted behind him. He grabbed the man's neck and twisted.

Snap!

Thatcher looked up at Watson in time to see her flinch. The grimace on her face spoke volumes about what she thought of his action.

"I had to," he said with his head down. "It was the only way."

She nodded.

"Help me," he said. "We need to move his body."

They used the stairwell and navigated the man's body toward a dumpster. A few minutes later, he was buried beneath a mountain of trash.

"Do you think anyone saw us?" she asked.

Thatcher shook his head. "This is not how I envisioned our reunion."

"And what exactly did you envision?"

"Perhaps us clinking our glasses together, saying cheers, and glancing at our feet during a high school reunion."

The corners of her mouth curled upward. "That's a far more boring story."

"Of course, this is one we can't tell anyone about," he said.

"I know."

"Let's go back inside. I need to show you something."

Thatcher followed Watson up the stairs. He had regular conversations with her in high school, but he never really *noticed* her. He couldn't help but notice her now, as her shapely figure swayed in front of him up the steps.

How did I miss her?

At the moment, it didn't matter. It was a nice bonus to the task at hand, which was solving who was behind the chemical attack in the Taliban compound.

Once they reached her apartment, he checked every room, looking under all the beds and opening each closet.

"Clear!" he said as he strode back toward the common area.

"So, what is this vial you were telling me about?"

"Wait a minute," he said. "You were almost killed and you don't want to talk about it."

She laughed and shook her head. "It wasn't the first time today. Perhaps it won't be the last. At the moment, I'm far more interested in *why* someone is trying to kill me. What has made me such a target?"

He handed her the vial. "Well, here it is. Can you tell me what's in it?"

She didn't open it, instead deciding to study it.

"It's not some historical artifact," he said.

She held up her index finger. "I know—but these markings are familiar."

He leaned toward her, excitedly. "You mean you've seen these before."

"I think so." She looked closer at the vial and then nodded. "Yep, I recognize this."

"Well, then, what is it?"

"I saw something just like this in our lab a few days ago. And if I remember correctly, these markings look just like the ones on the vials I recently investigated."

Thatcher's eyes widened. "Really?"

She nodded.

"Well, what did the liquid in the vials do?"

"They almost killed innocent people—including me."

CHAPTER 34

SENATOR THOR SIPPED HIS COFFEE and drew in a deep breath as he stared out at the sprawling green space behind his house in the posh D.C. suburb of McLean, Virginia, on a crisp Wednesday morning. He could hear the echoes of giggles and laughter coming from somewhere else in the neighborhood. The sound made him smile then grimace in pain. Those playful noises should have been coming from his yard too. Instead, only his bubbling water fountain provided a calming yet mundane soundtrack.

He glanced at the paper. The image of Staff Sgt. Thatcher in a parachute about to splash down into the Potomac River dominated the front page along with the headline: "Sordid Soldier or Frank Fighter?" The op-ed section contained a pair of columns with opposing views—one calling him a coward, the other anointing him a hero.

Thor's phone buzzed and he looked at the caller ID. It was Greg Holbrook, one of his friends from college who also happened to work in D.C. as a lobbyist for a prominent gun manufacturer.

"Did you read this morning's paper?" Holbrook said once Thor answered, dispensing with formalities.

Thor sighed. "I'm looking at it right now. God, this is

a nightmare!"

"Perhaps for some people, but there's something fishy going on—and you know it."

"The only thing fishy going on is you calling me this early at home to talk about work-related issues."

Holbrook chuckled. "What? I can't just call up my good buddy, son of Odin, and find out how he's doing?"

"You know I don't like to be called that."

Holbrook laughed again. "Exactly—that's why I do it. It's one of the many endearing things about my favorite senator, whom I've never voted for."

"And who's your favorite senator that you have voted for?"

Holbrook clucked his tongue. "You know I don't vote and tell. Besides, I think it'd be easy to figure out who my favorite senator is based on his voting record."

"What'd you really call about, Holbie Wan Kenobi?"

"Really? You're gonna go there? Of all the characters from Star Wars to be named after, you had to pick the old dude who gets sliced up by Darth Vader."

"Would a Chewbacca nickname derivative work better for you?"

"I'm gonna growl like Chewbacca if you don't stop."

"I'm gonna hang up if you don't answer my question. I've got a busy day ahead."

"Okay, okay, fine. I was wondering if you could tell me what is going on with this Sergeant Thatcher guy—like, is what he's saying true? Did the U.S. military try to have his entire squad killed to keep some secret?"

Thor sighed and contemplated his answer. "You know I can't really talk about that, right? Security clearance and all."

"I know, but I thought—"

"You thought what? That since we're old friends that I'd just tell you the truth about what's going on?"

"Yeah, but—"

"Look, I'll level with you. Nobody really knows what's going on yet. And until we're able to get him in front of a Senate committee and question him ourselves, we won't know. All I know is that he was taken into custody yesterday by an FBI agent—basically everything that was in *The Washington Post* article this morning."

"That's it?"

"I don't work for the CIA—and my security clearance only gets me information when I need to know it. Maybe I'll know more today, but it won't be anything I'll be able to tell you." He paused. "And why are you so interested in this guy anyway? This hasn't got anything to do with guns."

"I might be a lobbyist, Senator, but I'm an American, too. And if something like this is going on in our own country, I want to know about it so I can help stop it from happening again."

"Politics are often complex and—"

"Wait. Are you justifying the military's action against his troops?"

"Before you jump to any conclusions, we don't even know what really happened yet. However, the short answer to your question is no. But the long answer is far more nuanced and complicated."

"I'm not interested in nuance and complexities—just the truth. I want to know if these people I'm rubbing shoulders with on a daily basis are traitors or patriots."

"They're both and neither—at the same time," Thor

shot back. "I wish things here were black and white. If they were, it'd be much easier to invoke change. Before I came to Washington and took my oath to serve the American people, everything seemed black and white to me. But I now realize I live in a gray world, one where black and white is an ideology as much as it is a tattered dream from a bygone era. No one's hands are clean around here nor is anyone interested in washing up."

Thor signaled for one of his maids to bring him another cup of coffee. He mouthed, "Thanks, Lucy," to the woman as she picked up his mug. She smiled and headed toward the kitchen.

Holbrook remained silent.

"Are you still there?" Thor asked.

"Yeah. I'm here." He paused. "You know, I'm as cynical as anyone else in this town, but I thought there were a few sacred cows left in our country—like the military seeking to protect rather than serve its own interests, whatever those might be. Nobody should be trying to kill Sergeant Thatcher. What did he ever do to deserve such a thing?"

"Sometimes it's necessary to deal with traitors in an unconventional fashion."

"Ah-ha! So, you do know something," Holbrook said. "Don't hold out on me."

Thor measured his words as he responded. "I think I've made it clear to you that I can't tell you anything, Holbrook. But even if I could, I don't know what good it would do. I'd like to know what Sergeant Thatcher was doing in that upper northeast region of Afghanistan. It's not a place he should've been."

"Maybe he was just following orders."

"Maybe that's what he wants you to think."

"You remember the deserter who made big news after we traded Al-Qaeda operatives for him?"

"How could I forget?"

Thor looked up to see Lucy returning with a cup of coffee in her hand. He took it from her and nodded as a gesture of appreciation. "He claimed his innocence as well—but the man was a deserter. He abandoned his post and it cost several faithful soldiers their lives as they went looking for him."

"Are you suggesting that's what happened here?"

"Like I said, even if I knew, I couldn't tell you. All I can say is that people try to spin their tales in the most favorable light."

"Especially politicians."

Thor grunted. "I'll try not to be offended by that."

"You shouldn't be. You're a different breed of politician."

Thor chuckled. "Flatter me all you want but you're still not getting any information out of me—even if I had any."

"Fine. Be that way. You're just like everybody else."

"You can't even say that with conviction, can you? Just like a lobbyist."

"I'll try not to be offended at that."

Thor laughed again. "Look, Holbrook. You can stop by my office and we can discuss this over coffee some morning later this week, but I've got to get going."

"I'll be by later this week if I don't get the answers I'm looking for—don't you worry."

"What are you now? An investigative blogger looking for fodder?"

"Can't a citizen be concerned with the inner workings of his own government?"

"Most citizens can—but a conniving lobbyist?"

"Okay, enough already. But you better be ready to answer my questions. Clearance or not."

Thor hung up and shook his head in frustration.

If only running the government were as simple as he thinks it is.

He took another sip of his hot coffee, withdrawing quickly as he nearly burnt his lip. He once again scanned the pristine landscape in his backyard. It was his sanctuary, his haven—his spot where he could escape the endless Beltway chatter and just think.

His phone buzzed again. But as he reached for it, he felt a sharp pain in his chest. Instead of grabbing the phone, he clutched his upper body and toppled to the ground, dragging the outdoor glass table with him. The table shattered as it crashed down around him on the brick patio.

"Senator Thor! Senator Thor!" cried Lucy as she hustled toward him. She knelt down beside him and slapped his face a few times. "Senator Thor! Are you okay?"

He didn't twitch, much less move.

CHAPTER 35

FLYNN BURST INTO BANKS' ROOM without knocking. His actions stood in stark contrast to his usual gentlemanly nature and special attention to his grooming practices. Wearing nothing but boxers and a hairdo that appeared to be move-in ready for a family of birds, he shook Banks' feet as she sat up excitedly.

"What is it?" she asked.

"It's Thatcher. He's gone."

"What? How? Why?"

"He must've swiped your keys last night before bed."

She gestured for him to turn around so she could get dressed. He turned his back to her and closed his eyes.

"I never thought he'd do something like that. *We* are supposed to be protecting *him*."

Flynn cracked his knuckles. "Maybe he didn't trust us."

"How could he not? Doesn't he realize we're trying to save him?"

"In all fairness, we did drag him to a cabin in the middle of the woods all by ourselves."

"To protect him. And we treated him with nothing but respect and kindness."

Flynn laughed. "Speaking from experience here, but

telling the truth isn't easy—especially when you suspect everyone is trying to kill or silence you."

"If what he told us is true—all of it—his life is in serious jeopardy." She paused. "I'm done now. You can turn around."

Flynn spun to face her. "Whoa! You can roll out of bed and look like that?"

She put her hand up. "Let's keep this professional, okay?"

He nodded. "Fair enough." He took a deep breath. "We need to figure out where he is."

"Yeah, and I need to call my boss." She glanced around the room before rushing toward the kitchen.

"What is it?"

"My phone. I don't see it."

Flynn grunted. "Maybe he took it with him." He handed his phone to her. "Here. Call your phone."

She put the phone on speaker and let it ring until it went to voicemail. "That sneaky little bastard."

"Let me see if I can get us a cab up here. It might be a while."

"Try Uber."

"Out *here*?"

"Yeah, they have cars everywhere."

Flynn opened the app on his smart phone and located a cab only three minutes away. "I can't have a car coming to a CIA secret safe house."

"Let's meet him at that intersection about a quarter of a mile away."

Five minutes later, Flynn and Banks stood along the road at an intersection in the mountainside enclave, waiting to be picked up by an Uber driver. Flynn wasn't too fond of the social media taxicab service, but he decided to reconsider his position based on this experience. Within two minutes of alerting the Uber driver where they were, a man in a new Toyota Camry pulled up.

Flynn and Banks piled in and he struck up a friendly conversation with them.

"Car trouble?" the man asked.

"Something like that," Banks answered.

"I'm George Prescott the Third," the man said over his shoulder. He twirled the pair of fizzy black and white die hanging from his rearview mirror before he turned down the ranting of a talk show host on the radio.

"Jennifer."

"James."

Prescott froze. "Wait a minute—James? James Flynn?"

Banks looked at Flynn and rolled her eyes, while Flynn said nothing.

"The conspiracy theorist and journalist?" Prescott continued. "*The* James Flynn?"

"I haven't even said if my last name's Flynn or not."

A grin spread across Prescott's face. "Don't worry. You don't need to. I'd know that voice anywhere. I've heard you on *Coast to Coast* with George Noory more times than I can count. I'd know your voice anywhere."

"I hope you enjoyed the program."

"*Programs*," Prescott answered, emphasizing the *s*. "And, yes, I enjoyed them all."

"Glad to hear that."

They rode in silence for a few minutes while a newsbreak interrupted the talk radio program droning away in the background.

> *Officials are preparing for Russian President
> Alexander Petrov's appearance tomorrow in front
> of the U.S. Senate as they anticipate a large crowd
> of protestors. Security will be tight on Capitol Hill
> with multiple checkpoints. Officials are advising
> anyone planning on taking part in the protests to-
> morrow to arrive early and prepare for long lines
> for security screening. Meanwhile, the White House
> administration has backed off its earlier calls to re-
> voke Petrov's invitation, but has yet to extend an
> invitation for Petrov to meet with the President pri-
> vately while he's here.*

"Damn Russians. Always trying to stir something up,"
Prescott mumbled to himself. He turned off the radio.
"Well, since I've got you for a while, you're the perfect per-
son to talk to today. Have you been following the Super
Hero Soldier—you know, the one who parachuted into the
Potomac River the other day?"

"I'm familiar with him, yes," Flynn said.

"So, what do you think? Government conspiracy? Deranged lunatic? Somewhere in between? I'm dying to know
the truth."

"You and me both," Flynn said.

"I thought you were an expert at sniffing out such
crimes."

Flynn nodded. "Expert might be taking it a bit too far."
He sat forward in his seat. "I consider myself a journalist
first and foremost—the kind of journalist who prefers to

gather all of the facts first before jumping to any wild conclusions."

"What kind of journalist does that these days?" Prescott said, eyeing Flynn in the rearview mirror.

Flynn shrugged.

Before he could say another word, Prescott blurted out, "An unemployed one! Get it? The kind of journalist who doesn't sensationalize doesn't have a job."

Flynn waved him off. "Oh, I get it. It's just not that accurate. Outside of the tabloids, most journalists are committed to uncovering the truth. Some are better than others."

Prescott steadied the hula girl wiggling on his dashboard. "What about you, miss?" he said, shifting his eyes towards Banks.

"It's Jennifer."

The correction didn't rile Prescott in the least bit. "Okay, Jennifer. What about you? Are you a journalist?"

She chuckled. "Oh, goodness, no. I can barely stand to be around them."

"Yet here you are with one of the nation's most well-respected journalists."

She laughed again. "True, but Mr. Flynn's always going to be a spook first, journalist second."

Flynn scowled at her. "Look, I wish I could help you more, but don't know much more than you do and—"

Prescott held his finger in the air then poked the die. "*Much more.* No, no, no. You can't fool me, Mr. Flynn. I've lived in this city long enough to pick up on catch phrases for spinning a lie and making it sound like the truth. You do know something else that I don't know, don't you?"

Flynn took a deep breath and shifted in his seat.

"What's the biggest conspiracy that remains unsolved in our country's history?"

"Who shot JFK?"

Flynn waved him off. "And you call yourself a fan? I solved that last year. Try to keep up, Mr. Prescott."

"Area 51."

Flynn sat back in his seat. "You didn't hear that from me." He watched the rearview mirror as Prescott's eyes lit up.

Prescott slammed his fist on the steering wheel. "I knew it!" he said, flicking the hula girl shaking on his dashboard. He leaned down, getting on eye-level with the tottering toy. "I told you it had to do with aliens, girl. I just knew it!"

Flynn leaned over to Banks and whispered, "Are all Uber drivers like this?"

She pointed toward a sticker on the back window that read, "My other car is a UFO."

He shook his head.

"They're not all like this," she whispered back. "But then again, everyone is a conspiracy theorist, right?"

Flynn bit his lip, letting go of her not-so-subtle dig. In a matter of seconds, several comebacks popped into his head, but he decided he'd rather keep the peace than keep score with witty banter—at least with Banks.

He handed her his phone. "Why don't you try your phone again? Maybe Thatcher will answer this time?"

"I don't know why he would."

"Just do it, okay?"

She took the phone and dialed. After the third ring he picked up. "Hello?"

"Is this Special Agent Banks?" Thatcher asked.

"Yeah—and I wanna know what the hell you thought you were doing. That was stupid what you did last night."

"Actually, it was a stroke of genius—not to mention I saved my friend's life."

"What are you talking about?"

"I can't go into details now, but I'll tell you about it later. I just had to meet my friend who could examine the liquid in the vial I took from that compound in Afghanistan. According to her, it's not Korean."

"Look, let's not talk about this right now," Banks said. "Where are you?"

"I'm at my friend's lab downtown," he said before giving her the address. "She had to go to work this morning, so I tagged along with her."

"Stay right there and don't talk to anyone."

"Affirmative."

She hung up and gave Prescott the address.

"The Goldstein Group? This must be really juicy," Prescott said. "There are all kinds of rumors on conspiracy boards about that place."

"Don't hold your breath—we're just going to meet a friend who borrowed my car last night."

"Oh." He paused and thought for a moment. "This is how you do it, isn't it?"

"Do what?" Banks asked.

"Deceive the general public into thinking everything's okay when really there's a shit storm going on and we're all gonna die if you don't do something about it."

Flynn chuckled. "Man, you watch too many movies."

Prescott shook his head. "I thought you were one of

us, man. A true believer. But now I'm starting to doubt it all. I'm even beginning to wonder if you're a plant by our government to make sure nobody finds out the truth as you *investigate* everything."

Flynn leaned forward in his seat. "Here's what I'm gonna do for you, Prescott. I'm gonna attend a Q and A session that you host when my next book comes out. Invite your friends, your chat room buddies, your grandma—I don't care. And I'll come over and answer everyone's questions. How does that sound?"

A grin spread across Prescott's face. "You really mean it?"

Flynn handed him a business card. "I've never been very good at joking."

"Deal, Mr. Flynn. Wait until the guys hear this."

"But no disparaging me online, got it? That wouldn't be kind, now would it?"

Prescott shook his head. "No, sir. It wouldn't—and it'd be a lie."

Flynn sat back in his seat after patting Prescott on the shoulder. "That's right. It would be one big lie. And if there's anything I've learned about you during this ride, it's that you are all about the truth."

Prescott nodded and poked his fuzzy die again. "I know you'd bring me good luck today."

Banks rolled her eyes and looked at her GPS. They were almost at The Goldstein Group.

"This is fine here," she said.

"You sure you don't want me to take you all the way?" Prescott asked.

"Nope. We'll take it from here. Thanks for the ride."

Flynn and Banks climbed out of the car and watched it drive away.

"Now that was an experience," Flynn said.

"Is it always like that with you out in public?"

"What do you mean?"

"Nut jobs fawning all over you, telling you how amazing you are?"

Flynn shrugged. "I don't think he thought I was *that* amazing."

"You know what I mean."

"I get it from time to time—and it can be annoying. But it's also a good reminder that it's because of these people that I have my job."

"If I had a job only because of whack jobs—"

"Be careful what you say there, Special Agent Banks, because if it weren't for all the whack jobs who think they can outsmart you, you'd also be doing something else."

"And what kind of job do you think I'd have?"

"A model?"

She rolled her eyes.

"A Bond girl."

She shoved him playfully. "Please. I'm not into all that misogynistic garbage. Bond would be dead at the bottom of a river if it weren't for all those women."

"Or dead in his own bed."

"That, too." She stopped. "I mean, can't you think of at least one respectable profession I might have if I didn't work for the Bureau?"

"Martial arts instructor?"

"I'll take what I can get." She gestured toward the building. "We're here."

"This ought to be interesting."

Once inside, they asked the receptionist to ring Dr. Watson, who brought Staff Sgt. Thatcher with her into the lobby.

After brief introductions, Dr. Watson said, "You must excuse me, for I have an urgent errand that I have to run. I'll reconnect with you later and fill you in on everything."

She scurried out the door and into the parking lot.

Banks then leaned in close to Thatcher. "If you ever try to pull a stunt like that again—"

Thatcher put up his hand. "Save your threats. We're on the same side. I just wasn't sure I could trust you. I had to do some research on you two—and find out what was inside this vial. If I gave it to you to figure out, it would've entered some chain of custody protocol and we may have never found out the truth."

"So, what'd you find out?" Flynn asked.

Thatcher glanced around the lobby. "Let's not talk about it here. Plus, I'm starving. Are either of you up for an early lunch?"

"I could go for a bite to eat," Flynn said. "Banks?"

"Why not?" she said, holding out her hand. "But I want *my* keys in *my* hands before the count of three. One … two …"

"Three," Thatcher said as he placed them in her hand. "Happy?"

She growled and headed toward the parking lot.

As soon as everyone got inside the car, Thatcher leaned forward from the backseat. "I killed a man last night."

Banks looked over her shoulder. "You did what?"

"It was self-defense. I mean, for Dr. Watson."

She rubbed her face with both hands. "You better start talking."

"Last night when I got to Dr. Watson's apartment, the door was ajar. I entered slowly and found a man trying to wrestle her to the ground. I fought him for a few minutes— and when I realized he wasn't going to stop and leave her alone, I engaged him in hand-to-hand combat."

"And how'd you kill him?"

"I snapped his neck."

"What'd you do with the body?" Flynn asked.

"We put it in a dumpster and covered it with trash."

Banks sighed. "Did anyone see you?"

"We didn't see anyone else, if that answers your question."

"It doesn't."

"Well, I can't be certain, but I didn't see a soul on the streets while we were covering him up or in the stairwell when we were dragging his body down the stairs."

She shook her head. "I'll cover for you if I have to. But what we really want to know is what you found out was in that vial—and where it came from."

Banks pulled out of the parking lot and looked back at Thatcher as she headed down the street.

"We haven't found out anything yet. It's still running in the lab—but Dr. Watson suspects it's the same virus." Then he grabbed Banks' shoulders. "Stop the car!"

"What?" Banks said.

He pointed toward the other lane. "That's Dr. Watson's car."

In the opposite lane, a mangled vehicle flipped on its hood smoked as sirens wailed in the distance.

196 | **R.J. PATTERSON**

Banks pulled off to the side and stopped the car. The traffic prevented them from crossing the street quickly as paramedics arrived on the scene within seconds after they stopped.

Thatcher gawked at the scene before unleashing a guttural scream.

"Melissa!"

CHAPTER 36

KRAMER ENTERED THE BLACK SEDAN like a ghost. The man seated next to him spit out some of his coffee when he realized he wasn't alone."

"Geez, Kramer," the man said. "Can't you at least give me a little warning?"

"The second someone knows I'm coming, that's the second I fail."

"Well, I'm not a target, so enough with the spook tactics."

Kramer nodded and turned to stare out the window. "I need better intel if I'm going to achieve all your objectives."

"Perhaps if you were a better shot—"

Kramer's eyes narrowed. "I'm good, but not a god. In fact, I'm great—and you won't find anyone else better than me. So, let's dispense with the snide jabs."

"Fair enough." The man sighed. "Look, tomorrow is a very important day if we're going to carry out this plan. Operation Threat Level Five is now active."

"What does that mean for me?"

"A change of priorities, if you will."

"You want me to forget about Banks and Flynn."

"For the time being. Thatcher, however, must be dealt with swiftly."

"From the intel you gave me, all three of them are running around together."

"For the time being, though he escaped from their custody last night."

Kramer's brow furrowed. "How do you know this? You didn't even know where they were staying last night."

"Another operative was watching another target—and Thatcher met up with her."

"But Thatcher got away?"

"Thatcher killed our operative. Broke his neck and left his body in a dumpster."

"And the woman?"

"We took care of her this morning."

Kramer chuckled. "I see what this is all about. You're really scared of Thatcher—and you think that this is a suicide mission, so you want me to at least get him before Flynn or Banks take me out. Well, good luck to them. They're going to need it."

"Thatcher could bring down our entire operation if he's not skillfully eliminated."

"Piece of cake."

"All that bravado of yours might get you killed."

"It hasn't so far." Kramer grinned and slapped the man on the knee. "I'll be in touch, senator."

***

SENATOR RYAN TAPPED on the window with his cane, signaling for the driver to head toward their next destination. He picked up his phone and dialed a number.

"Time to move to Phase 2," he said before hanging up.

CHAPTER 37

WHEN WATSON WOKE UP, Thatcher sat at her bedside, holding her hand. He smiled as she stirred. Squinting, she propped herself up with her elbows and looked around.

"What happened? Where am I?" she asked.

"Everything's going to be all right," Thatcher said. "You were in an accident, but you're okay now."

"How did you know?"

"We saw your car along the road as we were leaving."

She glanced around the room before leaning closer to him. In a whisper, she said, "Do you think *they* know?"

"Who is *they* and what would *they* know?"

She scanned the room before answering. "Whoever has been watching me and sent someone to kill me last night—I think you can figure out what I'm talking about."

Thatcher stroked her hair. "I'm not going to let these bastards hurt you—whoever they are."

"It's got to do with what's in that vial. You know I can't go back to the lab."

"I'll keep you safe. Don't worry about that."

Her face fell. "I can't even go back to my condo." She buried her head in her hands. "What am I going to do?"

"Before we can formulate a plan, you need to get better.

That was a nasty wreck."

"What did the doctor say?"

The door swung open and a stocky male nurse swaggered into the room. "I can answer that question for you," he said. Offering his hand to Watson, "Nurse O'Connor."

"Nice to meet you," she said.

"You were in a terrible accident from what I hear, but you're going to be fine. A few bruised ribs and maybe a concussion, but nothing a little rest and some aspirin won't fix. The doc just wants to keep you in overnight for some observations."

"I don't remember anything," she said. "All I know is that one minute I was driving and the next I'm waking up here in the hospital."

"You'll be fine," O'Connor said, patting her on the leg. "Just don't let this guy keep you up too much. You need to get some more sleep."

Thatcher smiled and waved at the nurse, who hung up Watson's chart at the foot of the bed before exiting the room.

Thatcher turned his attention back to her. "You really don't remember what happened?"

"I think a car crossed the center line and struck me, but I can't be sure. It all happened so fast."

He leaned in close. "I don't think this was any accident either. Someone clearly wants to stop you from producing an antidote for this virus."

"Or they want to control it."

Thatcher cocked his head. "What do you mean?"

"I mean, I was assigned to come up with a vaccine for the virus. One of my colleagues was assigned to come up with an antidote."

"So. Somebody doesn't want you to succeed."

"I think they do. In fact, I think the same people who asked me to do this are now the ones trying to kill me. They got at least an antidote out of this and now they want to make sure I go away for good."

"What makes you think that?"

She sat up fully. "Some strange things have been going on recently at the lab. Unusual requests, more secrecy than I've even seen, unfamiliar visitors and observers in my lab. It makes me all very suspicious of what's really going on upstairs with management."

"Perhaps someone in The Goldstein Group is dirty."

She shook her head. "I think it's more than just a *someone*. Think about it. If you had a deadly virus on your hands but controlled the antidote *and* the vaccine, you'd control everything. People would give up their firstborn to get it if they caught the virus; they'd do anything for a cure."

"But that doesn't explain how the virus ended up in a remote corner of Afghanistan."

"Maybe the virus makers are claiming there's no cure—and The Goldstein Group purchased some in order to make an antidote."

"And now they want to control it?"

"It'd definitely be a financial windfall for them."

Thatcher frowned. "Profiting off another human's misery? That doesn't sound like the kind of company you ever would've worked for."

She looked down and sighed. "No, it's not what I ever envisioned for myself either. I wanted to do real good for the world instead of making antidotes to only stave off the evil that keeps popping up everywhere."

"Well, here's your chance," Thatcher said.

She looked at him, brow furrowed. "What do you mean?"

"Give away the antidote's recipe. Get all the major pharmaceutical companies to start producing the stuff now so we'll have enough when the virus strikes."

She threw her hands in the air. "I can't do that. They'd fire me. I'd never work anywhere like The Goldstein Group again."

"And why does that bother you so much?"

She nodded and smiled. "Good point."

A hard knock on the door interrupted their conversation and another nurse walked in, this time stockier than the first guy.

"Where's Nurse O'Connor?" Thatcher asked.

"Shift change," the nurse answered.

Without another word, he started to swap out her IV fluids.

"Excuse me," Thatcher said. "What are you doing?"

"My job," the nurse said.

"What's in there?"

The nurse froze and glared at him. "Are you always this pushy?"

"When it comes to my friend's health care, you bet I am."

The nurse sighed. "The damn Internet is ruining everything. Everybody thinks they know as much as the medical professionals because they read something on a website once."

Thatcher stood up. "You didn't answer my question."

The nurse ignored him.

Thatcher's voice rose. "I said, you didn't answer my question."

The nurse finished swapping out the bag and adjusted the flow of the liquid through the tube feeding into Watson's arm.

Thatcher ripped the tube out of her arm.

"Owww!" Watson cried.

"What'd you do that for?" the nurse asked.

"Just answer the damn question—what's in the bag?"

Without saying another word, the nurse leapt across the bed toward Thatcher, knocking him into the wall. He tried to put the soldier in a sleeper hold but his efforts were rebuffed.

An aluminum tray clanked to the ground as the two men tussled around the room. Watson fiddled for her call button but couldn't find it.

The nurse picked up a pair of scissors off the floor and lunged at Thatcher, who narrowly avoided the sharp blade. For several more seconds, they danced around the room—the nurse waving the scissors at Thatcher, while Thatcher steered clear. When the nurse lunged toward Thatcher again, Thatcher ripped off the IV tube and quickly wrapped it around the nurse, forcing him to drop his weapon.

In control now, Thatcher spun the man around and kneed him in the back, sending him to the ground. Thatcher knelt down, reaching under the man and put him in a sleeper hold.

"Is this what you were trying to do to me?" Thatcher asked.

But Thatcher couldn't hold it long enough. The nurse jumped to his feet and delivered a flurry of punches that sent Thatcher backward.

Watson continued feeling around her bed for the emergency call button. After a few seconds, she found it and pressed it.

The alarm didn't faze the nurse—or the FBI special agent standing outside her room.

CHAPTER 38

"ARE YOU SURE WE'RE DOING the right thing?" Banks asked as she stared outside the window at the mass of humanity going nowhere. The early afternoon traffic on the Beltway had ground to a near standstill.

"What are you talking about?" Flynn asked.

"Leaving Thatcher and Dr. Watson at the hospital."

He rubbed his chin and looked at the glowing taillights in front of him. "It's your people. You trust them, right?"

She hesitated while she drummed on the steering wheel. "Yes—well—I don't know." She threw her hands in the air. "Who can you trust anymore?"

"My personal list seems to shrink by the day—occupational hazard, I guess."

"I feel the same way."

"I'm sure they're fine. Thatcher can take care of himself."

"I guess the real question is whether or not I trust my boss."

Flynn turned and looked at her. "So, do you?"

She shrugged. "More so than some of the other people I work with—but that's not saying much."

"Life in espionage—it can eat away at your soul."

"Or wake you up to reality." She paused. "Nothing is as it seems."

"That's exactly why we need to find out what's going on here—I'm still hung up on the fact that the Russians were trying to steal Plutonium-238 from the U.S. in a brazen heist, not to mention that there's an assassin out there trying to kill us."

"Isn't that why we're meeting your handler?" she asked.

He nodded. "I hope he's got some answers."

The traffic started to move again and Banks squeezed between two drivers, the latter of whom was engrossed with his phone instead of paying attention to the crawling cars around him. He leaned on his horn.

Flynn turned around and eyed the man. "Whatever happened to common courtesy?" he said as he waved. The driver gave him the middle finger salute in return. "There's so much love in this city."

Banks laughed and stomped on the gas again, this time sneaking between a pair of cars to get into the HOV lane, which was moving twice as fast as the other lanes.

"Nice driving," Flynn said.

"Thanks."

"Only problem is, we have to get off at the next exit in order to meet Osborne."

She glared at him. "That would've been nice to know before now."

"You never asked."

The car lurched as she jammed her foot on the gas pedal and swerved to the right. A few more honks and middle-finger salutes later, Banks had successfully navigated her vehicle off the Beltway.

"Left or right?" she asked with a hint of sarcasm.

He winked at her. "Take a right."

Flynn led her toward an abandoned warehouse a couple of miles off the highway, but not before he made her follow the protocol for shaking any tails that Osborne taught him.

"You have one paranoid handler," Banks said after Flynn finally let her turn onto the road leading to the meeting location.

"Never know who's watching."

A trail of dust followed them until Banks finally parked the SUV and flashed her headlights four times as Flynn instructed.

A black sedan parked about fifty meters away flashed its lights back twice.

"That's him," Flynn said, wasting no time getting out of the car.

Osborne also got out and waited for the two agents to join him.

"Why all the secrecy all of a sudden?" Banks asked as she strode toward Osborne.

"There's a lot more going on beneath the surface— stuff I haven't even sorted out yet. But better safe than sorry, right?"

Flynn shook his head. "We've almost been sorry this week—and we most definitely haven't been safe."

"But you're alive. And right now, that's what's most important because we've lost several agents already this week, good agents."

Flynn folded his arms and tilted his head to one side. "What's going on?"

"I'm still working on it, but from what I can gather, there's a massive cover-up taking place among the top brass at the CIA."

"What kind of cover-up?" Banks asked.

"I don't know yet, but it's not good. Spies are secretive by nature, but there are a few things leaking out."

"Anything you can divulge to me?" Flynn asked.

Osborne shook his head. "Not yet. Not until I get confirmation."

Flynn sighed. "Have you found out anything about the mystery man trying to kill us?"

Osborne put his index finger in the air triumphantly. "Now, that's something I do have some information about—at least I think I do." He reached into his car and grabbed a folder from the passenger seat. He handed it to Flynn. "I learned about a clandestine group of assassins under the name 'Project White Out.' It's off the books, of course, but there is a record of at least a half-dozen former operatives and special recruits for the program that I could find information on." He paused for a moment. "Recognize any of these men?"

Flynn chuckled. "Cory Young is a member of a black ops CIA project?" He shook his head. "Now, I am afraid for the future of this country."

"Anyone else you recognize?" Osborne asked.

Banks looked over Flynn's shoulder.

Osborne encouraged her, pointing at the file. "You, too, Special Agent Banks. Don't be shy. This is a team effort at this point—this small team of three."

She shook her head. "None of these men look familiar."

"I'll keep digging," Osborne said. "But be on the lookout—and find some other place to stay. Someone is after you—and apparently, they're after Dr. Watson, not to mention Thatcher."

Osborne's phone buzzed and he fished it out of his pocket. "Oh, my god."

"What is it?" Flynn asked.

"It's Senator Thor—he's dead."

CHAPTER 39

WATSON WATCHED AS THATCHER struggled to shake loose the man who called himself a nurse. To her, it was clear that his mission was more about ending her life than saving it. She waited for several moments, but no one rushed into the room—not even the guard supposedly standing watch outside her door.

A bedside tray clanged onto the ground as the two men wrestled near her. Thatcher fought to gain an advantage, but he couldn't shake loose the man's grip.

However, once Thatcher managed to turn the man's back to Watson, she picked up her IV stand and started hitting him with it. At first, she couldn't muster much more than annoying jabs. Then after a few moments, she landed a blow to the head that knocked him off balance, giving Thatcher enough time to gain a more favorable position.

Thatcher wormed his way behind the man and jammed his knee into his back, this time without flinching. He then put the man in a sleeper hold and waited.

The nurse struggled for only a few seconds before his body went limp.

Thatcher scrambled over to Watson and started ripping the monitoring wires and devices off her body. He handed her a pile of clothes. "Here—put these on."

"What are you doing?" she said.

"Getting you out of here. Whoever is after you isn't going to stop until you're dead. And I'm not going to let that happen."

Watson hustled into her clothes and slipped her shoes on.

"Ready?" Thatcher asked.

She nodded.

He opened the door and found the FBI agent standing with his back to him. A doctor and two nurses were trying to get into the room, but he refused to let them in.

Thatcher gave the agent a shove and dashed down the hallway, Watson in tow.

They raced down the stairwell and outside where they found a cab parked along the curb. They both climbed inside.

"George Washington University," Thatcher said. "And step on it."

Watson looked out the back window and saw several people spilling out into the parking lot, searching for her. As long as the first nurse was telling her the truth, she had nothing to worry about—though her list of people she could trust was shrinking by the moment.

"What are we going to do at GW?" she asked Thatcher in a whisper.

"We're going to find out what's in this vial," he said, tapping his pocket.

Her eyes widened. "You brought it with you? Are you crazy?"

"I've been called worse—but I'm determined. I must

know what's going on with this stuff."

She sat up straight and stared at him. "I'll tell you what's going on—whatever is in that vial is gonna cost us our lives. You can't be toting it around like that."

He tilted his head to one side. "So, you would've preferred for me to leave it in your lab?"

She shook her head. "This stuff is dangerous."

"So are the people who are trying to control your antidote. We need to know what we're dealing with—and I need to know why the United States military turned on me."

The taxi driver's identification card dangled from the rearview mirror. Based on his name, it was clear to Watson that he wasn't born in the United States, nor was English his first language.

"Are you out of your mind? This could kill us all."

The driver whistled and pointed to the right. "Is this it?" he stammered.

Thatcher nodded. "Thank you." He threw the man a twenty-dollar bill and climbed out of the car. He offered his hand to Watson. She declined.

"You're going to get us killed, I hope you know that," she said, stomping onto the sidewalk.

"We're both living on borrowed time," he said. "Let's just make it count, okay?"

She glared at him and stopped. "It doesn't have to be this way. We can just walk away."

Thatcher shook his head. "You think they'll just let you walk away—after all you've seen? I know you're not that delusional."

"I was only trying to help," she said. "I was only trying to follow orders."

"Sometimes the people who give us orders only do so because they don't have the guts to do the dirty work themselves. Real leaders get in the trenches and show us how it's done."

They didn't talk as they walked toward the heart of campus, remaining silent for several minutes.

"Do you know where a lab is?" Thatcher asked.

"I thought you did," she shot back. "I know nothing about GW's facilities."

"But you know something, right?"

She shook her head. "Fine. I'll ask someone." She stopped a student and asked for direction to the university's research lab. Less than a minute later, they changed course and headed toward the intended destination.

"What if it's not what you think is in here?" Thatcher asked as he swirled the liquid around.

"Would you put that away?" she said. Her stern rebuke made him jam the vial into his pocket.

"I'm just curious. You don't have to bite my head off."

"I most certainly do," she said. "If that thing were to slip out of your hand and break, we'd have an epidemic on our hands—an epidemic that can only be stopped by the antidote I create, the antidote that hasn't been mass produced yet."

"I'm tired of fighting—just figure out what's in here."

After a few more minutes of navigating their way to the bioscience building, Watson wandered into a lab with a half-dozen students busy on their experiments.

"Hello?" she said.

Nobody moved.

"Hello? Can anyone help me?"

One of the students backed away from his microscope and looked up. He stumbled over his stool, knocking it over as he rushed over to meet her.

He offered his hand. "Noah Plimpton. I'm in charge of the lab here."

She shook his hand. "Dr. Melissa Watson."

"How can we help you, Dr. Watson?"

She glanced around the lab. "My assistant and I need to borrow some equipment—and I need to do it in a contained area."

Noah looked at Thatcher, who forced a smile. Noah returned his focus to Watson. "What's this pertaining to exactly?"

"I wish I could tell you more, Noah, but the fact is we're in a bit of a hurry and it's somewhat proprietary."

Noah cocked his head to one side. "Where did you say you worked again?"

"I didn't say, but I work at The Goldstein Group."

Noah's eyes widened. "The Goldstein Group? And you're *here* wanting to use *our* equipment? If I had a fraction of their funding and equipment—"

"Look, if you help me out, I'll put in a word for you— that is if you're interested in working there. I hear there may even be an opening soon. How's that sound?"

"Sounds excellent."

"So you'll help?"

"Absolutely. Just tell me what you need."

"Great. Let's start with hazmat suits?"

"Hazmat suits? Whoa. What kind of project is this?"

"The less you ask, the better."

"But I need to know if you're going to contaminate

my lab."

"Trust me. I'd never contaminate your lab. Just give us a contained space."

Noah sighed and then winked at her. "Okay—I've got just the spot for you."

Watson gave him a list of the things she needed. They waited patiently while Noah directed a few of the grad students to fetch the supplies.

"You sure you'll be able to figure this out?" Thatcher whispered to Watson.

She nodded. "I'd bet my life on it."

"Good—because I *am* betting my life on it. If this turns out to be a fake, I'm going to be forever cast as a pariah."

She glanced at him. "It could be worse."

"Nope. This would be the pinnacle—or rather, the worst possible position I've ever been in—in my life."

She waved him off. "Okay, okay. Knock it off. I get it. You're unhappy. Let's see if we can change that."

Once Noah finished setting them up, Watson thanked him. She and Thatcher then donned hazmat suits.

"You ready?" she asked.

"Ready as I'll ever be."

She put a drop of the liquid on a slide and placed it beneath a microscope. After a few minutes, she looked up. "Yep, this is it. Exactly the same."

"So, what do you suggest we do about it?" Thatcher asked.

"I say we stick to the plan, make them think we don't know anything."

"And then what?"

"We'll know when the time is right," she said.

"There's no good time to break bad news," he said. "There's no good time to let anyone run over you either."

"Good point," Thatcher said. "Let's get someplace safe and regroup."

"I agree," she said. "If this virus gets airborne before the antidote has been created—much less a vaccine—we're talking about a potential catastrophic loss of life."

CHAPTER 40

FLYNN RECLINED IN HIS SEAT while Banks kicked up gravel on her way out of the meeting site with Osborne. He closed his eyes and remained completely still, interlocking his fingers and resting them on his stomach.

"Hey," Banks said hitting him in the arm. "Wake up! This is no time for a nap."

"I'm thinking," Flynn said.

"Well, I need you to think with me instead of becoming one with the passenger seat over there."

Flynn smiled. "Just when this seat was starting to divulge all your secrets." He shook his head and sat upright. "Okay, fine. Let's just focus on what we know."

"It's quite simple really—someone tried to kill us, someone tried to kill Dr. Watson twice, Sergeant Thatcher claims the military tried to kill him, and someone just killed Senator Thor, the hawk senator."

"And the Russians tried to steal Plutonium-238 and the Russian President is speaking to the U.S. Senate tomorrow."

She brushed her hair back with her hand. "What are we missing here?"

"A common denominator and motive."

"Thanks, Captain Obvious—but I was looking for

something a little more specific."

"Me, too—but I can't figure out the connection yet, if there even is one. We could just be dealing with multiple random events."

She sighed. "Where are we headed anyway?"

"I'm glad you asked," Flynn said. "At least this time, you won't have to make any last-second exits."

He proceeded to give her directions to a studio apartment he kept in D.C.

"Does anybody know about this place?" she asked.

Flynn shook his head. "Not a soul. I bought it with cash under an alias."

"A government alias?"

He furrowed his brow. "Really? You think I'd keep anything the government gave me after what they did to me? Please."

"Just checking. You can never be too sure."

Banks tuned the radio to a news program that discussed the current events of the day. More violence in the Middle East, a celebrity said something offensive that turned into an Internet mob, depressing economic news that made pundits argue over whether it was good news or bad, and a report about an cat video that went viral on the web.

"I swear you could've played this news report every day for the past three years and I couldn't have told you what year it was," Banks said, shaking her head.

"The only thing that would've made it better was if there was a report about something stupid one of the Kardashians did."

Banks smirked. "That wouldn't be news."

A few minutes later, they arrived at Flynn's apartment.

He took a quick look around and determined it was safe.

"Looking for the boogie man?" Banks asked. "Didn't you say nobody knew about this place?"

"You can never be too sure, right?"

They sat down in the living area when Banks' phone rang. She didn't recognize the number. It rang again while she stared at the phone.

"Are you gonna answer that?" Flynn said.

She bit her lip. "I'm not sure who it is."

"Just answer it—or put it away."

She tapped on the green button to answer. "Banks."

"Hi, Special Agent Banks, this is Sergeant Thatcher. I wanted to let you know that Dr. Watson finally had a chance to analyze the liquid in the vial."

Banks pushed a button on her phone. "I'm putting you on speaker so Flynn can hear you. Go ahead."

"So, Dr. Watson says the vial I have contains the virus that she was developing a vaccine for. I already figured this, but she said based on her experiments this virus is deadly."

Flynn piped up. "But she created a vaccine for it, right?"

"No, she created an antidote instead, but she doesn't know what's being done with it. She gave it to her boss— and now it looks like someone wants her dead."

"Can you get the formula from her?" Banks asked.

"I'm going to have her email it to your phone right now. And then you can get it in the hands of the appropriate people."

"No, don't email it. Just have her write it down and hide it in the George Washington lab. We can't let that information fall into the hands of the wrong people—and I've got no idea who is monitoring my emails."

"She's already working on it," Thatcher said.

"What else do we know about this virus?"

"She said that once it gets airborne, it can wipe out hundreds of people in a matter of minutes. And once you catch it, you don't have long. In her limited test group, no monkey lived past twenty-four hours. But it's not a large enough sample to determine anything, she said."

"Okay, great. Now, find a safe place and I'll get in touch with you soon enough."

Banks hung up the phone and slumped on the couch.

"This is getting more interesting by the minute," Flynn said.

"I wish this was simpler, not interesting."

Flynn's phone rang. "It's Osborne."

"Flynn."

"Have you found out anything new?"

"Hang on. I'm putting you on speaker so Special Agent Banks can hear."

"Okay."

"So, to answer your question, yes. We have found out something new. The vial that Sergeant Thatcher brought back from Afghanistan matched what Dr. Watson was working on. She created an antidote for it, but who knows what The Goldstein Group intends to do with it."

"I hope they're already producing it."

"No way. Not this fast," Flynn said.

"If it's longer than twenty-four hours, it's far too long."

"What are you talking about?"

"We just got some chatter about an attack tomorrow on Capitol Hill. Our best intel indicates it's going to happen during President Petrov's speech."

"Can you stop it?"

Osborne sighed. "If we do, it'll look political. The White House administration has already expressed how much they dislike Petrov doing this."

"But if this threat is real and he dies, it's going to start a war."

Flynn smiled. "Not that Americans would care about either Petrov or a bunch of senators exiting this world a little early."

"Enough with the wise cracks."

"Do you think the administration fabricated a rumor about the attack to keep Petrov from speaking?"

"It's possible, but they were the ones who told us that this situation is a lose-lose for them—and they want us to ensure that the least amount of damage is done."

"Which is obviously keeping everyone alive."

"Exactly."

"Let me talk to Dr. Watson about how these terrorists might go about making the virus airborne and get back with you."

"Excellent. But make it quick. We don't have much time to secure the senate chamber."

Flynn hung up and looked at Banks. He watched her eyes widen as the sound of someone clapping slowly echoed off the brick walls.

"Well done, you two."

They turned around to see a man with his gun trained on them.

"Well done. Too bad you won't be able to do a thing about it."

CHAPTER 41

THATCHER WANTED TO GET his story out there, one that could exonerate him and help him eliminate the motive for some secret government assassin trying to keep him silent permanently. He considered putting his story out on social media, but he didn't even believe half of what he read on there anymore. People created sites to fact check others—and now there were fact checking sites for the fact checking sites. He needed a trustworthy source, a source people would believe before dismissing him as a crazed soldier or deserter who wanted to turn himself into a hero.

"Banks and Flynn told you to get someplace safe?" Watson asked as they got into her car.

"The television station," he said.

"What? Excuse me?"

"Let's go to the television station."

"You think that's safe?" she asked as she turned the ignition.

"I can't think of any place these people can't get us, but if we don't get this story out there, who knows what will become of us. I don't know about you, but I can't live my life like this, always looking over my shoulder every ten seconds to see if someone is going to put a bullet in my head.

I chose that life overseas as a member of our military so I wouldn't have to live that way when I was home."

"You think anyone will listen to us?"

"I think my return home made quite a splash in the media—pun intended. I don't see why they wouldn't want to interview me."

"Channel 9 isn't that far from here."

"Sounds good to me. Let's go."

A half hour later, they entered the WUSA building and asked to speak to a producer. The security guard at the front desk was anything but compliant.

"Everyone's already gone home for the evening," he said.

"There's an eleven o'clock news program. I know people are in there."

The guard stopped. "Hey, aren't you that soldier guy, who—"

"Yes, Sergeant Thatcher. And I want to speak to a producer. I don't think they'd take too kindly to finding out that you turned down the hottest news story in D.C."

"Okay, okay. Just a minute."

The guard made a phone call and less than a minute later, a squatty man with a thin ring of hair surrounding his baldhead rushed into the lobby.

"Staff Sgt. Thatcher?" the man asked.

Thatcher nodded. "In the flesh."

The producer offered his hand. "John Finkle, producer for the eleven o'clock news. To what do we owe this honor?"

"I need to tell my story," Thatcher said.

"Wonderful. We can schedule something for tomorrow."

Thatcher shook his head. "That'll be too late. I need to do this now—or else I'll go find another network that will take my exclusive this evening."

Finkle put his hands up. "All right. Come with me. This may take a bit of juggling. We've only got about an hour and a half before we go live."

Thatcher and Watson followed Winkle down the hall.

"And who's the young lady?" Finkle asked over his shoulder.

"This is Dr. Watson."

"Wonderful," Finkle said. "Pleased to meet you. I'm normally not this rushed—" He paused. "Oh, who am I kidding? I'm always in a rush. But maybe more so than usual after this curve ball."

They stood in the wings of the set and watched Finkle scurry across the floor toward one of the women who appeared to be on-air talent. Her face lit up as she listened to Finkle deliver the news. She nearly tripped over one of the wires on the studio floor as she rushed over to introduce herself.

"Hi, I'm Rosalyn Booker," she said, extending her hand to Thatcher and then Watson.

"Pleased to meet you," Thatcher said.

She gestured toward a couple of director's chairs nearby. "So, why all the urgency? What's this all about?"

"Well, I know you've heard my story that I got out when I was in Germany, but ever since I've been back, no one knows the truth about what really happened to me—and I want to make sure it gets out there."

Booker narrowed her eyes and cocked her head to one side. "But why tonight? Why *right now*?"

228 | **R.J. PATTERSON**

"I can't tell you *everything*, Ms. Booker, but I can tell you that if I don't get on the air and talk about this tonight, I'm liable to end up dead in some mysterious suicide or car accident or some other weird form of death in the next day or two. It's for my own protection."

"You think sharing your story will protect you from the people who are trying to kill you?"

"Absolutely. If anything, it will make it more difficult for them."

"How so?"

"Once I share my story on-air, the people who are trying to kill me will have a dark cloud of suspicion over them if I wind up dead."

"And what's her role in this?" Booker said, pointing at Watson.

"I'm trying to keep her safe, too."

"Well, this sounds like it has the potential to be an incredible interview. Why don't you tell me a little bit first so I can craft some questions that will be helpful? Let me just go get my pad so I can take a few notes."

Once Booker got up, Watson's phone rang.

"It's Banks," she said.

"Put her on speaker," Thatcher answered.

"Hi, Special Agent Banks. What can we do for you?"

"Thatcher mentioned that you made a copy of the working antidote."

"Yes, I hid it."

"Okay. We need it as soon as possible."

Watson furrowed her brow. "Why? What's going on?"

"There's a rumored attack going to take place tomorrow—and if we don't make the antidote, some very important people could die, not to mention the turmoil it could throw this country into."

"Okay. We're down at Channel 9 and Sergeant Thatcher is about to go on the air in an interview at eleven o'clock. Just come on down here and I'll give it to you. I've got the formula committed to memory."

"See you soon."

Watson hung up and looked at Thatcher. "What have I got myself into?"

He put his hand on her shoulder. "Don't worry. Hopefully once I share my story, we'll get out of this together."

***

KRAMER EYED HIS TWO CAPTIVES and grinned. "Well done, Special Agent Banks. I had no idea that you could be so compliant."

Kramer dragged Flynn's two kitchen chairs to the center of the living area and placed them back-to-back. "Now, why don't the two of you each have a seat."

Neither Flynn nor Banks moved.

"Not all at once now," Kramer said.

They both remained still.

"Do I need to take away a chair and start playing music to get you to move? Or should I just shoot the last one to sit down? Decisions, decisions."

They both walked toward the chairs and took a seat.

"That's better." He knelt down beside them and started to tie them up. "Now, I bet you're probably wondering why I haven't killed you yet. Maybe you think I'm some crazy assassin who wants to play mind games with you." Kramer chuckled. "But I'm neither. I'm just like you—an American follow-ing orders. Unfortunately, you just happen to be in my way."

He finished tying them up before setting up a small camera in the kitchen.

"Now I've got a guy in a car outside watching this cam-era. If he even sees you trying to move, he's going to come in here and put a bullet in your head. Understand?"

They both nodded.

"Well, then. I'll see you soon—and it won't be pleasant when I do. I owe you two quite a bit."

Kramer dashed toward the door. He picked up Banks' keys. "I'll take these, since you won't be needing them."

The door rattled as he slammed it shut. Then he locked the dead bolt.

Banks groaned. "I swear this day couldn't get much worse."

A few more clicks and turns. They both looked toward the door as Kramer strode back in. He held a syringe in one hand, the cap to it clenched in his teeth.

"I almost forgot about this," Kramer said. "This'll keep you sitting tight for a long while."

Flynn twisted his neck to elude Kramer's grasp, but it didn't last long before he felt a firm hand grab him. "If you move, it'll hurt more than it has to." Kramer sunk the needle into Flynn. Five seconds later, his head slumped down.

"Now your turn," Kramer said, sliding around in front of Banks. She struggled for a moment. "Didn't you learn anything from your partner over there?" He grabbed her. "Now, hold still and say goodnight."

Kramer slid the needle into her neck and walked out of the apartment.

***

"WE NEED TO TAPE THIS," Finkle said, looking at Booker and Thatcher. Neither moved. "Now."

"Right now?" Booker asked.

Finkle nodded. "We can do a short interview now, sort of a tease to a special for tomorrow's six o'clock news. Then we'll do a longer interview after the broadcast ends tonight." He paused and looked directly at Thatcher. "As long as that's all right with you, Sergeant Thatcher."

Thatcher nodded. "Fine by me. Let's get this show on the road."

A woman came over to him and started dusting his face with makeup.

"Is this necessary?" he asked.

Booker giggled. "It is unless you want to look like a ghost. High definition television is very unforgiving."

Thatcher relaxed in the director's chair as the woman continued to prepare his face for the bright studio lights.

"One more thing, Ms. Booker," he said.

"Oh? What's that?"

"We have some friends who are coming down here to meet us. They need to talk to Dr. Watson about something— and it's very important. Can you let the guard at the desk know so he can let them in and not hassle them like he did us?"

She smiled. "Sure. Let me make a call downstairs." She turned and walked away, her heels clicking on the smooth polished floor.

Thatcher turned to Watson. "Have you heard from them yet?"

She shook her head. "I'm sure they'll be here soon. Just stay focused on getting the message out about what's happened to you over the past few days." She took his hand and squeezed it. "You're going to do great."

Thatcher looked up at her and smiled. "Thanks for believing in me."

"Like I had a choice. It all made too much sense for me not too."

"I still appreciate it."

Booker walked back across the floor with a big smile on her face. "It's all taken care of," she said. "Your friends will be treated like VIPs."

Thatcher nodded and lifted his chin for the woman still decorating his face.

Before anyone could say another word, a loud pop followed by a complete loss of power sent the building into a frenzy.

"What the—" Thatcher said.

Three seconds elapsed until the emergency floodlights kicked on, enabling just enough light to keep people from running into one another. A few choice expletives filled the air along with shrieks and people questioning the source of the blackout.

When Thatcher's eyes adjusted, he looked to his left where Watson had been standing.

"Melissa?" he said. "Melissa?"

Moments later, the lights came back on—and she was nowhere to be seen.

Booker walked back toward him, wearing a big smile on her face. "Now that was strange."

Thatcher stood up. "Have you seen my friend, Melissa?"

Booker shook her head. "She's probably downstairs meeting your friends."

"No. She was right here."

"She'll show up."

Thatcher scanned the room, looking for her amidst the chaos of people preparing for the forthcoming broadcast in the aftermath of the brief power outage. She was nowhere to be seen.

"Ready to do this?" Booker asked, putting her hand on Thatcher's arm.

He shook her off. "No. Not now. Not until I find Melissa."

CHAPTER 42

KRAMER CARRIED DR. WATSON's limp body over his shoulder down the stairwell and laid her on the backseat of his car. He nodded at the security guard as he exited the parking garage and headed toward The Goldstein Group's lab.

His phone buzzed. "Yeah."

"Did you get her?" the man asked.

Kramer glanced in the rearview mirror and saw Watson still lying there, motionless. "Yeah. We're on our way to the lab."

"Excellent. We'll be ready for her."

Kramer hung up and sped through the surface roads, the streetlights flickering off his windshield. Babysitting a doctor wasn't in his plans, though if he were honest, he only had himself to blame. If he hadn't been so lazy, he could've eliminated the other FBI agent and her journalist friend back on the Columbia River. But he was paying dearly for his carelessness, something his employer had little tolerance for.

A detour sent him down a side street that was unfamiliar to him. The orange cones and flashing lights forced him into a single lane—and then a sudden stop. He craned his neck to see what the problem was. Unable to see what was going on, he decided to put his car in reverse only to see another car roar up behind him.

Just my luck. The assignment that will never end.

The car in front of him rolled forward and he followed suit, easing forward. He checked the clock again. It wouldn't be long before he'd get another call, wondering where he was and what happened to him.

Then Kramer noticed the flares on the road and realized he was in line for a sobriety check. He looked at the clock again and made some quick calculations in his head. He figured Watson wouldn't wake up for at least another ten minutes.

The minutes ticked by as the cars rolled through the checkpoint.

Come on, come on.

He banged the steering wheel and let out a string of expletives. Then his phone buzzed.

"Yeah."

"Where are you?"

"I'm in line at a sobriety checkpoint."

"And the doctor?"

"She's still out."

"How much longer?"

"Depends on how this check goes. I'd guess five minutes."

Kramer hung up and rolled forward. He tapped on the steering wheel as he inched closer toward the checkpoint.

When the police officer handed the license back to the driver in front of him, the car eased forward.

Kramer took a deep breath.

Stay cool.

He rarely interacted with people on his assignments,

much less police officers. He preferred to do his work from a long distance away behind a rifle and a scope. Yet here he was, trying to keep from blowing his cover.

"License and registration," the officer said once Kramer rolled down his window.

The flashlight blinded him for a moment, forcing him to shield his eyes. Kramer handed the proper documents to the officer and placed both hands on the steering wheel.

The officer directed his light onto the documents Kramer handed him. He seemed to linger on it for a while, forcing Kramer to get nervous. He was a killer for hire, not a stone-cold killer. To him, there was a difference. And the last thing he wanted was to shoot a cop and start a citywide manhunt for him. His employer wouldn't appreciate all the attention—and he likely wouldn't last a night or two in jail before someone came to "take care of the problem." His job was already lonely enough without having to be all alone on the run.

Just hand the damn thing back to me.

After a few more seconds, the officer put Kramer's license and registration between his index and middle finger and handed them back.

Kramer coolly took them and nodded at the officer, who was about to let him go until his flashlight fell on the backseat. Instead of waving Kramer on, the officer held his hand up.

"Hang on a minute."

The officer put his nose against the glass of the backseat window and shined his light on the woman sprawled out.

"What's this all about?" the officer asked.

Kramer shook his head. "A little too much to drink.

She lost her job this afternoon and didn't stop drinking until I offered to take her home."

"So you know her?"

Kramer nodded. "Unfortunately. She can be a bit needy sometimes, if you know what I mean."

The officer smirked. "Well, good luck with that. And have a good night."

Kramer put his car in drive and started to roll up his window and a moan erupted from the backseat.

And then a scream.

Watson started banging on the back glass and yelling. She saw a flashlight fall on her as Kramer stomped on the gas. Then the light disappeared.

She started slapping him on the head. "What are you doing to me?"

Kramer raised his arm and shoved her back with his elbow. He slowed down for a red light and brandished his gun. The sight of the gun sent her scrambling further into the backseat.

"Sit tight, Dr. Watson. I don't want any trouble out of you. My employer won't be very happy if I drop a dead body on his doorstep."

"Your employer? Who's your employer?"

Kramer shook his head. "It's best that you don't bother yourself with such things since it won't matter if you aren't willing to give up the rest of the formula."

"Is that why I'm here?"

Kramer remained silent and kept driving.

"Answer me, damn it. Is that why I'm here?"

Kramer wheeled into The Goldstein Group parking lot. "You'll have all your questions answered soon enough."

CHAPTER 43

THATCHER CAUGHT A CAB and asked to be let out two blocks away from The Goldstein Group. Based of his best estimate, if this is where they took Dr. Watson, she had to have arrived at least twenty minutes ahead of him. However, he wasn't overly concerned yet. If they wanted her dead, they would've killed her by now—whoever *they* was.

On several of his tours, he'd been involved in rescue missions, which taught him the art of extraction. And like any good art, there were a few non-negotiable rules, starting with the first one—only act if you have good intelligence. The second one was to have a good plan, while the third one was to proceed with caution in case rules one and two weren't adhered to.

Thatcher didn't have time for rules or art—and he doubted Watson did either. Once they got the antidote formula out of her and found out it worked, she was expendable. No, she was more than that: she was a loose end, something that necessitated being tied up and disposed of. And he needed her to prove that the Taliban outpost he attacked in Afghanistan had the same virus she was tasked with creating a vaccine for. He wanted to stay at Channel 9 and tell his story on television—but it would be dismissed as fantasy if he didn't have Watson to corroborate what he was saying.

He noted a guardhouse at the main entrance to the facility along with a pair of armed guards patrolling the perimeter.

Since when did a research facility require armed guards?

He needed a way in without drawing too much attention, which required some thought. He crept behind a row of bushes and sat down while he formulated a plan. Satisfied that his plan could work, he got up and headed toward the guardhouse.

When Thatcher tapped on the guardhouse window, the startled guard sat up.

"Can I help you?" he said, his face turning red from embarrassment.

Thatcher nodded. "Yeah, I'm lost and I was wondering if you could tell me where The Goldstein Group is."

"This is The Goldstein Group," the guard said. He stood up. "Are you sure you're all right?"

Thatcher sized him up.

Perfect.

Thatcher squinted and cupped his hand behind his ear. "What did you say?"

"I said—" the guard opened the door and walked outside. He turned to face Thatcher, who hadn't moved. "I said this is The Goldstein Group, but I don't have any visitors expected tonight. Everyone's gone home."

Thatcher cocked his head. "Have they?"

The guard's eyes narrowed. "What are you—"

A quick jab to the guard's nose with the bottom of Thatcher's palm sent the man sprawling backward. Thatcher punched him again and shifted behind him to catch him. He put the guard in a sleeper hold.

It took Thatcher less than two minutes to strip the man and change into his clothes. He tied up the guard and locked him in the guardhouse after stripping out all communications. The holstered handgun disappointed Thatcher but it would have to suffice.

He stole near one of the doors and shielded himself by crouching at the corner. Heavy footfalls fell on the sidewalk nearby—and Thatcher prepared himself.

With the patrolman getting closer, Thatcher exploded from around the corner and kept his head down, driving the man into the ground. Two quick punches knocked the patrolman out and Thatcher lifted the access card off the man. He dragged the man's body into the bushes and continued to work his plan.

Thatcher utilized the access card to open a side door. Since Watson gave him a tour of the facility earlier, he knew the general layout. He headed straight for the stairwell leading to the basement and Watson's lab.

He carefully opened the door leading to the main hallway. It was clear. He continued down the hall until he reached the door to Watson's lab. He peered inside and saw only one other man, who appeared to be armed. The man paced around the room while Watson mixed several elements together in between looking at a microscope.

Thatcher waited until the man moved close to the door. He swiped his access card and used the door to batter the man, forcing him to the ground. A few more quick punches put the man out and Thatcher began tying him up.

"What are you doing here?" Watson said as she rushed

242 | **R.J. PATTERSON**

over to him. "They're going to kill you if they find you here."

"They're going to kill you as soon as you complete that antidote for them. It's the only thing that's kept you alive this long."

"I know—but I figured it might buy me enough time to get a message out of here or escape."

"I like that second option." He grabbed her hand. "Let's go."

They got up to leave the room when someone hailed the guard on his walkie-talkie.

"Status report, Gordon," crackled a voice over the small device.

Silence.

"Gordon? Gordon? Are you there, Gordon?"

Thatcher looked at Watson. "We've gotta go now."

They crept into the hall and dashed toward the stairwell. Thatcher opened the door and staggered back when he felt a stiff blow to his head. He slumped to the ground and looked up to see Kramer with his gun trained on him.

"Trying to break the help out?" Kramer asked. "She's still got a job to do." A grin spread across his face. "And you and I are gonna take a ride."

CHAPTER 44

DR. WATSON'S HANDS TREMBLED as she squirted some of the antidote she'd made into a test tube and placed it in the centrifuge. She glanced over her shoulder at the two men with their guns trained on her, while three men in suits talked quietly. One of the men was Dr. Franklin, her boss. But she didn't recognize the other two.

"How much longer?" Franklin bellowed.

"A few more minutes," she said. "I need to check a few things first and add one more thing."

"This better work, Dr. Watson," he said. "Your life depends on it."

She already knew she was as good as dead the second they verified it worked, but she wasn't going down without a fight.

"Dr. Franklin, would you be so kind as to fetch something for me in the quarantine room?"

He laughed and shook his head "Are you crazy?"

"Fine. I'll do it myself."

She donned the hazmat suit.

"Is all that really necessary, Dr. Watson?" he asked.

"Better safe than sorry."

He rolled his eyes. "The antidote better be right this time."

She'd put up a good front in the lab ever since she arrived. While she was grateful for Thatcher and his rescue attempt, she had already formulated her own escape plan—one she worked methodically.

Doing research in a lab that had strong ties to the U.S. military meant odd items often showed up around the lab. Lethal viruses, rare ingredients—all just another day at the office. But Dr. Watson knew how to create plenty of chemical compounds and what to do with the oddities that ended up in her lab, including capsaicin.

Inside the quarantine area, she found what she was really looking for—a hand-held aerosol spray pump and an emulsifier. She mixed the water with her emulsifier and the capsaicin.

Voila! Pepper spray!

When she exited the quarantine room, she continued to work her plan.

"I'm not sure the virus is cleared in there," she said.

"Why not?" Franklin asked.

She watched as the guards and the other men crowded toward a corner away from her. "Just a feeling."

They all eyed her carefully and backed farther away as she edged closer to them.

"Do I stink?" she asked with a coy smile. "Because if I didn't know better, I'd think you guys were trying to steer clear of me."

Do it now!

Watson then held up her aerosol pump can and started to spray. The men screamed as they fell to their knees and groped in her general direction, trying to apprehend her. She kicked Franklin in the head and snatched the keys out of his pocket. And she was gone.

She shed the hazmat suit in the stairwell and raced out of the building. She needed to find Thatcher before it was too late.

CHAPTER 45

THATCHER GRIPPED THE DOOR HANDLE as Kramer drove his car onto Connecticut Avenue. He tried to control his breathing and put up a courageous front. He never feared death in battle. At least there, he had a fighting chance. But this was different—this was an execution.

"Afraid to die?" Kramer laughed. His gun, trained on Thatcher, bounced on his knee as he laughed. "I never would've guessed such a tough soldier would have a hard time with the finality of his own life. You've trained for this."

Thatcher shook his head. "A soldier's trained to survive—and kill—not die."

"I guess that explains it."

They rode in silence for a few minutes until Thatcher spoke up.

"Why are you doing this?"

"Doing what?"

"Carrying out someone else's bidding—you know, doing the dirty work?"

"You mean, like you do in the desert in the guise of freedom?"

"I'm protecting this country."

Kramer laughed. "From some heroine addict on a

camel? Really?"

Thatcher sighed. "And what are you doing?"

"I'm doing the same as you, though I'm protecting us against a real enemy, not some contrived threat to grease the skids on the war machine and feed the masses the illusion that they're safe."

Thatcher stared at the skyline against the night sky. "And what exactly is that threat?"

"If you think that we don't live under a constant threat in this country and that people like me are ensuring these threats never materialize, you're naïve at best."

"Yeah—so, you kill innocent Americans? A noble cause, indeed."

"I don't do this for nobility—I do it for freedom."

"This isn't the kind of freedom I want."

Kramer chuckled. "Good thing since you won't be around to experience it."

With that, Kramer slowed down and pulled off onto the right shoulder just before the beginning of the Taft Bridge. It was quiet—and empty.

"What are you doing?" Thatcher asked as Kramer pulled him out of the car.

"You don't think I could just shoot you, do you? A soldier returns home and accuses his own government of killing his entire squad—and then dies of a gunshot wound? Not a story that my employer wants to get out. It's much easier to fake psychiatric evaluations and sell a story that you were a delusional and troubled soldier."

"The kind of soldier who leapt to his death?"

Kramer smiled. "Now you're catching on."

Thatcher slowed his pace, anything to buy more time.

A car, a pedestrian, a cyclist—anyone. He needed to be seen. And he needed to be seen right now.

The roar of an engine pierced the night air. Thatcher turned to look and saw a pair of headlights racing down the bridge toward them.

CHAPTER 46

MELISSA WATSON PULLED into a gas station and started to fill up. She spotted the green ATM sign in the window and grabbed a baseball cap out of her backseat. The last thing she wanted was surveillance footage of her splashed across the television and Internet. She hustled inside while gas continued to course into her car. With the hat pulled down over her eyes, she withdrew her maximum daily limit and kept her head down as she exited.

She left the city and headed south. After driving for fifteen minutes, she found a hotel just off the highway and decided it would be a safe place to stay for the night.

"I need a room for tonight," she said to the clerk.

The clerk sighed and glanced at the clock on the wall behind him. "Would you like a queen or a king room?"

"Whatever is cheapest?"

"Queen it is." He typed on the keyboard and asked for Watson's name.

"Meg Ryan."

The clerk looked at her and rolled his eyes. "Seriously? Can I see your driver's license?"

"I'd like to pay cash."

"Fine, but I'll need a credit card for incidentals."

Watson shook her head. "I don't have one."

"Look, *Meg*. Everybody with a pulse has a credit card—and I can't check you in unless you've got one."

She slapped a hundred-dollar bill on the counter. "I'm sure you can make exceptions."

He snatched the bill and slid it into his pocket. "You know what? I think we can."

Ten minutes later, Watson settled into her room and used a private search to get online and find out if there was any news of note regarding Thatcher. *The Washington Post* website was full of conjecture as to Staff Sgt. Thatcher's whereabouts, as their requests with the feds to interview him had been rebuffed.

She snickered aloud.

You can't interview him because even they don't know where he is.

There was an article about Russian President Petrov's speech before the U.S. Senate in the morning. Another teased of an entertainment blog post about something scandalous a Kardashian had done. Just like usual—nothing that mattered to her.

She composed a letter detailing everything she'd done along with what she observed and gathered while working for The Goldstein Group. She wanted to send it to someone for insurance purposes. But she knew if she did, whoever was watching her might find out where she was.

Instead of communicating through traditional means, she decided to create a dummy email account and send it to someone who just might believe her: Channel 9's Rosayln Booker.

She hit send and closed her computer before collapsing onto the bed in exhaustion. She said a quick prayer for Thatcher and fell asleep.

CHAPTER 47

TODD OSBORNE REVIEWED a slew of reports on his desk about possible terrorist attacks on American interests in various regions of the world. It was late and the words on the page seemed to run together. If the coffee pot in the break room hadn't been turned off hours ago, he would've gritted his teeth and poured a cup of the substance that had surely turned to tar by now. But he wasn't that desperate to stay—not yet anyway.

He combed through the pages, looking for something, anything. While the report would've made a conspiracy theorist's year, he'd been with the CIA long enough to discern potential threats from imminent ones. As he combed through the reports, he searched for the one nugget that might give him a clue to what was happening, specifically to James Flynn.

He conceded that Flynn had made plenty of enemies for blowing the whistle on unethical practices within the agency in Africa, but Flynn's stature of prominence would give anyone pause before murdering him in a gruesome fashion. Yet, someone was very much trying to kill him, though the brazenness of the attack on the Columbia River led Osborne to believe either Flynn wasn't the intended target or

254 | **R.J. PATTERSON**

he was dealing with a different kind of terrorist with a different kind of mission. Whatever the reason, he couldn't seem to find one why Flynn might be in someone's crosshairs—nor had he heard any chatter before or since from his agents embedded in Russia about the theft of Plutonium.

He loosened his tie and flipped through a few more reports before he decided to start again the next day. After tidying up his office, he locked up and headed downstairs. There wasn't a soul there—or so he thought.

When he reached the corner of the hallway, he noticed a light still streaming from Don Vandenberg's office and overheard part of his phone conversation. Once he edged within earshot, he froze, mouth agape.

"Is everything set for tomorrow?" Vandenberg asked.

Osborne held his breath and waited.

"Do we have enough antidote for everyone?"

Antidote? What the—

"Whatever we do, we can't let Petrov die—not yet anyway."

Osborne's eyes widened as he started to put everything together. When he'd heard that an attack on the Senate floor was imminent, he believed it—he just didn't know who was crazy enough to pull it off. He never dreamed it was someone within the agency.

Osborne tiptoed down the hall and exited through a stairwell on the other side of the building. He pulled his phone out of his pocket and called Flynn.

Come on, come on. Pick up.

The call went to voicemail.

Damnit, Flynn. Where are you?

CHAPTER 48

THE CAR SCREECHED TO A HALT in front of Thatcher and the door flew open. Thatcher bent over and peered inside. Despite the glow of the streetlights, he couldn't make out who was inside.

"What are you doing?" the man asked Kramer.

"Following orders."

"Plans have changed. We need him alive."

Kramer shoved Thatcher toward the open door. "What about the others?"

"Eliminate them, but make it look like an accident. We don't need to draw any unwarranted attention."

"That's my specialty," Kramer said with a smile. "So you have the antidote now?"

"We brought in another scientist who figured out what ingredient the good doctor was withholding from us. The antidote works."

"And the doctor?"

"We have ways of discrediting her. But if you are feeling bloodthirsty tonight, knock yourself out. You won't hear me complain."

Thatcher slid into the limousine and took a seat across from the man, whose face seemed familiar.

"Do you know who I am, Sergeant Thatcher?" the man asked, catching himself as the car lurched forward and started to move down the street.

Thatcher shook his head.

"For the moment, I'm your savior."

Thatcher folded his arms. "Do you want me to tell you thank you?"

"I'd hold off on that just yet. You likely won't thank me by the time I'm finished with you."

Thatcher leaned forward and glared at the man while the streetlights flashed behind him. "I could break your neck right now."

The man glanced down at his pocket and moved what appeared to be a gun. "I'm sure you wouldn't get far before I put two bullets in you."

Thatcher sat back. "What do you want from me?"

"I want to make you a hero."

Thatcher furrowed his brow. "A hero? I'm already a hero?"

"Not quite," the man said as he threw a copy of *The Washington Post* at him. The article headline spoke volumes about how people felt about him: "Source: Army Deserter Abandoned Squad in Time of Need."

"Lies," Thatcher said, tossing the paper back at the man. "Nothing but lies."

"This is the twenty-first century, sergeant. One man's lie is another man's truth."

"Nobody believes this garbage."

The man threw the paper back at him. "Check out the poll at the bottom."

Thatcher scanned the page until he found a small

graphic with a question: "Is Staff Sgt. Thatcher a hero or a traitor?" Only twenty-two percent saw him as a hero, while sixty-five percent said traitor. He shook his head and slumped into the seat.

"Like I said: one man's lie is another man's truth."

Thatcher crumpled up the paper and threw it down. He growled before he gathered his composure and looked at the man with a forced smile. "So, what is it you want me to do?"

"I want you to be a hero tomorrow."

"And what am I supposed to do, exactly?"

The man smiled and leaned back in his seat, tapping his cane on the floorboard. "I thought you'd never ask."

CHAPTER 49

SENATOR RYAN HOBBLED into his office about an hour before President Petrov was scheduled to make an appearance in the Senate chamber. He had an appointment to talk with his campaign director, one that had been on his calendar for five months.

"You're not going to hear President Petrov?" one of his aides asked him during their morning briefing.

"It's an election year, kid," Ryan said, lightly tapping the aide on the head with his cane. "Nothing is more important than holding onto power—and that includes listening to mindless speeches from the leaders of other world powers."

"Sorry, sir. I guess I'm a bit more idealistic than you."

"Stick around D.C. long, kid, and that'll change."

Ryan smiled as he leaned back in his chair and tucked his hands behind his head. His plan was coming together perfectly. America was in danger, even if the general population had no idea. But she was—her freedoms, her potential, her future. Lurking across large bodies of water were people who hated her, who envied her, who loathed her. And if the country's defense wasn't vigilant, everyone who was an American citizen would pay a heavy price. In Ryan's opinion, America had paid enough already. She was going broke beneath the burden of policies enacted to make everyone equal, unaware that the pursuit of equality would lead to the destruction of the country's basic freedoms. And Ryan was going to stop it, no matter what it required. He had no intention of leaving behind a world for his children and grandchildren that was destined to fail or worse—succumbed to the rule of some tyrant from the Middle East.

His phone buzzed and he picked it up.

"Yes."

"Senator Ryan, Maggie Jordan from *Time* magazine is on the line for you. She had an interview scheduled for you at this time."

"I'm ready for her," he said. The line clicked and his secretary hung up. "Hi, Miss Jordan. What can I help you with today?"

"Thanks for talking with me today, Senator. I am working on a piece about the rise of terror threats in the Middle East on many different fronts and I wanted to get your perspective on things."

Ryan's eyes lit up. "Of course. What do you want to know?"

Over the next twenty minutes, Ryan pontificated about a number of subjects, including national security, homeland defense, the U.S. military's presence in the Persian Gulf, and the future of the country's long-range missile defense system. Nothing he said deviated from his party's platform—though they were milk-toast opinions compared to the ones he espoused in private. But he ended strong.

"If we're not careful, America is going to wake up one morning and realize that she's not only in danger but that there are real threats who might just obliterate nearly two hundred and fifty years of freedom."

The line went silent for a few moments before Jordan spoke again. "And who exactly are these threats?"

"They're everywhere you look. We're under siege and if you look closely, you'll see who they are. We must be vigilant to protect our people and their freedoms and whatever cost. Otherwise, we might end up under Sharia law—or worse!"

"Aren't you being a bit of an alarmist, senator?"

"Someone must sound the alarm or else we'll all end up enslaved or dead. This isn't something to nuance through political channels. We must be forthright and honest with the American people. Otherwise, they'll never forgive us."

The reporter asked a few more inane questions before hanging up.

Ryan, pleased with his performance, leaned back in his chair. It wasn't close to the performance set to take place in the Senate chamber in about thirty minutes.

Once he unleashed the virus on the Senate floor, he'd be considered a prophet—and everyone would turn to him. He'd be the Winston Churchill of the twenty-first century.

It wouldn't be long now.

CHAPTER 50

FLYNN JERKED AWAKE and glanced around the room as the sunlight streamed in through the floor-to-ceiling windows. He tried to move, which proved to be a more difficult task than he first thought. The ropes binding him to the chair gave little, if at all. He moved his head back, bumping Banks.

"Owww!" she said, awaking startled. "What the—"

Flynn tried to turn in her direction when he noticed they weren't alone.

"Well, well, well. Welcome to the land of the living," Kramer said. He strode across the room and stopped in front of Banks, stroking her face with the back of his hand.

She spat at him. "You think you'll get away with this? Think again."

Kramer threw his head back and laughed. "Think? I know I'll get away with it. One federal agent and a former federal agent in a shoot out."

He jammed a gun into each of their hands.

Banks pulled the trigger. *Click*. Nothing happened.

Kramer ripped the gun out of her hand. "I can't believe you were so helpful, Special Agent Banks. Thank you for pulling the trigger. Now, I can pin several murders I've committed in the last week on you. They'll paint you as the rogue agent. Brilliant." He pause and took a deep breath. "Of course, you'll never hear any of it. It'll all be posthumously bestowed upon you. But that's the immediate future of your legacy. Kinda shocking, isn't it?"

Banks struggled to get free, managing to do nothing but inch the chair toward Kramer's direction.

Flynn sighed. "Keep it together, Banks. He's just trying to get inside your head."

Kramer plodded toward Flynn. "Oh, I'm doing more than that—I'm creating a narrative, one that must stand up to our twenty-four hour news cycle. 'The troubled federal agent and the jaded journalist,'" he said, making his way around to Flynn and pointing at him for emphasis. "This is coming together far more easily than I predicted, though I would've preferred you both died on the Columbia River."

"Who are you working for, you sick bastard?" Banks growled."

"Now, now. No need for name-calling. We're all civil here." A grin leaked across Kramer's face. "I'm especially civil right before I kill someone. It's only fair, right?"

"You'll never get away with this!" Banks screamed.

"I already have," Kramer said as he put on a mask and popped open a canister. He punched in a few numbers on the canister's keypad and stood up. Without breaking stride, he kicked a box toward them and closed the door as he exited the room.

"What is that thing?" Banks asked.

"If I had to bet, I'd guess it was the virus," Flynn said. "I have no idea how much time we have left, but I'd guess it isn't much. We've gotta get outta here."

"And how do you suggest we do that?"

Flynn snickered. "I've been in worse situations—believe me. This is nothing."

"Well, do you mind getting us out of this nothing situation before we die?"

"It'd be my pleasure—just follow my lead."

Flynn scooted toward the fireplace, quickly getting Banks in sync. He positioned them close enough so he could rub his bindings on the poker. After about a minute, Banks spoke up.

"Still think this is gonna work?"

"Patience," Flynn said, still moving his bindings over the iron cast poker. "These things take time."

"That's a commodity we don't have much of at the moment."

"Wait for it—wait for it." Then, *snap!* The rope shredded after Flynn's persistent sawing. He untied himself and then worked on Banks' bindings.

Once loosed, she dashed toward the front door, Flynn right behind her. Before the door shut behind them, they heard a click and a hissing noise.

"Is that what I think it was?" Banks asked.

Flynn didn't flinch, reaching for the fire alarm on the wall and yanking it down. The sprinklers overhead sprayed water everywhere as grumpy tenants spilled into the hallway trying to figure out what was going on. Flynn and Banks hustled down the stairs ahead of the rush.

He stopped once they got clear of the building. "That should take care of it, but we've got more important things to do right now—like ruining the plans of Kramer and his cronies."

Banks' eyes narrowed. "What makes you think he has cronies?"

"He doesn't strike me as the type of person who could pull this off on his own. Do you feel differently?"

Banks shook his head. "Nope—I think he survives on brute strength, not wits."

"My thoughts exactly."

"Well, let's shock them all. We're running short on time."

CHAPTER 51

MELISSA WATSON AWOKE to a blaring radio. A DJ explained the rules of his contest where the eighth caller could be entered to win a cruise to the Bahamas if they could correctly identify the clip he played. Watson rolled over and moaned, covering her head with the pillow. Not that it did any good.

Lauryn Hill crooned the words to an ominous song.

I know this one.

"So, Jessica, can you name that tune for a chance to win a cruise to the Bahamas?"

She said nothing for a few moments. "Is it Ashlee Simpson?"

"You are—incorrect. Sorry about that, Jessica." The DJ's apology was anything but heartfelt. "The correct answer is Lauryn Hill. That was 'I Get Out.' But hold on the line and we'll hook you up with a Q107 prize pack."

She stumbled toward the shower and contemplated her next move. With everything going on, she wanted to stay low, hide out for a while. She doubted she'd be able to sustain her incognito lifestyle for long. Eventually, they'd find her one way or another—and she knew it.

She was over halfway through her shower before she

267

remembered the email she'd sent Rosalyn Booker. That put a quick end to the personal grooming. She rinsed the rest of the soap off and wrapped a towel around herself. Without another thought, she rushed toward her computer and opened it. She tapped on the keyboard to check her email and found a reply from Rosalyn Booker.

TO: Kim Welch (kwelch3693@gmail.com)
FROM: Rosalyn Booker (rbooker@c9wusa.com)
RE: Information

I'm covering President Petrov's speech on Thursday morning. Meet me on Capitol Hill after his speech. I want to hear more. Just look for the WUSA Channel 9 news van and I'll find you.

Warmest regards,
Rosalyn

It didn't take long before she had gathered all her belongings in her suitcase and exited the hotel room. She slid her keycard to the clerk on duty and announced that she was checking out of her room.

"What room?" the clerk asked.

"Room two forty-two," she said.

"Do you want a receipt, miss?"

Watson didn't look back. She strolled out of the hotel and headed for her car.

CHAPTER 52

FLYNN BOUGHT A BURNER PHONE at the cell phone store on the corner, while Banks flagged down a cab. The taxi pulled up to the curb and they both piled in. The smooth reggae rhythms of Bob Marley pumped through the speakers. He liked Marley's music, though he wasn't in the mood to listen to it at the moment. Reggae was for the beach with a beer in your hand—not what you listen to when you're trying to stop mad men from killing some of the most powerful men in the country.

Flynn checked his watch. Thirty minutes until Petrov was supposed to speak. Traffic ground to a halt. He tapped on the back of the front passenger seat nervously.

"What's going on?" Banks asked, putting her hand on top of Flynn's. She gave it a squeeze.

"Probably some dignitary in town," the cabbie grumbled.

Flynn glanced at the meter and tossed the man fifty bucks and opened his door. "We'll get out here." He tugged Banks' arm. "Let's go. We've gotta hustle."

Flynn turned on his phone and called Osborne.

"Where have you been?" Osborne asked. "I've been trying to reach you."

"It's a long story, but we're alive and headed for Capitol Hill."

"Look, I don't know what you plan on doing, but this is gonna be tricky."

"That goes without saying."

"No, what I mean is that this is an inside job."

Flynn stopped. "An inside job?"

Banks froze, too, and stared at Flynn as he listened to Osborne.

"Yeah, this just got really complicated," Osborne said.

"The CIA has been behind this?"

"Not sure how high this goes to the top, but I overheard Vandenberg last night on the phone when I was leaving the office—and they definitely plan to release the virus."

Flynn laughed. "Won't make much difference to us?"

"Come again?"

Flynn took a deep breath. "The assassin who's been hunting us tied us up and released the virus in the room. We've got twenty-four hours to get the antidote into our system."

"Well, what are you doing going to the Capitol? Go get some medical help."

"There's only one person who knows how to make the antidote—and I have no way of contacting her."

"I wouldn't be so sure she's the only one who can make it."

"What makes you think that?"

"I heard Vandenberg talking about the antidote and having enough for everyone in the senate."

"This is gonna be a disaster."

"Not if you can stop it. I'll try to send some agents

over to help you out, but it's going to be tight."

"Banks and I will handle it. Just be prepared for the political fallout."

Flynn hung up and looked at Banks. "Still got your badge?"

She held it up. "Let's move."

CHAPTER 53

DR. WATSON climbed the steps of the Metro station at the Archives exit. She didn't want to keep Rosalyn Booker waiting. Sharing everything she knew with a television reporter was her Hail Mary. It might be enough to raise suspicion in the intelligence community—as well as keep her alive. But nothing was certain. The attention of the public could change as swiftly as some Hollywood starlet walking down the street and making a scene. She could be forgotten about in two hours or worse—she could be dead.

"Miss Booker!" she yelled as she hustled toward the reporter standing near the Capitol.

"You made it," Booker said. "I was just about to give up on you."

"Thank you for staying. This is really important."

"I hope you'll stay longer than Sergeant Thatcher did last night."

Watson looked down and shook her head. "So you didn't get a chance to talk to him?"

"Not on camera. He was too worried about what happened to you."

Watson didn't want to reveal all her cards at once. As much as she viewed Booker as an ally, she needed to make sure first. "Yeah, I had to leave in a hurry."

Booker cocked her head and furrowed her brow. "Is everything okay?"

"It is now. Thanks for asking."

"Good. So, let's get down to business. I don't have much time before I have to go cover the Russian president's speech."

Watson gave Booker permission to record their conversation on camera. She went on to detail everything—from her original assignment to create a vaccine for the virus, to working with Mosley to make an antidote, to her contact with Thatcher, to the vial he brought back from the desert, and finally to her abduction the night before."

"How'd you escape?"

Watson smiled. "Never leave a good chemist in a lab full of active compounds."

Booker laughed. "This is absolutely fascinating. Can anyone else corroborate your claims?"

"Thatcher can—once you find him."

Booker's eyebrows shot up. "You don't know where he is?"

She shook her head. "I wish I did. One of the agents took him last night. I haven't been able to reach him, though I must admit I've been reluctant to find him—at least until I talked to you."

"Well, good luck. And when you find him, let me know so I can interview him. Finkle won't let me run with your story unless I can verify it independently."

"I understand. I'll get you in touch as soon as I find him."

CHAPTER 54

KRAMER SNEERED AT THE GUARD who begged for his life. His pleas about having a family and a two-year-old daughter almost seemed to move Kramer, who hesitated for a moment. But only for a moment.

Bang! Bang!

Two clean shots to the head sent the guard tumbling to the floor in a bloody mess.

"Nice shot," Kramer said as he looked at Staff Sgt. Thatcher.

"You sick, bastard," Thatcher growled. "You'll never get away with this."

Kramer held up his index finger. "No, *you'll* never get away with this—because I didn't shoot him. *You* did."

Thatcher struggled to get free from the bindings that kept him tethered to the chair in the large storage room on the second floor of the Capitol.

Kramer knelt down and attached a device to the ropes on his ankles. "Don't worry. You'll be freed just in time for you to get caught." He slid the gun near the body of the guard lying still in a growing pool of blood. "And no one will believe your story, so you might want to save your breath."

"I'm gonna hunt you down and kill you," Thatcher said.

Kramer laughed. "Now, that'd be a trick even Houdini couldn't pull off. But, hey, a person can dream, can't he?"

Thatcher struggled again, feeling the rope burn his wrists, and he tried to break free.

Kramer shook his head. "It's sad, really. A war hero turned traitor. Pathetic." He turned and headed for the door before pausing once he put his hand on the handle. "I've still got more work to do—your work. But don't worry. Ten more minutes and it'll all be over." He winked at Thatcher and closed the door behind him as he exited.

CHAPTER 55

OSBORNE PUNCHED THE NUMBERS on his phone and waited as the phone started to ring. He rehearsed in his head what he was going to tell the security agent who answered the phone, though he wasn't sure it would have much effect.

"This is Todd Osborne from the CIA," he said. "I need to talk to the head of security right now. It's urgent."

"He's a little preoccupied at the moment," said the man who answered the phone.

"This is a matter of national security. I suggest you get him immediately."

The guard sighed. "I'll see what I can do."

Click.

He put me on hold? He put me on hold? Are you kidding me? What kind of agents are we training in the twenty-first century? This is ridiculous.

After about thirty seconds, the line clicked again. "Agent Osborne? Are you still there?"

"I'm here."

"He's in the middle of preparations for the Russian President's speech here in a few minutes."

"That's exactly why I'm calling, nimrod. We have

credible evidence of an attack on the Senate chamber this afternoon and I need to speak to him now."

"He asked me to take a number and said he'd call you back when he got a chance."

"If I could climb through this phone, I'd put both hands around your neck and strangle you."

"That's not exactly how you win friends over here, Agent Osborne. Why don't you go ahead and give me your number so I can pass it along?"

Osborne hung up the phone and screamed. "Imbeciles!"

He dialed Flynn's burner phone back.

Flynn didn't answer.

CHAPTER 56

FLYNN WALKED UP THE STEPS of the Capitol and checked his watch. President Petrov was scheduled to take the podium in less than ten minutes. It wasn't much time to find the canister containing the virus, but it wasn't impossible.

Banks flashed her badge at the security guards standing in front of the entrance. He nodded at the guards before he felt a firm hand in the center of his chest.

"Not so fast, tough guy," a guard said. "I need to see your credentials."

Banks turned around. "He's with me."

"I don't care if he's *with* the President of the United States—I need to see his credentials," the guard said as he glared at Banks.

"I'm with the press," Flynn said.

The guard pointed to his right. "Press entrance is that way."

"We don't have time for this," Banks said as she grabbed Flynn's arm and pulled him up the steps.

"I'm sorry, but you better make time unless you want to create a scene—not to mention ruin your career," another guard said.

"People are gonna die if we don't get inside *now*," she said.

"Sorry. Not my problem," the guard replied.

Flynn put his hands up. "It's no big deal," he said. "I'll take care of it, Banks."

He hustled to the right and found the press entrance. He flashed his credentials, drawing a suspicious eye from the woman checking her list of approved media.

"I don't seem to see your name on here," the woman said.

"Check again," Flynn said.

When the woman looked down, Flynn dashed toward the door to get wanded by a guard at the entrance.

"Hey!" the woman yelled. "Come back here."

Flynn disappeared into the crowd and looked for Banks. He felt a tap on his shoulder.

"Oh, there you are," he said as he turned around.

"Stick with me. We can't lose any more time until we find that thug."

"I want him."

"He's all yours," she said as she took the stairs two at a time.

They searched the upstairs as quickly as possible, but they weren't finished when they heard a strong applause echoing in the hallway.

"And now without further adieu, I present President Petrov," said a voice over the speaker.

Flynn stopped and looked at Banks.

"Don't look at me now," she said. "Keep checking these rooms before they release the virus."

Before they could take another step, a hissing noise filled the hallway of the Capitol.

"We're too late," Flynn said.

CHAPTER 57

SENATOR RYAN WATCHED the opening lines of President Petrov's speech and smiled. His plan had gone off without a hitch. Even if they stopped the attack, he didn't care. The damage had been done.

He hoisted his right foot up onto his desk and leaned back in his chair.

President Petrov looked sharp on the screen—like a real leader. His English was perfect and he used his idioms properly.

"In this day and age, we must look to those who have experience shepherding people toward a great goal—one that serves the greater good. Gone are the days of the blind leading the blind. This is where the rubber meets the road and true leaders must rise up to embrace the challenges facing us in the twenty-first century and push through until we reach the tomorrow we've all dreamed of. That's how we've managed to secure a bright future in Russia—the kind of future we'd like to see worldwide. In our shrinking world, it's not good enough for one country to excel above others. We must all pull each other up, all striving for a better tomorrow."

If only America had a President who acted half as much like a leader as Petrov.

He dragged one of his feet off the desk and spun around to pour himself a glass of bourbon. When he reached for the glass, it tumbled onto the floor. He picked it up and froze once he saw the country of origin etched on the glass. "Made in Korea." Three harmless little words, yet one of them made Ryan's stomach convulse—a physical pain brought out by an emotional one. Korea. He hurled the glass across the room. The glass shattered as it hit the bookcase.

One of his aides knocked on the door. "Are you okay, senator?"

Ryan limped toward the door and opened it. "I'm fine. I just need another tumbler. Think you can find me one made in China or Indonesia.

The aide nodded. "I'll do my best, sir."

Ryan staggered back to his seat and slumped into it. Then he smiled as he returned his attention to Petrov's speech. He wanted to watch his plan unfold in all its glory—and horror.

In a few minutes, revenge will be mine.

CHAPTER 58

FLYNN STUMBLED TO THE FLOOR as a handful of agents rushed past him down the hall. They stormed into a room he hadn't cleared yet. His head felt light and dizzy. He squeezed his eyes shut, hoping to clear his head. It didn't work.

"Are you okay?" Banks asked.

Flynn's eyes widened. He started to say something but stopped and blinked hard.

"Flynn?"

He stood up and then tumbled back to the ground.

"Do you need some help?"

Flynn held up his hand and slowly stood up. "I'll be all right. Let's go."

Whatever was bothering him physically, started to affect him mentally. At the very least, it was knocking him off his game. Somebody, somewhere in this building was unleashing a virus that could kill everyone in the Capitol, depending on where it was placed. And with his mind spinning, he struggled to think where to look that security scouring the building hadn't already checked.

Then a moment of clarity—the boiler room.

Kramer's canister threw him off, as Flynn presumed

that would be the method of delivery—seemingly harmless canisters. Perhaps they'd be disguised as cans of food or other common commodities scattered about the building. Using a timer, they'd release a gas laced with the virus. It would've been a brilliant plan, though one requiring months of detailed planning and plenty of foreknowledge about the day's events. But the placement of the canisters could have tipped the hand of the conspirators. Instead, shove the virus into a ventilation system and let fate sort it all out.

Flynn looked at Banks. "I know where he is. The boiler room. Where is it?"

She pointed and took off running, Flynn right behind her. They rushed down two sets of steps in a stairwell and headed down a long hallway. Once they turned the corner, they skidded to a stop and watched Capitol Hill police storm into the room.

Banks started toward the boiler room at a slow pace but increased it with each step. Flynn didn't move—not until he heard Sergeant Thatcher's voice piercing the heavy air.

"Get out now," Thatcher screamed. "You're all gonna die!"

Flynn took off in a dead sprint and was met with a forceful forearm by one of the police on the scene once he reached the entrance to the room. Jolted by the hit, Flynn stumbled backward but maintained his balance. He peered over the handful of officers huddled around Thatcher. However, what Thatcher saw jarred him more than the blow he suffered to his chest.

Thatcher sat on the floor, blood smeared all over his shirt and pants. A few feet away was an opened canister—along with a gun and the body of a dead Capitol Hill police officer.

"Get up, scum," one of the officers said as he yanked Thatcher to his feet.

"You're not listening to me," Thatcher protested. "You're as good as dead."

"So are you, asshole," another officer said. "Now move, you traitor, before I shoot you right here and save the government a lot of money on your pathetic life."

Thatcher shuffled forward before an officer shoved him in the back. "I said move it!"

As the officers walked him out of the room, he locked eyes with Banks. "Special Agent Banks, help me out. You know I've been set up! I would never do this."

One of the officers glared at her. "You know this piece of garbage?"

She nodded. "I wouldn't jump to conclusions too hastily."

Thatcher stopped walking, locking his legs. "They released the virus through the ventilation system. Everybody is in danger."

The officer pushing him forward froze. He looked back at Banks. "Is what he's saying true?"

Banks looked down. "I wouldn't march him outside if I were you—not unless you want to be responsible for creating an outbreak."

"So, you're saying you believe him?"

"I don't have to believe him—I know just how dangerous that virus is. And we've likely all got it by now."

The officer's face turned pale. "How long do we have?"

"Twenty-four hours, if we're lucky."

The officer turned Thatcher around and pushed him

back into the boiler room. "Get comfortable, men. We're going to be here a while."

One of the officers looked up at Banks. "Is there anything we can do?"

"Yeah," she said. "Pray."

CHAPTER 59

MELISSA WATSON SCRUNCHED her nose and forced the palm of her hand onto her steering wheel and held it there. She knew it wouldn't achieve anything other than add to the cacophony of bleating horns outside the Capitol. It had been fifteen minutes since her car last had the room to move forward more than a foot.

She rolled her window down. "C'mon, move it. Let's go!"

Another motorist ambled down the stagnate traffic toward her. Watson's open window served as an invitation for conversation.

"That won't help," the man said after he stopped by Watson's car.

"It makes me feel better," she said. "I've got to get somewhere in a hurry."

"Good luck with that. I doubt we'll be moving any time soon."

"Why? Did something happen?"

"Oh, you haven't heard? A biochemical attack on Capitol Hill today during the Russian president's speech. It's got the whole city gridlocked. It's all over the news."

Watson's eyes widened and she covered her mouth with her hand.

"You all right, Miss?" the man asked.

Watson rolled up her window and got out of her car. She locked it before breaking into a dead sprint toward the Capitol building.

"Miss, don't leave you car like this," he called.

Watson didn't hear her. She knew exactly what happened—and who was behind it. And that hundreds of people were going to die if they didn't get the antidote soon.

In a matter of minutes, she reached a blockade that created a perimeter of two hundred yards around the Capitol building. Out of breath, she tried to flag down one of the law enforcement officers standing guard.

"What happened here?" she asked.

"Ma'am. You need to evacuate this area immediately. There's a potential bio hazard in the Capitol and we're trying to secure the area."

She took a deep breath, letting it out before continuing. "I know. That's why I'm here. I'm the only one who knows how to make an antidote. I need to talk to someone in charge."

He waved her off and rolled his eyes. "Get outta here, lady. Save yourself while there's still time."

"I'm not lying. Get me your supervisor right now."

He held his hands up. "Ma'am, I'm not gonna ask you again."

Watson nodded and walked away from the guard, moving parallel with the blockade. Then she hopped the blockade and sprinted up the Capitol steps.

Before she advanced more than a hundred feet, one of the guards pounced on her, tackling her on the cement stairs.

The guard slapped handcuffs on her and grabbed her arm, pulling Watson to her feet. "You're coming with me, lady."

"Hopefully, we're going to go meet someone important," she said. "Everyone in there is going to die if you don't let me help them."

Watson marched ahead of the guard until they reached a temporary command station set up about five hundred yards away from the Capitol building doors.

"I caught this lady jumping over the barricade and babbling about how everyone inside is going to die," the officer said to his supervisor.

The supervisor, whose thin gray hair made Watson guess he was in his late 50s, waved off the officer. "Thanks. I'll take it from here." He looked at Watson and took off her handcuffs. He offered his hand. "Captain Zelinski."

She stuck her hand out and shook his. "Dr. Melissa Watson."

"So, ma'am, what do you know that we don't?"

"I know what's going on in there—and if you don't let me talk to somebody inside to find out more about what's going on, everyone is going to die."

He folded his arms and leaned back, eyeing her cautiously. "Is that so? What are you—a mystic healer? I certainly wouldn't figure you for a cold and calculating terrorist, but I've been wrong before."

"I am—*was*—a research scientist for The Goldstein Group. I developed an antidote for the virus that I think was released in there."

"How do you know a virus was released in there?"

"It's all over the news."

"Mmm, hmm." He looked past her at the scene unfolding behind him. Incident response units roared through their barricade to get closer to the Capitol.

She turned around and shrieked. "You can't let them do that," she said. "That virus is highly contagious."

"Yet, you sprinted straight toward the Capitol, according to my officer. It must not be *that* contagious."

"I'm immune. I almost died but had to develop an antidote to save my own life. You have to believe me."

"What was your name again?"

"Dr. Melissa Watson."

"And what was that outfit you said you worked for?"

She sighed. "The Goldstein Group—but they're trying to kill me. If you contact them, don't breathe my name. I'll be dead before you know it."

He chuckled. "This is quite a tale you're spinning, *Doctor* Watson."

"Every word of it's true."

"Is it now? You claim to be a doctor, but I can't verify that because someone might kill you. You run for the building containing this deadly virus but claim you're immune. You're not giving me much to work with here."

"Look me up on The Goldstein Group website. Look me up in the Yale database. I'm not some nut job. I want to help—in fact, I might be the only person who can help you right now."

"Give me a minute," he said.

Captain Zelinski turned toward one of his lieutenants and whispered in his ear.

Watson tapped her foot and sighed as she watched a hive of activity swirling behind the captain. She bent her ear to the conversations and tried to pick up as much as she could. Her heart sank when she overheard chatter on the scanner about the arrest of Sergeant Thatcher for the murder of one of the Capitol Hill police officers.

She rubbed her face with both hands and sat down in a nearby chair. She knew he was set up—and if they could set Thatcher up, what would they do to her?

Ten minutes later, one of the officers returned and tapped Zelinski on the shoulder.

"What is it?" he asked.

The officer leaned in and whispered something to him. Zelinski turned around, his eyes narrowed.

"What did you say your name was again?" he asked.

"I already told you twice before—it's Dr. Melissa Watson."

"Well, *Doctor* Watson, you don't appear to exist—at least according to Yale or The Goldstein Group. Do you have any identification?"

She shook her head. "I left it in my car."

"Is that right? Well, at this time, I'm going have to detain you for your little stunt up there."

Another report cackled over the radio. *Our best estimate is that we've got more than two thousand people quarantined in the Capitol building right now.*

"You've gotta let me help," she pleaded.

Zelinski held up his index finger as he listened to the rest of the report.

A few people are already starting to show symptoms of something that has to pertain to the virus. Bloody noses out of nowhere, people complaining about a sharp pain in their stomach.

Watson grabbed Zelinski's arm. "Come on. If this is

what it sounds like, everybody in there is in trouble. Besides, what's it gonna hurt to let me have a look? Send some of your officers with me."

He looked at her hand gripping his bicep and then at her. "Take your hand off me." He paused. "And I don't repeat myself. Sit down."

Watson settled into her seat and glanced at the clock. Nearly an hour had already elapsed since the incident occurred. It was one hour less to create an antidote that could save everyone inside. One hour less to prevent the plans of madmen from gaining ridiculous control.

CHAPTER 60

THERESA THOMPSON GRABBED the remote control and cranked up the volume on the television hanging in The National's offices. She sank down into an empty chair right behind her next to one of her political reporters. The report painted by the reporter inside wasn't a pretty one—but it was raw and real. With a quaking voice, she detailed the attack and how they'd learned that the virus was a deadly one that could kill them all.

"This is unreal," she said to anyone who'd listen. "How do people pull off something like this? How can anyone expect to be safe if we can't even keep our own Capitol building free from terrorist attacks?"

"Petrov was here today," said one of the reporters.

Thompson threw her hands in the air. "But that'd be crazy to let him die while speaking to U.S. senators. It's almost guaranteed to start a war, even if he survives."

"Maybe that's the point."

She rolled her eyes. "No way. There's something else going on here."

Before Thompson could utter another word, the anchor on the news desk interrupted the analyst. "Sorry to cut you off, Ben, but we've got some breaking news about the origin of the virus. It appears to be a biological weapon developed by the North Koreans. Again, I repeat, the viral attack appears to be North Korean in origin."

"The North Koreans? This is unreal. They just wanted to piss everybody off at once, didn't they?" Thompson said.

"Guess they wanted to get more bang for their Won," another reporter said.

A smile flashed across Thompson's face. "That'd be a funny tweet if people weren't going to die—and anyone in our celebrity-obsessed culture knew what the hell a 'won' was."

"I guess if I have to explain it, it's not funny."

Thompson nodded. "You got that right." She turned her attention back to the television.

Senator Ryan was on the air, talking with the anchor about the attack.

"Why weren't you there this morning, Senator Ryan?"

Ryan closed his eyes and shook his head. "I have principles, which include not listening to some deranged lunatic of a leader address our country's most influential legislators. I'm just not interested, not to mention I think it was disrespectful to our own president for members of my party to invite him."

"Guess it pays to stick to your principles, huh?" the anchor said.

"This wasn't about sticking to my principles as much as it was about honoring our president, who has some tough decisions ahead of him in the days ahead."

"What kind of decisions are you referring to, senator?"

"The kind that could lead to war."

The anchor squinted and cocked his head to the right.

"What exactly are you referring to, Senator? The president has been adamant about the fact that he's not going to engage our troops in any more needless conflicts."

"You call this needless? We just experienced the first direct terrorist attack on one of our most iconic government buildings in well over a decade. I'd say he needs to make a statement—and make a forceful one."

"Senator, are you suggesting we go to war with North Korea as a result of this attack?"

Ryan put his hands up. "I'm not suggesting anything at the moment—but I am *saying*, not just suggesting, that if it's proven that the North Koreans are indeed behind this, then we need to let them know this kind of brazen terrorist attack will not be tolerated. We need to strike back."

The anchor swung back over to one of his embedded reporters, who gave an update that didn't provide anything new—other than they had less time than when the report began.

Thompson stood up and returned to her office, shaking her head the whole way. She struggled to believe that North Korea was capable of pulling off such a feat. Pyongyang contained the noisiest saber rattlers on the planet. But when it came to action? They proved to be cowards time and time again.

However, it didn't stop her inbox from blowing up with article pitches from foreign relation analysts and journalists wanting to write about the seeds of war that had been supposedly germinating in North Korea for a while.

Where's Flynn at? I know he'll be able to make sense of this ridiculousness.

Times like these were when she appreciated having a

former CIA operative and analyst on her payroll.

She dialed his number and waited. Straight to voice-mail.

Thompson stood up and closed the door to her office. She needed to clear her head and think—and develop a semblance of an editorial plan for her staff. Undoubtedly, users would be scouring *The National* website for answers. It was where the nation always turned for truth in reporting. But at the moment, she had nothing.

One of her section editors knocked on her door.

She motioned for him to enter. "What's on your mind?"

"Do we have a coverage plan yet? This is the biggest thing since 9/11. We need to get on top of this first."

"First, we need to gather some facts before we start writing anything. We hardly know what's going on yet."

"We know the what and the who—just not the why."

Thompson looked down at some papers on her desk and scratched out a few notes. "You think we know the *who* already?"

"You're right. Maybe we don't. I'm not quite as cynical as you when it comes to government officials—though I never interviewed Senator Ryan either. You probably have some unique perspective on all this after that piece you wrote about him fifteen years ago."

Thompson leaned back in her chair, her mouth agape. "I almost forgot."

"You almost forgot that you interviewed him?"

Thompson shook her head. "No, I almost forgot his story—and I'm not believing for one second that it's the North Koreans."

"Then who did it?"

"Get outta here. I've got some phone calls to make."

The editor stood there. "That still doesn't tell me how we need to direct our reporters."

"Just give me a minute."

Thompson watched the editor leave and close the door behind him. She picked up her phone again and dialed Flynn's number. After the third ring, he answered.

"Oh, thank God, I reached you. Where have you been?"

"It's a long story."

"We need to talk. Where are you now?"

"In the Capitol building. There's a little bit of a biological scare—hopefully you've heard about it by now."

Thompson gasped. "You're—you're in the Capitol building right now?"

"Quarantined and everything."

"Well, look. I think I know who's behind all of this."

"I'm glad someone does because it sure as hell isn't Sergeant Thatcher."

"I know. It's a far worse situation—it's Senator Ryan."

CHAPTER 61

FLYNN SAT ON THE FLOOR against the wall in the hall-way outside one of the offices commandeered by the Capitol police. He heard through the walls Staff Sgt. Thatcher's repeated pleas of innocence, but there wasn't much he could do about it at the moment. The evidence displayed in front of the Capitol police when they stormed into the boiler room pointed toward Thatcher's guilt. There was no denying that, not even for the most ardent defender of the Army survivor.

"Think they'll find him guilty?" Banks asked.

Flynn shrugged. "May not matter. We might all die in here."

"Have you tried to reach Dr. Watson?"

He nodded. "I haven't been able to reach her. All my calls go straight to voice mail." He shook his head. "She's our only hope of surviving this thing—and she's probably dead in a ditch somewhere."

"I doubt they'd bother to even throw her in a ditch."

"So, who's behind all this?" she asked.

"Senator Ryan."

She jerked back from him as her eyes narrowed and her head tilted to one side. "The old senator that hobbles around on a cane? *That* guy?"

"So my editor says."

"And you believe her?"

Flynn shrugged again. "I've got no reason not to. She's not one to create conjecture without a solid hunch or lead."

"What does she have on Ryan?"

"A feeling."

Banks laughed. "A feeling? If only I could make arrests based on that without consequences."

"For what it's worth, she said it was a *strong* feeling."

"Oh, a strong feeling. Well, then, that changes everything. Let me call my boss. We'll have him picked up right away for terrorist acts against the United States."

Flynn sighed. "Now, now. No need to get snarky. I'm just relaying a message."

"I hope there's more to the story."

"There always is—but for once, I'm not concerned about the story."

"Oh?"

"I'm concerned about surviving." He felt a strong twinge in his chest and doubled over in pain.

"Flynn? Are you okay?" She reached over and put her hand on top of his. "Do you need medical attention?"

He grimaced. "I'll be fine." He staggered to his feet. "But we need to find Dr. Watson—or I won't be fine. None of us will be."

CHAPTER 62

WATSON DUG HARD into her leg with her fingernails. The pain smarted as blood started to trickle down her calf toward her ankle. She collected some of the blood and hunched over to avoid being seen.

She sat up and screamed. "Oh, my god. What is happening?"

Zelinski turned around and his mouth fell agape. He backed up, hitting the side of the tent as he put his hands out. "Stay right there. Don't move." He then raised his voice. "Everybody, out of here now!"

The assisting officers glanced over at Watson and scrambled out of the tent.

Less than a minute later, Zelinski stuck his head back inside the tent. "We're going to quarantine you in one of our police vans."

"I don't need to be quarantined—I need to get the antidote."

Zelinski's eyes narrowed. "I don't have time to argue with you right now. I'm dealing with a crisis situation and you need to do what I say or else it won't be pleasant for you."

"If everyone in there dies, it's going to be very unpleasant for you."

Zelinski pointed toward a surveillance van. "Not another word. In there now."

Watson trudged through the tent. Two officers flung the side doors open and sprinted away from the vehicle. She climbed inside before they slammed the doors.

She mouthed, "Help me," to the officers, but they backed away and returned to Zelinski, who shook his head before turning his back.

Watson surveyed the scene again. No officers were paying any attention to her. She glanced at the van and noticed the keys still in the ignition.

Perfect.

She jumped into driver's seat and turned the key as the engine roared to life. She looked to her left to see if anyone noticed what she was doing. They were all absorbed in the crisis at hand.

She eased out onto the road and gave one more quick glance in her rearview mirror. Her getaway was clean.

Who's gonna want to arrest me anyway since I have the virus?

She smiled and wiped the blood off her face.

Easier than I thought it would be.

Several minutes later, she pulled onto the George Washington University campus and raced to the biosciences building.

She threw the doors open to Noah Plimpton's lab.

"Dr. Watson?" he said as a grin spread across his face. "To what do we owe this privilege?" Then his face dropped. "Are you okay?"

"I need your help, Noah, and I need it right now."

"I've got a class that I have to teach in a few minutes."

She ran up to him and grabbed his shirt. "Hundreds

of people are going to die at the Capitol if you don't help me."

"Okay, let's go."

"You drive," she said.

They piled into his car and tore out of the parking lot.

"Where are we going?" he asked.

"The Goldstein Group."

"The Goldstein Group? What's going on?"

"I have to level with you, Noah. This is very serious—and The Goldstein Group isn't exactly the kind of place you want to work."

"But you work there."

"*Worked* there."

"What happened?"

"Those people are evil—the kind of people I never wanted to associate with. They only want to use science to further their twisted agenda to wage wars for profit and power."

"What are you talking about?"

"That virus I looked at in your lab was deployed this morning in the Capitol while the Russian president was speaking. It's highly contagious—"

"And you brought it into *my* lab?"

"I know how to handle it. Your lab is clean. But that's not important right now."

"So, what are we doing?"

"We're going to break into The Goldstein Group and steal the immunogen we need to make the antidote for the virus."

The car lurched forward as he pumped the brakes for a red light. "You want me to break into The Goldstein

Group lab? Are you out of your mind?"

"Quite possibly, yes. But there are some very important people who need saving right now—and we might be their only hope."

He sighed. "Okay. Just tell me what to do."

As they approached the lab, she asked to be let out.

"Just drive up to the guardhouse and ask to see me. Keep him preoccupied until I give you the signal. And then go park on the street. When you see me come out, blast through the gate and come pick me up. It's simple really."

He chuckled. "Simple?"

"Maybe not, but it'll get the job done."

"Are you sure about this?" Noah asked.

She shook her head. "No, but what choice do I have?"

Noah's stunt brought the guard out of his hut for their conversation. Watson snuck up to the guardhouse and dashed inside and snatched an access card lying on top of his desk. She flashed a thumbs-up sign to Noah and sprinted toward the building.

In a matter of minutes, she was inside the building and in her lab. She'd produced extra immunogen as a precaution and placed it in the back of her fridge. If Franklin thought for once that she might return to try and retrieve the immunogen, he would've surely moved it.

Never underestimate a mad scientist.

She collected enough immunogen to make a sufficient amount of antidote for everyone in the Capitol building, based off what she heard the police saying. It required careful handling and several large containers. She packed them into a crate with heavy padding and attached it to a hand truck. Using the stairwell, she exited through a fire exit on the side of the building.

She looked around and saw no one in the parking lot—just Noah parked on the street like she instructed him. She waved for him and moments later his car tore through the guard gate. He skidded to a stop near her and she immediately hoisted the crate into the backseat.

She slapped the dash. "Let's go!"

He stomped on the gas and the car roared toward the exit. The guard stood in the way with his gun drawn. He held up one hand and was pleading with them to stop.

As Noah bore down on the exit, the guard put both hands on his gun and aimed at Watson. The windshield shattered as two shots ripped into the car. The guard dove out of the way as Noah barreled past.

Watson turned around and looked at the backseat to see if the immunogen was damaged.

She sighed. "Thank God, the immunogen is okay."

Noah's eyes bulged as he looked at her. "The immunogen might be okay, but you're not."

"What?" Watson looked down. Her arm was covered in blood.

CHAPTER 63

FLYNN FOLLOWED BANKS into the makeshift holding cell for Staff Sgt. Thatcher. Banks flashed her badge to the officers guarding him. She asked for privacy and the two men stepped outside and pulled the door shut behind them.

Thatcher sat on the floor, hunched over in the corner. His lips quivered as he tried to speak, but no sound came out. A tear streaked down his face as he looked up bleary-eyed at his visitors.

Banks squatted next to him and put her hand on his shoulder. "It's going to be okay. We'll help you get through this."

Thatcher's eyes widened. "You mean, I'm not going to be charged for this crime."

She shook her head. "That's a problem we'll have to let the legal system sort out. Right now, nobody believes you."

Thatcher clenched his fists and pounded the floor. He kicked at the air and screamed in frustration. "I wish Kramer would've just thrown me from that bridge."

Flynn sat down on the floor next to him. "He was going to throw you from a bridge?"

Thatcher wiped his nose with the back of his sleeve.

"Yeah. He was just moments from tossing me to my death when some man pulled up in a limo and said they had other plans for me."

"Did you get a good look at him?" Banks asked.

He shook his head. "It was dark and before I had a chance to study his face, I got hit in the head. The next thing I knew, I was holding a gun over a security guard in the boiler room of the Capitol Building. You've gotta believe me. I didn't do this."

Flynn grabbed Thatcher's arm and squeezed. "I believe you. We'll exonerate you no matter what it takes."

Thatcher sighed. "If you're still alive."

"Just keep your chin up and your hopes high—it's all we've got right now."

Thatcher's head dropped. "I'm a patriot—not a traitor. I was willing to give my life for this country, but I hate the idea that I might be remembered as someone who tried to kill innocent people."

Flynn stood up. "If I have anything to say about it, we'll make sure that people not only know you're a patriot, but that you're a real hero."

Then Flynn crumpled to the floor in pain.

***

BOOKER COULD ALMOST FEEL the excitement in Finkle's voice after he answered the phone. She wanted to revel in her journalistic triumph, but a professional victory felt hollow when death appeared imminent.

"This is fantastic," Finkle said. "You're going to win an Emmy for this."

"If I do, I doubt I'll be there to receive it," she muttered.

"How are you feeling?"

"Not the greatest, but if everything Dr. Watson told me earlier today is true, it won't be long before everyone starts to feel the effects of the virus."

"Well, you can't be sure everyone contracted it."

"I guess not, but they're not letting anyone in here to find out yet—and this place is getting crazy." She wasn't interested in staying on this subject. "Did you get my other footage from my interview with Dr. Watson?"

"That's a heckuva story, but I can't run that yet."

"Why not? It's obvious that she was telling the truth."

"Or maybe she's behind it all."

"Oh, come on, Finkle. You're not really that cynical, are you?"

"I'm accurate and I'm not running anything you can't verify with multiple sources—otherwise we become TMZ. And I refuse to let that happen on my watch."

"You have to admit that it sounds plausible."

"Perhaps, but you need to get someone other than Staff Sgt. Thatcher to verify it."

"Why not? He's the key to this story."

"Or the conniving mastermind."

"I've met him. *You've* met him. Does he strike you as a psychopath?"

"Psychopaths never strike anyone as a psychopath until the damage is done—and sometimes not even then. I'll happily pull some footage for you to prove my point. No one ever says, 'Yeah, this doesn't surprise me. My neighbor was always a scumbag.' What do they say? 'He was such a nice guy. I never would've guessed he would do anything like that.'"

"So you're saying this story is dead in the water?"

"Unless you can verify it some other way, yes."

"Whatever—I can't do any more work in here. I'm not feeling up to doing any more today."

"Can you do one more live feed for us in ten minutes?"

She sighed. "I guess."

Ten minutes later, Booker went on the air describing what she'd seen earlier inside the Capitol. Her cameraman panned down the hall behind her to show some of Capitol Hill's most prominent power players slumped against the wall, pale-faced and sickly. One senator threw up as the picture tightened in on his face.

Once her report ended, Finkle got back on the phone with her. "Excellent work as always, Booker."

"You better run that interview with Dr. Watson. You're going to wish you did once the smoke clears from this investigation."

"I'll consider it." He paused. "In the meantime, we just got some word about the antidotes since I last spoke with you."

"Oh? What is it?"

"It doesn't look like there's going to be any—at least not enough for everyone. And there's not enough time to test everyone, according to a report from the CDC."

"I feel weak," she said, collapsing to her knees and then slumping onto the floor.

"Booker? Booker? Booker!"

CHAPTER 64

ONCE WATSON AND NOAH returned to the lab at George Washington, she took his undershirt and made a tourniquet for her arm. She sucked in a breath through her teeth and scowled. With her good arm, she swept everything off one of the lab tables and pulled up a stool.

"Are you sure you can do this?" Noah asked.

"I don't have a choice. Everybody on Capitol Hill is going to die if we don't make enough antidote for them."

He nodded. "Well, let's get to work."

They started to create the antidote from the immunogen they'd taken from the lab.

Noah sighed. "Is this the kind of work you thought you'd be doing when you started your career in immunology?"

Watson laughed and shook her head. "Not even close. I was more of an idealist who wanted to save the world."

"So what changed?"

"Nothing really. I thought I could change the world working at The Goldstein Group. With all the resources and funding they had, I thought I might be able to create some vaccines that might eradicate some awful diseases."

"But that wasn't the case?"

She shrugged. "I probably could have if I shut up and followed orders. But I'm just not that kind of woman. What they were doing was wrong, not to mention a violation of my conscience."

Noah stopped and tilted his head to one side. "But aren't there always sacrifices in the name of science?"

She put her hands on the table and leaned forward. "True sacrifice happens when a person chooses it for himself, not when sacrifice is chosen for him. A scientist may choose to make a sacrifice in order to create something for the good of the whole, but a test subject who isn't privy to his or her own so-called sacrifice? That's not sacrifice. It's not even ethical science."

"What would you call it then?"

"Evil."

"Even if something good emerges from it?"

"I call that redemption, the moment when evil is plucked from sure death and given a new purpose, a purpose to bring healing and hope."

"Is that what we're doing here?"

"We're doing what we have to do. We're morally obligated to do this." She glanced at her arm. "Bloodied bicep and all."

***

THE SUN MADE ITS first glorious appearance on Friday morning as Watson completed production of the antidote and started preparing the syringes. She glanced at Noah, who was working on his fourth cup of coffee since they began their quest.

"How are you doin'?" she asked.

"I'll be doing much better once I get some sleep."

"This will all be over with soon."

He looked up at her. "And you think they're going to let you just waltz right up to the Capitol steps and start injecting people with this antidote?"

"There's only one way to find out."

A few minutes later, they gathered up the antidote-filled syringes and headed for the door.

Once they drove up to the Capitol, it remained as she had left it—cordoned off and heavily guarded.

Watson grabbed a tray of antidote syringes and looked at Noah. "Here goes nothin'."

As they approached the perimeter, several guards surrounded them.

"Hands in the air, on your knees—now!" one of the guards growled.

They complied before Watson started talking. "I have an antidote that will ensure that everyone inside lives."

The guards said nothing.

"You're going to have the deaths of every person in the Capitol on your conscience if you don't let me in."

Zelinski rushed up to her. "Nice stunt, *Doc.*"

"This hasn't been a stunt. I've only been concerned about one thing—and that's trying to save the people behind those doors," she said, gesturing toward the building.

"Hands up," a guard said.

She put her hands back in the air.

"And how do you expect to do that?" Zelinski asked.

"I've got the antidote."

He squatted down in front of her and looked her in

314 | **R.J. PATTERSON**

the eyes. "And how can I trust you? I can't even find any proof that you're a doctor."

Before she could say another word, Zelinski's radio crackled with a message.

It's getting pretty bad in here, sir. Quite a few senators are complaining, doubled over in pain. If what we heard is true about this virus, this is about to get really ugly.

Watson looked up at him. "What do you have to lose?"

Zelinski stood up and ran his hands through his hair as he let out a long breath. "I still need to verify your credentials—find out if you are who you say you are."

Watson glanced at her watch. "I don't know how long that will take, but if you don't let me in there soon, you're going to be dragging out dead bodies—bodies of very important people. And I don't think you want that."

He paced around for a moment. "Fine. I'll have one of my men on the inside meet you."

Watson and Noah clambered to their feet. "Have some of your men get the rest of the antidote doses out of the van. And hurry—we're running out of time."

CHAPTER 65

FLYNN AWOKE IN George Washington University Hospital with tubes weaving across his body. He blinked hard twice and pushed himself up in the bed. The afternoon sun shone brightly into his room. He then looked to his right and noticed Banks seated at his bedside.

She leaned forward and put her hands on top of his. "You're finally awake."

"What happened?" he asked.

"You passed out."

"So, how'd I end up here?"

"Dr. Watson created the antidote and administered it."

"Did anyone die?"

"Not so far. It looks like she made it just in time."

He smiled. "Well, that's good."

A doctor walked into the room holding Flynn's medical chart. "Congratulations, Mr. Flynn. Looks like you cleared the virus," the doctor said.

"That's good news."

The doctor smiled. "Very good news, indeed." He paused. "So, can we expect to see this conspiracy plot tackled on one of your shows in the near future?"

Flynn furrowed his brow. "I wasn't aware that this was

a conspiracy."

The doctor clicked his pen a few times. "Oh, don't play coy with me. You know this was a coordinated effort by someone to kill the Russian president—and our entire congress at the same time."

"We could use a purge in the Senate," Flynn said. "But I'm not sure this was the right way to go about it."

"So it was a conspiracy? I *knew* it!"

"I never said that," Flynn said before he cracked a wry smile. "Just keep watching for me on television. I'm sure I'll have a special on this sooner or later."

"Well, congratulations on clearing the virus. I'll be back to check on you later," the doctor said before exiting the room.

Banks tilted her head and stared at him. "Look at you, Mr. Popular. Getting some special treatment from the doctor."

Flynn waved her off. "He was just being nice."

She shook her head. "No, I saw one of your books on his desk. He was clearly doing more than just being nice. *You*, on the other hand, are trying to be modest."

"Yet, it's so difficult."

She pushed him playfully and looked away. "I think you're definitely fine now."

"And what exactly did you mean by *fine*?"

She rolled her eyes. "Do I need to call the nurse back in here to give you a sedative?"

He chuckled before his face fell serious. Images of the Capitol flashed on the screen. "Turn that up," he said, pointing at the television.

Banks obliged and sat back in her chair.

Staff Sgt. Dan Thatcher has been charged today for his role in the plot that unleashed a deadly virus in the Capitol today, nearly killing scores of U.S. Senators, the Russian president, and other high-ranking officials. Staff Sgt. Thatcher, who levied harsh allegations against the U.S. Military just days ago after he claimed his entire squad was killed in an attack by a U.S. drone, parachuted into the Potomac River on Tuesday and was supposedly in custody of the FBI. No formal statements about his whereabouts had been made until he was charged Friday morning for the biological terrorist attack on the Capitol. Officials insist that he didn't act alone but have refused to give any clues as to who might have aided Staff Sgt. Thatcher in the attack.

"Are you kidding me? They still think Thatcher did this?" Flynn asked.

"I tried to talk to my boss about it, but he said the evidence was overwhelming."

"We need to prove that Senator Ryan was behind this."

Banks sighed. "So, we're back to that again? Your editor's strong *feeling?*"

On cue, another news report started with Senator Ryan's face filling the screen.

This is just another reason why we need to increase our spending on defense instead of decreasing it like the current administration is calling for. These kinds of terrorist acts are unacceptable. No American should be forced to live in this country under a burden of fear. Such terrorism strikes at the very heart of the principles upon which this country was founded—and I'm not going to stand for it.

Banks whipped her head toward Flynn. "Still think he's

the one behind all this?"

"After seeing that, I almost guarantee it."

"*After* seeing that? Did we just watch the same clip?"

"Where's your investigator instinct?"

"Where's your reasonable doubt? Because I have plenty."

Flynn ripped out the tubes from his body and started getting dressed.

"What are you doing?" Banks asked.

"I'm going to prove you're wrong."

"How exactly are you going to do that?"

Flynn's phone buzzed with a call from Osborne. He held up his index finger.

"Flynn? Are you okay?" Osborne asked.

"I am now. What's going on?"

"I broke a few laws and might get fired for what I just did—but I have a suspect and a smoking gun."

"So, who's behind this?"

"You won't believe it."

"Try me."

"Senator Ryan. I'm going to arrest him now. Meet me at headquarters in an hour. I want you to be there for the questioning."

Flynn turned and smiled at Banks. "It'll be my pleasure."

CHAPTER 66

SENATOR RYAN REMAINED STOIC once Todd Osborne entered the interrogation room. Ryan tapped the foot of his good leg and slumped in his chair, arms folded. He leaned to the side and looked past Osborne, staring at his reflection in the glass. He knew that other agents stood behind it watching his every move. He'd been here before.

Ryan controlled his breathing. At the moment it was one of the few things he could control along with his temper, though he doubted he'd control that much longer.

If I last a minute, it'll be a monumental feat.

Osborne sat across from Ryan and didn't say a word. He sifted through thick folders full of papers and jotted down a few notes on a yellow legal pad.

"Would you like to call your lawyer?" Osborne asked.

Ryan shook his head. "I haven't done anything wrong."

Without responding, Osborne continued to situate the papers in his file folder.

"You mind telling me what this is all about?" Ryan said.

Osborne didn't look up. "I was hoping you could tell me, Senator Ryan."

"I don't play games."

Osborne looked up slowly as he pursed his lips. "Neither do I."

Ryan took a deep breath and looked to his left, avoiding eye contact with Osborne.

"I suggest you start talking," Osborne snapped.

Ryan didn't move.

"Now!" Osborne banged his fist on the table and leaned in close.

Ryan turned his gaze back toward Osborne. "I've got no idea what this is all about," he said, his voice rising with each passing moment. "I was simply trying to unwind after a very trying day where I nearly lost some of my closest friends in this world when you showed up with your S.W.A.T. team like I'm some gun-toting, blood-thirsty bank robber. When we're through here, I'm going to make sure you're *through* here, too."

Not bad. I made it ninety seconds.

Osborne slid the folder aside and folded his hands. "Senator, there's no need for idle threats."

Ryan's eyes narrowed. "This isn't a threat. This is a promise, so listen closely—I will destroy you."

"I doubt you'll find anyone climbing all over themselves to help a traitor."

Ryan slouched and leaned back in his chair. He held up index finger. "First, I'm not a traitor. Second, you'd be surprised at the help I have."

Osborne shrugged. "You'd be surprised at what I know."

"You know nothing. You're barely wet behind the ears."

"And you can barely hear. I'd say we're even." Osborne

cracked a smile. "What I doubt you know is that we know who your help is and we're going to flush him out."

Ryan laughed and shook his head. "I don't work with amateurs. But I doubt you'll find him anyway."

Osborne stood up. "Look, let's cut the crap, Senator. There's a giant elephant in the room—and it's the evidence that you colluded to release a bio weapon on Capitol Hill today."

"I have no idea what you're talking about—and quite frankly I'm insulted that you would insinuate as much."

"Oh, really? Is there a reason why you didn't come to the senate chamber today?"

"I had a meeting with one of my campaign advisors. It's been on the books for weeks."

Osborne looked at his folder. "That proves nothing—other than the fact that you knew in advance this was going to happen."

"It doesn't prove I had anything to do with it—especially since I didn't."

Osborne held up his index finger and wagged it. "Not so fast. I did a little digging and found out that you scheduled that conference call on the day Petrov's speech was finalized."

"Mere coincidence."

"Perhaps, but I doubt any jury would see it that way once I present all the evidence."

"You're crazier than you look if you think any of this will ever reach a court room. You're in over your head, kid."

"I'm not sure you know what we have, Senator."

Ryan waved him off and laughed. "You've got a lot of conjecture and a prayer. Nothing that could ever win a conviction. Quite frankly, I'm surprised anyone with any authority let you bring me in."

"I don't need anyone's permission to bring in anyone—but there's not a person in this building who would give me any pushback once I presented the evidence from this." Osborne pulled a plastic bag out of his pocket that contained a cell phone.

Ryan's eyes flashed wide for a moment. He pointed at the phone. "I've never seen this phone before in my life."

"That's odd since it had your prints all over it. Not to mention that when we triangulated the position of this phone and your regular business cell phone, they were almost always in the same place."

"And yet somehow it came into your possession?"

"We swapped it out earlier today while you were speaking to the press."

"It's no crime to have two cell phones."

"True. But it is a crime to conspire to kill a federal agent."

Ryan chuckled. "You're going to be in the funny farm by the end of the weekend if you keep concocting such cockamamie theories."

"I doubt any jury will believe it's a coincidence that calls placed from this burner phone were to a phone near the location of our agents, often several minutes before they were attacked."

Ryan's face fell. "I didn't place those calls."

"I doubt that, sir. Your fingerprints were the only ones on the phone. There wasn't even as much as a smudge of another person's prints."

"I'm being set up," he screamed.

Osborne shook his head. "No, you're being nailed as a traitor." He paused. "But perhaps there's a way we can make the end of your life in prison a little more comfortable."

"I didn't do this."

"Maybe this audio clip will make you stop acting like a fool and trying to play me for one."

Osborne tapped a few buttons on his cell phone and a recording of Ryan's voice blared in the room.

I don't care how you do it—I just want Banks and Lang dead.

"Just so happened to have one of your staffers under surveillance on a different case and had permission to put a bug in your office. Who knew it would come back to haunt you?"

Ryan hung his head and said nothing.

"And then there's the death of Senator Thor, God rest his soul. You had him killed too. And for what? His patriotism was too over the top for you? He didn't see eye to eye with you on the role of the military?" He paused. "Thor happened to be a good friend of mine, a man who dedicated himself to his work. And you snatched that away from him."

Ryan remained still and silent.

"I have half a mind to shoot you right here, but it wouldn't be justice. You need to pay for what you did and spend the rest of your miserable pathetic life in prison." Osborne paused. "However, I can make things a *little* more comfortable for you."

Ryan finally looked up and shook his head. "You have no idea what you're dealing with—or who you're dealing with."

324 | **R.J. PATTERSON**

"Enlighten me, Senator."

"There are powerful people out there—people more powerful than the President—who won't like what you're trying to do."

"And what am I trying to do exactly?"

"Bring down one of the CIA's top clandestine programs."

Osborne flashed a wry grin and cocked his head to one side. "That's what you'd like for me to believe, but I know better. This program has nothing to do with the CIA, though it does involved a fair number of people within the CIA."

"You're going to regret this."

Osborne picked up the bagged burner phone and slammed it down in front of Ryan. "*You* are going to call your killer, tell him that you need to meet. No funny business. If he doesn't show or runs, I'll make sure the twilight years of your pathetic little life are the most miserable you'll ever endure. You got that?"

Ryan grumbled as he pulled the phone out of the sack and punched a few numbers in.

"On speaker," Osborne said.

Ryan pushed the button to put the call on speakerphone and waited as it rang. It rang four times before someone answered.

"What do you want now?" the man asked.

"We need to meet."

"When?"

"One hour at our regular location."

"See you there—and bring me some cash and a new passport. I have a feeling the feds are going to be coming after me."

Ryan turned the phone off and buried his head in his hands.

"That wasn't Sergeant Thatcher now, was it?"

Ryan shook his head.

"What was that? I can't hear you. I need you to speak up for the record."

"No."

Osborne slapped a pen down on top of a blank legal pad and slid it across the table toward Ryan. "Write down the address of the meeting place and the protocol."

Ryan scratched a few notes on the pad and slid it back.

Osborne grabbed the pad off the table. "If anything goes sideways, Senator, I'll make sure the only sunlight you ever see again is in a picture." He walked toward the door, stopping and turning back toward Ryan once he put his hand on the knob. "So, why'd you do it, Senator? Why risk everything and try to kill your colleagues?"

"I never meant to kill my colleagues or Petrov."

Osborne's eyebrows shot upward. "Then what did you mean to do?"

Ryan cleared his throat before he began to talk. "Our world isn't nearly as safe as we think it is—and our government is playing fast and loose with the truth when it addresses the public about our security. If we don't do something about this, our country is going to be overtaken in the middle of the night."

"So, hiring Russian mercenaries to steal nuclear material from our own facility or trying to kill the Russian president and the entire U.S. Senate with a bio terrorism attack will change all that?"

"It might just wake Americans up from their slumber.

They need to know the danger they are living in. If I could pull this off, just think what a terrorist hell-bent on murdering innocent people could do."

Osborne shook his head and looked down. "I can't even tell the difference between you and the terrorists any more. You disgust me."

***

FLYNN AND BANKS NODDED knowingly at one another as Osborne exited the interview room and opened the door leading to the observation room where they were.

"You nailed him," Flynn said to Osborne as he entered.

"Thanks but we're not out of the woods yet. We still need to get Kramer."

"And what's your plan to do that?"

"I was hoping you'd ask—I'm going to need both of you."

CHAPTER 67

FLYNN TOOK HIS POSITION in West Potomac Park. Through his binoculars, he watched the body double for Senator Ryan shift back and forth on the bench situated near a paved path facing the water. He tapped his cane a few times and looked around.

Settle down, buddy. Don't blow this.

He checked his watch. Two minutes until Kramer was supposed to show.

"You ready, Banks?" he asked into his radio.

"Ready to string this thug up and make him pay for killing Lang."

Flynn chuckled. "You might need to take a number and get in line behind the federal government after his stunt yesterday."

"They'll be lucky if there's anything left of him after I'm through."

"Just stay calm and focused, okay? This isn't a revenge mission."

"No, it's far more than that to me. It's personal."

Flynn scanned the area again with his binoculars. "Remember, he tried to kill me, too. I'd consider that as personal as it gets." He paused. "But we want to bring him in, not take him out."

"If things go awry, I won't hesitate—"

"I understand. Just stay cool, all right? This nightmare will be over with real soon."

Flynn saw a man walking alone toward the bench. "Kramer," he said to himself. Then into his radio, "I've got eyes on the target. Dark jacket and jeans, wearing a Yankees baseball cap."

"I've got him, too," Banks said.

"Patience, Banks. Patience."

As Kramer neared the meeting place, he coolly veered away from the bench and toward the water while ambling along the path. The body double glanced over his shoulder.

"He's been made," Flynn said. "Don't lose him."

Flynn left his position and moved onto the path. So far, Kramer proved to be unpredictable—and the last thing Flynn wanted was to pursue a scared and volatile assassin into a crowd of innocent people.

"Are you tracking him, Banks?" Flynn asked.

"I haven't taken my eyes off of him."

Kramer glanced over his left shoulder, then his right. His pace quickened—and before Flynn knew it, Kramer broke into a sprint.

"We've got a runner," Flynn said.

He pumped his arms and picked up his legs as fast as he could to keep pace with Kramer.

"Banks, where are you?" he asked.

"I'm going to corner him," she said.

Flynn watched Banks run past a smaller monument and disappear well away from the Lincoln Memorial and the heart of the park where most of the people were.

"Banks, I lost him. Where are you?"

Nothing.

Flynn kept running toward the last place he saw Kramer. "Banks? Do you copy?"

Still nothing.

"Where's my backup?" Flynn asked.

"Coming to you," one voice crackled on his radio.

"I'm heading your way, too," said another agent.

"Does anyone have eyes on Kramer or Banks?" Flynn asked.

"Negative."

"Negative."

As Flynn rounded the corner of the monument, he stopped almost instantly, the scene horrifying him.

Kramer held a knife to Banks' throat. "Make another move toward me and I'll have no qualms about cutting her throat." Banks struggled to break free but couldn't. Kramer jammed his knife closer to her throat. "Sweetheart, I wouldn't suggest that if I were you."

Flynn held up his hands. "What do you want?"

"I want to disappear and never be heard from again."

A sly smile spread across Flynn's face. "Finally something we can agree on—though I think we have vastly different ideas as to how we can accomplish that."

"I'm warning you—I'm not going to prison—not without taking someone down with me," Kramer growled.

Flynn watched Banks' eyes widen, appearing glossed over with the distinct look of fear. "Let's don't act too rashly." He moved, attempting to force Kramer into the open.

"Stop right there," Kramer said. "I know what you're doing. I know exactly where your snipers are and how much time you have left. I've got all the same training you do. So, let's take this nice and easy so you don't lose any more agents."

Flynn looked at Banks, who winked at him. "Did you think I was still with the agency?"

"Stop trying to stall. Stay where you are. I'm leaving right now."

Before Kramer could say another word, Banks elbowed him in the stomach.

"Now!" she said. Her sharp jab to his abdomen created just enough space for a breakaway attempt.

Flynn knelt down and pulled a knife out of his boot, hurling it at Kramer. Flynn's aim was true as the knife struck Kramer's throat and lodged there.

Kramer's hands went immediately around his neck in an effort to stop the bleeding. But it was a lost cause.

The two other agents and Osborne rushed up behind them around the same time.

"What'd you do?" he asked, mouth agape staring at Kramer.

"What you pay me to do."

"I didn't want you to kill him. We still need him to testify against Senator Ryan. I think we'll have everything we need to convict Senator Ryan."

"It's a little too late for that," Flynn said as they watched Kramer stop struggling and breathe his last.

Banks looked down at Kramer's dead body and shook her head. "That was for Lang—and all the others you terrorized as an assassin. May your soul never find rest."

Flynn walked over to Banks and put his arm around her. "It's over," he said. "We got him."

CHAPTER 68

FLYNN PULLED THE CHAIR out from underneath the table for Banks and waited for her to sit down. She shot him a look and rolled her eyes before putting her hands on her hips.

"I'm fully capable of pulling out my own chair," she said, stamping her foot.

"I know what you're capable of, but I'm obligated to be a gentleman."

She sat down. "How refreshing."

Flynn pushed her chair in and then moved around to his side of the table and took a seat. He leaned in as he scooted his chair closer to the table. "So, how are you?"

"Probably not nearly as good as you after getting all the national attention for your story on Senator Ryan and that whole fiasco. You'll probably end up with a Pulitzer before it's all said and done."

Flynn held his hands up. "Let's not get ahead of ourselves here. I'm just pleased that the story has received a lot of attention because people deserve to know the truth."

She nodded and smiled.

Flynn leaned in again. "So, how are you *really*?"

She shrugged. "Good—I suppose. I haven't had any

nervous breakdowns on my own, though my new partner has been giving me fits."

"I can't believe it's already been two months since we got justice for Lang."

She shook her head and pursed her lips. "Justice isn't always satisfying."

"No, but it can bring closure."

"I don't know if I'll ever get over Lang's death. He was such a good partner. We worked well together, but I just don't know if I'll ever find a good partner like that ever again."

Their waiter came to their table and poured a pair of complimentary glasses of wine.

Flynn picked up his glass. "I think we need to toast something."

"Such as?"

"How about to Staff Sgt. Thatcher—the man who brought the twisted actions of Senator Ryan to light—and to Dr. Watson—the woman who created the antidote to save all the senators in our crooked capital."

"Here, here," she said, tapping her glass to his.

"Also to Dr. Watson and Staff Sgt. Thatcher on their recent engagement. I can't believe it only took them three months to decide they wanted to marry after this disaster."

"Sometimes adversity draws people together."

Flynn nodded. "Very astute observation."

"Well, that's a good start for our toasts."

Flynn's eyebrows shot upward. "A good *start*? Do you have anything else?"

"Osborne offered me a job."

"At the CIA?"

She nodded.

"Are you going to take it?"

"I haven't decided yet, but I don't think it would be wise for me to go back to the bureau. I may have burned too many bridges over there with what I did on that case."

"Makes sense. Did he tell you what you'd be doing?"

"Working on some special cases." She paused. "He said we may even work together on some future cases that you consult on."

Flynn picked up his glass and held it suspended in the air until Banks could grab hers and clink them together for another toast. "And you thought you'd never find another great partner again."

"You'll have to prove me wrong—and it won't be easy."

Flynn smiled. "I love a good challenge."

THE END

Acknowledgments

GETTING TO WRITE a story that practically started in my backyard proved to be more fun—and challenging—than I thought possible. However, I still needed to lean on the assistance and expertise of plenty of people in cobbling together this tale.

For starters, without readers who have found my work—and enjoyed it—I never would have trudged on with the arduous task of writing novels. Just knowing that you're out there, enjoying the diversions created by my books, inspires me to press on and work diligently to refine my craft.

The good people at The Experimental Breeder Reactor I in eastern Idaho helped me gain a better understanding of the terrain and environment from which this story launched.

David Doeringsfeld, the port manager at the Port of Lewiston, was patient in explain the inner workings of port life along the river at Idaho's only seaport.

Kelly Stimpert and some of her colleagues at the CDC equipped me on how to write intelligently (I hope) about the creation of vaccines and antidotes.

As with almost all my writing projects, Jennifer Wolf's editing helped make this a better story. Without her, this novel might be more confusing, not to mention full of female characters wearing horribly matched clothes.

Dan Pitts crafted and conceived another brilliant cover.

Bill Cooper continues to produce stellar audio versions of all my books — and have no doubt that this will yield the same high-quality listening enjoyment.

And last, but certainly not least, I must acknowledge my wife and her gracious soul for allowing me to once again immerse myself in a world of my own making while I wrote this story, one I hope you truly enjoyed.

About the Author

R.J. PATTERSON is a national award-winning journalist and award-winning author living in the Pacific Northwest. He first began his illustrious writing career as a sports journalist, recording his exploits on the soccer fields in England as a young boy. Then when his father told him that people would pay him to watch sports if he would write about what he saw, he went all in. He landed his first writing job at age 15 as a sports writer for a daily newspaper in Orangeburg, S.C. He later earned a degree in newspaper journalism from the University of Georgia, where he took a job covering high school sports for the award-winning *Athens Banner-Herald* and *Daily News*.

He later became the sports editor of *The Valdosta Daily Times* before working in the magazine world as an editor and freelance journalist. He has won numerous writing awards, including a national award for his investigative reporting on a sordid tale surrounding an NCAA investigation over the University of Georgia football program.

R.J. enjoys the great outdoors of the Northwest while living there with his wife and three children. He still follows sports closely.

He also loves connecting with readers and would love to hear from you. To stay updated about future projects, connect with him over Facebook or on the Internet at www.RJPbooks.com.